Ace Books by Denise Vitola

QUANTUM MOON
OPALITE MOON
MANJINN MOON
THE RED SKY FILE

The Novels of Denise Vitola

QUANTUM MOON

Ty Merrick is a twenty-first century detective investigating the death of a powerful district councilman. But Ty must deal with an even greater danger, for when the moon is full, she changes . . .

"Add Vitola to your list of names to watch for."
—*Science Fiction Chronicle*

OPALITE MOON

Three members of a secret sect—known as the Opalite—have been murdered. Ty must venture into the frozen fringes of a bankrupt society where only a lycanthrope would feel at home . . .

"Vitola's strong suit is taking the problems of today and projecting them onto the fun-house mirror of the future."
—*Contra Costa Times*

"A cleverly intricate tale of intriguing possibilities."
—*Romantic Times*

"[Vitola] is able to knit all the various elements (mystery, science fiction, and the fantastic) together into a coherent whole, for a unique and satisfying read."—*SF Site*

MANJINN MOON

Three agents from the Office of Intelligence have massive strokes—simultaneously. Ty uncovers an assassin with strange powers and deadly cunning: the Manjinn. And it's up to Ty to bring him down . . .

"A neat mystery wrapped up in intriguing speculation—just the kind of reading in which connoisseurs delight."
—*Romantic Times*

"A lot of fun."—*Press/Review*, Philadelphia

"Vitola's knack for punchy dialog and intriguing characters makes this SF-noir mystery crossover a good choice for most SF or mystery collections."—*Library Journal*

THE RED SKY FILE

DENISE VITOLA

ACE BOOKS, NEW YORK

This book is an Ace original edition,
and has never been previously published.

THE RED SKY FILE

An Ace Book / published by arrangement with
the author

PRINTING HISTORY
Ace edition / April 1999

All rights reserved.
Copyright © 1999 by Denise Vitola.
Cover art by Cliff Nielsen.
This book may not be reproduced in whole or in part,
by mimeograph or any other means, without permission.
For information address: The Berkley Publishing Group,
a member of Penguin Putnam Inc.,
375 Hudson Street, New York, New York 10014.

The Penguin Putnam Inc. World Wide Web site address is
http://www.penguinputnam.com

Check out the Ace Science Fiction & Fantasy newsletter
and much more at Club PPI!

ISBN: 0-441-00601-9

ACE®
Ace Books are published
by The Berkley Publishing Group,
a member of Penguin Putnam Inc.,
375 Hudson Street, New York, New York 10014.
ACE and the "A" design are trademarks
belonging to Charter Communications, Inc.

PRINTED IN THE UNITED STATES OF AMERICA

10 9 8 7 6 5 4 3 2 1

To Violet and Lewis Vitola
Thanks for everything.

THE RED SKY FILE

ONE

Lily Chamberlin had always wanted to be a member of the Black River Delta Patrol and now it was finally a reality—her first run down to the big water and back again to the District One Main Docking Facility. She would see things she'd only dreamed of—and she would do it as the pilot of the Patrol Cutter *Delora*.

A cutter carried two pilots for day and evening shifts and being the new pollywog made Lily the candidate for night duty. She did it willingly, but at the moment she was more than a little frustrated. The *Delora* harbored in a dark cove in the river, waiting for the light of day so its crew could successfully navigate through a section, dangerous with sandbars. Since the boat wasn't cruising, she was assigned the task of spotting for trouble along the junk-strewn shoreline with a powerful halogen flood lamp.

It was like nothing she'd ever seen. The banks of the river were full to bursting with a continuous shantytown. People had scavenged rocks, sticks, rusted metal, and mud to make their dwellings, and the farther toward the delta you got, the more bizarre the structures and the tighter the population. It was all hard to believe; her first tour of duty

followed the current straight through the biggest prison labor camp in the locality.

She'd heard the penal colony was big, but the scuttlebutt
hadn't done it justice. They said it went on for hundreds of
square miles and the perimeter was laced with thousands
and thousands of land mines. Lily recalled one instructor
back at the academy who'd claimed that it was impossible
to walk more than three feet into this death zone without
setting off an explosion. Whether a bogus story or not, it
seemed to keep the inmates inside the corral.

Lily took a deep breath and was instantly sorry that she
had. The water stank and this sulfuric perfume seemed to
cling to the soft tissues of her sinuses. It was hard to believe
several hundred thousand people drank this stuff. From now
on, it was rainwater for her. Not that the acid levels would
be any kinder to her liver, but for some reason, she felt
better about it.

She had to admit, her ideas of life on the river were
overromanticized and overrated. Years had passed with
these private fantasies, and in the end, they were all that
sustained her, but the truth was a little thick to the tongue.
These waters held dangers she'd not imagined, and the lines
between myth and superstition had blended with those of
reality. When she'd been piped aboard the *Delora,* Captain
Hazelton had taken her aside and told her the awful truths
of this tributary.

Lily shivered as she remembered his warnings—warnings that had included hard, cold facts. For lack of funding,
only one in three guard towers were manned and only one
aide station was open. Each cell block could support no
more than three hundred armed guards, and there were no
available medics on site. Manpower was an ever-present
shortcoming and the rivermen, as outgunned as all the rest,
were the keepers of the cage.

Lily glanced at the carbine propped against the nearby
bulkhead. This simple act bolstered her courage, yet it did
nothing to protect her from her notions about her own life
expectancy. Either she bought it while navigating the river,

or she bought it later. For her, and thousands like her, the question was only when she died, not how.

Her mother had often called her a fatalist, but the scuttlebutt running around the world suggested that anarchy was beginning to prevail in far-off districts and Lily knew her insights of a chaotic future would play out with precision. Three localities had already been lost to new thinking, but the majority of bureaucrats quoted in the news did nothing more than spout the party line, attend posh banquets for humanitarian rights, and continue to fiddle and diddle quietly under the table. There would come a day when the officials would find themselves on the inside of the jar looking out. Unfortunately, the people who would suffer the most would be those too poor in matter and spirit to do much more than hold on until society's latest purge stormed through their ranks.

Lily continued to scan the ragged, muddy edges of the cove, staring hard into the night. It was late summer, and in the cooling temperatures, her beam caught the brilliant twinkles of insect life. They were beautiful and mysterious. Admiring a large moth tracking the edge of the light, she enjoyed herself for a brief moment until she remembered Hazelton's additional warnings about these tiny creatures.

He had reminded her just that evening to bathe in bug repellent to keep the mosquitoes from biting, because the bloodsuckers along this tributary carried an unpleasant disease called dengue. Untreated, it turned into hemorrhagic fever. She wasn't sure what hemorrhagic fever did to a person, but the captain had one of those serious looks on his face, so she took his orders to heart and practically drank a can of DEET to protect her skin and her life.

The boat creaked as a sticky wind puffed down the river. She heard footsteps coming from the lower companionway, and pausing to listen, she tried to recognize their rhythm. They had a dragging quality to them, a heavy plod similar to her father's walk. Beyond that, though, she couldn't put the feet to the person, and not thinking much about it, she turned to check the cutter's security cameras.

Port and starboard were quiet, as well as the stern. The

computer monitor assigned to perimeter reconnaissance showed nothing out of the ordinary, but to make certain, Lily aimed the halogen's beam beyond the gnarled trees and wavy cattails to focus it upon the ruins forming the penal colony. Squinting, she satisfied herself that she didn't see any lurking figures.

She'd pushed the main hatch ajar just to get the breeze circulating throughout the bridge and now clearly heard the squeak of someone climbing up the ladder. It was probably Russo wanting to bum one of her smokes, and as if to make them even in his mind, he would tell her another story about the lost souls of Davy Jones's locker or a tale of the phantom ship known as the *Flying Dutchman*. He'd bothered her for three hours the night before, polishing off an entire pouch of her tobacco before he scuffled away to his bunk. Well, that grizzled, old pollywog wouldn't get off so cheap this time. If he wanted to twist a cigarette from her stash, then he would have to take part of her watch in return. She could use an hour of sack time after squinting at the river's shoreline for so many hours.

Lily turned back to the floodlight. She waited until she heard Russo step onto the bridge before announcing her intentions: "We make a deal tonight, Stan. You want smokes, you have to pay the price."

"I've already paid the price," came the eerie response. "Many times over."

Lily froze, panic edging her thoughts. That was not Russo. In fact, it was no voice she knew. With trepidation, she turned to see who spoke with the unearthly tone, but she'd darkened the lights to make observation of the riverbanks easier. The only thing she saw clearly was a huge, hulking form standing in the deep shadows.

Her patrol training told her to reach for the carbine, but the surprise at this blatant intrusion stunned Lily into asking a stupid question. "Who are you?"

It didn't answer. Instead, it raised its arm.

She abruptly cranked the lamp around to blind him. Her idea was a momentary success, and in this harsh illumination, Lily saw a beastly visage crowded beneath the rag-

ged hood of a wet, wool cape. Seconds later the events
played out like a prayer wheel spinning in slow motion.
She reached for her gun, but it was already too late.

The monster bellowed. It was a sorrowful cry, as horrible
in its intensity as it was in its timbre. His piercing scream
made her drop the rifle and grab her ears. The beast took
control of this frightening moment to fire a powerful stream
of glistening water, hitting her square in the chest. Even
before Lily collapsed to the deck, she knew this demon had
opened up a hole in her body big enough for the full moon
to fit through.

TWO

The thing about the water flowing through the Black River is this: You can put some into a bowl, strike a match to it, and cook an eight-course meal on the fiery burn-off. I thought about this as I stepped gingerly across the rickety pier leading to the boat, where I was supposed to find my partner, Andy LaRue, as he worked our latest crime scene.

We're marshals for District One and usually confined to land operations. I was a little sore over this newest gig, especially since I'm not fond of water—no matter how many chemicals it's laden with—but my watch commander insisted we take the case. Insistence, of course, being at the barbed end of a threat. So, here we were, looking into the River Patrol's underwear drawer, sure to find the fragrance of an illegal sachet.

The River Patrols have been around a long time. They were formed by our great humanitarian dictator, Vivian Duvalier, after he sank a contingent of UN peacekeeping vessels. This particular act brought him final victory over the world, and being thoroughly enamored of these boats and ships, he created an elite corps of water guardians to serve upon them. In the beginning, their mission was to answer the needs of the people living along the canals and estuaries, as well as monitoring the fishing and wildlife habitats surrounding these areas. The crews were touted as planetary ecologists and thought of themselves as the stewards of the future.

Yet, as it is with all noble enterprises, greed and hatred intervened. In this case, Duvalier's dream didn't work out exactly like it was supposed to. People started protesting, complaining, and running amok. Civil unrest became such a problem that our beloved leader was inspired to develop the labor-camp penal system to contain all the dissidents. The Ministry of Criminal Justice had to have a security force to mind these prisoners, and so the proud River Patrols were slowly turned into unwilling wardens of the politically persecuted.

I saw LaRue wave at me from the deck of the boat. His waist-length, sepia-colored hair blew wild in the breeze and for a moment I could see him fitting snugly into a pirate novel. Give him a sword as sharp as his wit and LaRue could bugger with the best of them.

He met me as I stepped aboard the cutter *Delora*. My partner is rarely at a loss for words and I could tell by the set of his jaw that he was ready to deliver a fresh lecture. I expected a greeting laced with metaphysical balderdash, but he surprised me by saying: "Did you know that in one of the old Romance languages the name *Delora* means 'pain' or 'suffering'?"

"Andy," I answered, "I don't care. I just don't want this bastard to sink. Now, what do we have here?"

"A juicy one, Ty."

"Is that juicy as in interesting, or juicy as in bloody?" I asked.

"Both." He used his chin to point the way toward the crime scene. "The crew swears that a bogeyman is responsible."

I stopped to stare at him. "This boat floats through the middle of a gigantic prison yard full of killers, rapists, and sleazy politicians. Is it necessary to load the explanation with paranormal crap, too?"

He shrugged, but didn't reply.

It seems that since my personal life has become a mixed bag of supernatural elements, I've been confined to a series of cases mired in the etheric glue of demons, poltergeists, and fairies. You see, I'm a lycanthrope. That's right—a werewolf. This illness came on me one night when carbon monoxide from a faulty furnace rearranged the molecules of my brain. I don't turn into a beast or routinely chew people up. I do change, though, and there have been times when I've acted with a carnal lust serious enough to get me into deep trouble.

We entered the bridge and I was banged on the nose by the familiar scent of death. You know the smell if you've ever stumbled across the rotting corpse of an animal. It burns your eyes and tans you sinuses until you're sure the delicate membranes in your face have been turned to leather. From this stench, I knew immediately we were dealing with an old murder. The area was full of personnel, each tech busy collecting his Baggie's worth of evidence, while the medical examiner, Frank Wilson, bellowed orders concerning the samples. We met our watch commander as she clasped a paper mask to her face while studying a body.

She glanced up when we approached, but laid a frown specifically on me. "Merrick," she said, "where have you been?"

"Today is my day off," I answered. "I had a doctor's appointment and then had trouble getting over here. Do you know the cross-district bus system cut out three more runs during the day?"

"Getting around is getting impossible," LaRue muttered.

"It's those new environmental laws," I answered. "If this keeps up, we'll need flying brooms for transportation."

Our banter was enough of an excuse for Julie to shake her head dismally and return her attention to the corpse, but I interrupted her before she could focus once more. "Why were we called out on the case? Doesn't the River Patrol keep their own investigators?"

"We're here as an interagency courtesy," she answered sharply.

"Oh," I said. "Which means there's a reason my shorts are fluttering over this."

Julie tried to hide a small smile creeping across that stern old face of hers. "Merrick, shut up and listen. We have five confirmed murders, time of death within the same hour. According to the captain, these bodies were found a week ago. He left the situation undisturbed and returned immediately to dock."

"Must have been a long trip for him," LaRue muttered.

"Undoubtedly," Julie answered.

"Where are the other bodies?" I asked.

"They were found stacked in the aft of the boat. Pointing to the wreck before her, she continued her review: "This was Riverman Recruit Lilith Chamberlin. It was her first tour of duty and she was straight out of the academy. She had the bridge watch—apparently by herself."

"The others were on evening watch?" I asked.

"Yes. Four men. All are in this woman's condition. Whoever dispatched these people accomplished it without raising an alarm. The crew was not found until the watch changed." She glanced past me. "Wilson, I need you over here."

He nodded, and tucking his fingers between his paunch and utility belt, he stepped over to smear color into the conversation. "That little girl there used to be a cute kid with a perky nose. Now look at her."

I did. She lay in a pool of sticky dried blood. The flies had already started feasting on her flesh and birthing their young in the moist fissure made when someone had slit her throat. Her uniform was split open down the front, exposing her small breasts and a large, circular hole in her chest. One hand was sawed from her wrist and missing, as were her ears and the tip of her nose. It appeared to be a case of killing for the trophies.

"Did the others lose body parts?" I asked.

"Yes," LaRue said.

I tossed Wilson a look. "So, Frank, what got them—the short shave with a long blade or the hole in the chest?"

"My guess is the nice-sized cavity through her sternum.

Her heart was completely blown out of her body." He pointed toward the far bulkhead and a blood-splattered stain there. When he spoke, his voice held a trifle bit of morbid glee. "The force launched it ten feet. It might have blown farther if it hadn't smacked into the bulkhead."

I tried to appreciate Wilson's awe concerning the trajectory of fleeing hearts, but failed miserably and so turned back to study the corpse. "That means she was standing when the shot was fired and her throat was an afterthought. What did it—a rifle blast?"

"No," Julie said. "We don't have any discharged rounds, no powder burns. Besides, conventional weaponry would produce extensive tissue damage. It would mangle everything in the process."

"What was it, then?" LaRue asked.

"It looks like a high-velocity water rifle," Wilson answered.

I glanced at LaRue and found myself shaking my head at this latest audacity of the modern world. A water rifle combines electricity, H_2O, and oxygen to create a firing stream more powerful than a laser and much easier to control.

Wilson continued. "I once saw one of those babies drill a hole through a solid steel door."

"You'd need a couple of gel-cell batteries to make it work," LaRue said. "Those things are heavy."

"That's right," Julie answered. "And the RP claims they don't use water rifles and never have."

I nodded and took a step back to look over the bridge. It was a gray-lined room with large square portholes on all four sides. Monitors and battered computer equipment composed the wealth of the conning helm, but rather than relying solely upon these electronic miracles, someone had used paper charts to navigate the waterway. The maps were strewn across the deck, damp and curling at the corners. Continuing my survey, I realized the cutter was like everything else in our humanitarian society: worn-out.

A sense of hopelessness pervades our lives and so the people have turned to the only things they can—superstition and invisible magic. You can shop anywhere on the backdoor market and find love potions, fertility keepers, and cures for lumbago that include swallowing seven golden coins with a teaspoon of turpentine as a chaser. It apparently was no different aboard this boat, for in the short space of the bridge I counted five charm sacks, ten good luck ribbons, and a couple of cornhusk voodoo dolls.

Julie pulled my attention quickly back to her. "The Patrol brass is not going to decommission the *Delora* for our investigation. Instead, they're going to outfit her with a skeleton crew, which will be composed of those volunteers not too frightened to go. I want you and LaRue aboard this boat when it next ships out."

I groaned. "Julie, I can't swim."

There was no getting any sympathy out of her. "Wear a life jacket."

"You can't even get her to wear her Kevlar vest," LaRue snorted.

He huffed to silence when I pierced him with a glare. "When do we leave?"

"This evening," she answered. "We'll clear out as soon as we can and they'll swab down the boat, provision it, and bring in the standby crew." She paused to study me, and perhaps to gauge the effect her next words would have upon me. "Gibson will be coming with you."

Dr. Lane Gibson. Gifted physician and skilled neurologist. He was my friend, my teacher, my lover, my tormentor, and my ever-present pain in the patooty. Do you recall when I mentioned that my lycanthropy had gotten me into a professional jam or two? I had an inordinately violent confrontation with a murderer during a full moon and it had ultimately landed me in Gibson's medical custody. With his help, I'm allowed to keep my job and my Class-A designation, while he searches far and wide for a cure or control of my paranormal disease. His responsibility doesn't extend much past a momentary compassion for my problems, though. He's busy trying to formulate new brain technology that the government might buy for fun and profit, and he's using my gray matter to come up with the idea that will launch him into this fame and fortune.

As we stretch this odd arrangement into a personal relationship, we focus upon our inadequacies until we both
lie bleeding from constantly sticking it to each other. Not
only could I not swim, but now I would have an uninter-
rupted fortnight to spend with Gibson. There would be no
escaping the good doctor and his latest treatment for my
lycanthropy.

"Why is Gibson coming along?" I asked Julie.

"Because he's had some experience with penal colonies.
The folks upstairs want an independent observer present."

"Why? Don't they trust the RP to take care of us?"

"I'm not told everything, Marshal Merrick." She stood,
and I heard her knees crack as she did. "I was told one
thing, though. The prison population has a strong belief in
karmic magic."

Past-life piddle. People have taken the principles of reincarnation and made magical practices out of them. A hundred years ago the concept of karma addressed the effect
of a person's actions during his lifetime. It was a force that
shaped his decisions, choices, and ultimately his fate. Yet
in our hapless society, these ancient ideas of life after life
have exploded from theological supposition to be redefined
and reworked. Karma, once an immutable power of spiritual faith, has become a pliable energy source, and with the
right magical spell, people believe it can be manipulated.

Even LaRue was guilty. For weeks he'd been harping
about how Gibson and I were soul mates down through the
ages, having been reborn again and again to work on the
karmic lessons of conflict and turmoil. In his mind, our one
saving grace was our love for each other. It didn't matter
that Gibson and I fenced with our affection, stabbing each
other every chance we got, because LaRue always recommended a charm sack, hex, or spray that would solve our
karmic differences.

"I thought this was a government facility that followed
strict rules and regulations," I said.

Julie shook her head. "This penal colony is a disaster
just waiting to happen. The District Council has let the ball
drop. And apparently, it happened years ago."

THREE

LaRue and I were back aboard the cutter *Delora*, just before moonrise. Gibson was there, but rather than displaying his customary intensity, the good doctor looked like he was ready to take a trip on the *African Queen*. He wore a set of black cammies displaying the Marshals Office insignia, as well as the gold caduceus of the medical corps. His long, sandy-blond hair fell loose from beneath the uniform cap and the sidearm he wore on his thigh looked mighty out of place.

"What is this?" I asked, pointing to his getup.

He smiled sheepishly. "My labor-insurance coverage is being picked up by the Marshals Office instead of the Planetary Health Organization right now. So, to do this, I have to be temporarily assigned to the homicide unit. Your vigilant watch commander is obeying the terms to the letter and I'm here as one of you."

LaRue grinned. "Yeah, but can you handle that blunderbuss you're wearing?"

"This blunderbuss is an Ansi-410 Repeater. It shoots rubber bullets."

LaRue's expression evaporated into suspiciousness. "That isn't standard issue."

It was Gibson's turn to smile. "That's right."

"Ah, but your Hippocratic oath won't let you shoot."

"Try again. I don't want to die at the hands of a whacked-out convict."

"Whacked out?" I asked.

"Yeah. Half of the prison population is mentally unstable."

"How do you know that?"

"Because they always are."

I glanced at LaRue, now knowing why Julie assigned us to this case. We were experts in the criminally insane, having dealt with more than our fair share.

"How many ammo cartridges do you have?" LaRue said.

"Ten," he answered. "Everything I had in stock." Slowly, Gibson chucked his attention from my partner to me. "I'm here to help you with this case, but I'm also here for you, Merrick. I intend to continue the investigation of your lycanthropy right into the full moon. The cutter has a very nice medical unit and lab, and an accommodating boat's doctor. I've got the run of the place, so don't think you're going to escape me in any way."

"This isn't going to be a cruise, Gibson," I said. "We've got an energetic killer on the loose. Maybe several. You should be peeing your shiny new pants instead of giving me orders."

"There's time enough for that," he said with a smile. "The late dinner bell is going to sound in fifteen minutes and the captain will meet us in the chow hall to brief us. If you want to stow your gear, it's down that ladder and to the right. The three of us are sharing the same bunk room. It's the only guest quarters they have."

"Just don't use my toothbrush," LaRue said as he tugged me along by the strap on my duffel bag.

We dumped our stuff off and headed for the crew's mess to meet the tour-of-duty officers Captain Jonathan Ritter and his exec, Lieutenant Wilhelmina Dacey, a pretty, young woman who preferred to be called "Wil."

Ritter had one of those faces that immediately put my

lycanthropic sensibilities on alert. It had too many rubbery
parts to it and twisted into too many needless expressions.
This fact caused me to stare at him as we dined on fish
sticks and red-eye gravy.

"You wouldn't believe how difficult it is to patrol this
penal colony," he said. "If you ask me, the government
has lost control over the whole labor-camp issue. The bureaucrats have filled the outpost until they can't squeeze
another rat into the place. We have problems every day
because of overcrowding."

"Things are just getting worse," Dacey said.

LaRue was apparently enraptured by her beauty and he
kept his eyes upon her while speaking to the captain.
"What is the *Delora*'s specific duty?"

"Security," she answered. "We also transport prisoners
and supplies. It's a full-time job on a limited staff, especially since the district has stopped airdropping provi-
sions."

"The district is running out of airplanes," LaRue said.
"They closed another manufacturing plant recently. It only
leaves one factory running on the whole continent."

Dacey nodded. "It just complicates the job."

"What about the dredge this thing carries?" I asked.
"What do you use that for?"

Ritter's face reminded me of a kitten caught inside of a
big sock. The muscles seemed to move under the skin while
his mask of self-control floated on top. "We use it for whatever we need. It comes in handy now and then—boats get
stuck in the muck this time of the year and we occasionally
have to deal with shifting sandbars." He paused. "The RP
is in the midst of reclaiming the Black River delta region
and we run out new equipment to them with each tour.
When we get there, we'll unhook the dredge and take on
a used one ready for servicing."

"What kind of problems do you get from the prison population?" Gibson asked as he speared a piece of cucumber.

"Lately we have had a lot of unrest," Ritter answered.
"This is an all-male population, Marshal. They've been

castrated both literally and figuratively, and recently their numbers have swelled with politicos.''

"The politicos are causing the unrest?"

Ritter nodded, shoving more food into his mouth. "They're behind it. I'm sure of it." He stopped once more to take a large bite of moldy bread. As he chewed he spewed. "The guard units assigned to the cell blocks are part of the problem."

"Explain that, please."

"The penal colony hasn't been run like a traditional prison for many years. Because the population is so extensive, you have a situation where an independent society has emerged."

"What kind of society?" I asked.

He paused, clearly uncomfortable with the information he was about to impart, but in a moment continued full speed ahead. "They've developed hierarchies based on the beliefs of witchcraft."

"Watering witching, to be more specific," Dacey said.

Well, hang me by the yardarm and bleach my bones white in the sun. "We're talking about the folks who dink up spells, curses, and the odd hex or two?"

Dacey nodded. "The one with the baddest magic is also the baddest man in the cell block."

"So, each person diddles with the karmic energy," I said. "If just enough to protect himself."

"Scam artists," Ritter added. "Every one of them. Dangerous, too. Half the bastards don't have any leg irons, but they have more goddamned weapons than you can shake a magic wand at."

Dacey jumped into the conversation. "The inmates hate the RP. They do everything they can to make life miserable for the units assigned to this labor camp. It's easy for them to trust a man who claims he can do big mojo and help them out of their troubles." She leaned across the table and spoke in a conspiratorial tone. "I've heard they have secret meetings to plot their nefarious acts, and then when they're done discussing the next attack, they gather together and sacrifice animals."

Ritter slopped some gravy on his shirt as he nodded his concurrence. "They don't always use animals, either."

"And we think some of them are actually cannibals," Dacey said.

"How do you know that?" I asked.

"The garbage scows," Ritter mumbled.

We stared at him until he realized we were functioning with landlubber brains.

"A scow is a flat-bottom boat. The RP has a bunch of them cruising the river. They collect trash and bodies."

"Bodies?" LaRue said. "Do they show signs of having supplied the evening meal?"

"Well, they've been scavenged, that's for sure. The inmates are directed to pile the cadavers at various points along the river, and when the scow comes along, it collects the corpses."

"What happens to the bodies?"

He shrugged and pushed in more gravy. "I understand they go to the Factory Disposal Recycling Project."

That was a fancy way to say the corpses stoked the flames at the smelting plant. "So, there have been an inordinate number of bodies piled at the piers?"

"Nope. Bodies without heads."

Dacey delicately spooned her dinner, nodding steadily. "They've found about twenty bodies over the last two months."

"And you think the prisoners are scooping out the brains for pan bread?" I asked.

"They don't keep the fact a secret. They call them soul cakes."

"Soul cakes?" I asked.

"Yes, Marshal Merrick. They mix the brains with flour, polluted water, and the occasional bird egg. Then they bake it up over a dung fire while they chant a spell over it."

"What kind of spell?" LaRue asked.

"The wheel-of-life stuff," she answered.

"You're talking about reincarnation," he said.

She nodded and scooped at her food. "I'm not exactly sure what the spells are all about. I imagine they're aiming to improve their karma. God knows, they could use it.''

Ritter tossed her a mean look. ''Don't feel sorry for them, Wil. I've told you about that. Your compassion is misplaced.''

''I would have to agree with Captain Ritter,'' I said.

She swallowed her bite, but didn't challenge this sage advice.

''Has anyone suggested a possible connection between water witch rituals and the murders on the *Delora*?'' LaRue asked.

Ritter poured a cup of coffee and sucked food from his teeth before answering. ''Sure. They were missing body parts. I figure the killer dined on his trophies.''

Already weary of this supernatural scenario, I decided to steer it back toward science and reason. ''Captain Ritter, does the cutter's arsenal contain water rifles?''

The kitten wiggled across his cheeks as he drew down a surprised expression. ''No. I already explained that to your commanding officer.''

''This is a penal colony. You can't honestly expect us to believe the guard units don't use water rifles as well as rocket launchers to control this population. What about the tower sentries?''

''I don't know. All I can tell you for sure is what goes for the cutters. No WRs. Lots of carbines and a couple auto weapons and that's about it. If you ask me, the RP doesn't give us near the firepower we need.'' That said, he dipped down for another spoonful of gravy.

Just as I followed suit by forking mashed potatoes into my mouth, Riverman Harvey marched up to the table. ''Marshals Merrick, LaRue, and Medic Gibson are requested in the radio room, sir. There's a marine communication from Medical Examiner Frank Wilson.''

I sighed and tossed a weary expression at my partner. ''Why does he always call when I'm eating a gourmet meal?''

LaRue shook his head and stuffed two fish sticks between his lips as he rose. Gibson and I were close behind, provisioned with our own greasy twigs.

We shuffled through the main companionway and down toward the bow of the ship, where we found the *Delora*'s comlink. A crewman showed us how to put it on speaker and a moment later we were listening to Wilson crunch into one of his wife's famous pickle sandwiches.

Wilson had just received the bonus of his career by having his personal forensics kingdom outfitted with the latest technology. It was a temporary arrangement, as everything is in our world, but he was determined to use his new computers with verve for as long as they would be his.

"What have you got for us, Frank?" I asked.

"Blood analysis, Merrick. According to the crew manifest, there were twenty people on board who were either type A or type O. We uncovered a small amount of type AB negative by the main hatch of the bridge. There was also a sample of mucus that corresponds to the blood."

"So, the pus came with the red. What else?"

"The initial workup on the samples showed inordinate levels of heavy metals, especially mercury."

"You think our killer has been trudging through polluted water?" LaRue asked.

"It's a good possibility. Of course, that only leaves you to sort through ten thousand inmates. I'm running a background check to see how many people incarcerated there have AB negative. That will limit the field somewhat, but I'm sure it won't be enough." He paused and we heard the rattle of a paper bag. Then: "Damn! Charlotte didn't pack me any butter cookies. Again."

"Frank, will you stop worrying about your stomach?" I asked, thinking of how badly I wanted to return to my own food. "Is there something else here that we need to know?"

"Yeah. I'm getting to it, Merrick." A moment more of mumbling and fumbling and he finally spoke. "The samples showed a bacteria. One that we don't recognize."

Gibson stormed into the communication. "Can you tell if we have an infectious situation?"

"Negative. We're working on it, but we had to call in a

specialist. He won't be here until later. ETA unknown. That means we're on ice until then.''

The creeping shrillness of my voice felt like it jabbed the back of my eyeballs on its way out. "What about all that fancy machinery you've been bragging about?"

"There's nothing we can do," he answered. "I can tell you, though, that the bacteria resembles *mycobacterium leprae*."

It was meaningless to me, so I deferred to Gibson, who growled at the speaker. "I could have sworn you said *mycobacterium leprae*."

"I did," Wilson said.

"What is it?" I demanded.

Gibson flicked his gaze at me. "It's leprosy, Merrick."

I tossed him a stunned look in return. "You're kidding. Right, Frank?"

"Wish I were."

"Hansen's disease was wiped out completely thirty years ago," Gibson said.

"I didn't say it was Hansen's," Wilson snapped.

"You said it resembled it. How so?"

"There's a couple extra compounds present we can't account for. Until we get this thing locked down, if we ever do get it locked down, I suggest you guys not kiss anyone. And mind the cook, too."

"Why?" I asked, hesitantly.

Gibson answered for him. "Because if this bacteria is contained in blood and mucus, it will be present in sweat and spit."

FOUR

Upon hearing this urgent word from Wilson, Gibson immediately contacted the boat's doctor and together they proceeded to test every crew member for anything resembling Hansen's disease. While he was busy in the sick bay LaRue and I decided it was time to conduct an interview or two. Ritter had room cleared for us in the mess, sending in Chief Riverman Bard Neilson to satisfy the order.

He was a big, burly, red-cheeked fellow, who looked like he was strong enough to hoist the mainsail by himself. Yet, as he took his seat, I noticed he moved with a certain grace and fluidity.

I opened the interrogation. "Mr. Neilson, you were aboard the *Delora* when it was attacked. Is that correct?"

"Yes, ma'am," he answered in a tiny voice.

"What are you duties?"

"I'm a maintenance pollywog. I keep the vessel spit-shined according to regulation. Of course, the old gal has seen better days."

"Her age is showing, huh?"

"Well, that and the pounding she takes."

"What do you mean?"

His rosy complexion blanched out when I asked the question. "Well, you know."

"No, we don't," I answered. "Please tell us."

Though no one else was in the room, he leaned forward and whispered, "It's the water witches' curse upon us."

I glanced at LaRue, hoping he was ready to stoke this particular boiler of superstition. He didn't let me down. In fact, he spoke in a genuine tone of voice. "Dealing with curses can be a bitch, and as marshals we've run up against our share. Can you tell us about the one you're referring to?"

"The one licked up by the Coven," he answered quietly.

"Who is the Coven?"

"A big group of water witches."

"Why did they curse the *Delora*?"

"Why do witches do anything? Revenge, I suppose."

"Revenge for what?"

He shrugged. "I don't know for sure. The brass don't trust us pollywogs with information. You can't expect the person who does the scrubbing and waxing to hear all the secrets."

"But you have heard some."

Neilson paused to smack his lips and point to the coffeepot. "Might I have some jo?"

I rose and flipped a chipped, white cup from a nearby rack, and sliding it onto the table, I left my hand poised around the rim. "Why was this boat cursed?"

He hesitated, staring at my hand. Then, after a ten-second standoff, he answered. "It was a bad deal that went down between one of the tour-of-duty officers and the Coven. I never did find out what the curse was all about, but I did discover that it was a putrefying spell. After it got flung on us, things just started breaking down around here. All at once."

I released his cup and sat down while he poured his drink.

"A putrefying spell?" LaRue asked. "I've never heard of that one."

"Yeah, neither did I till I came to the river. I hail from

a district where witches got the power over the birds and skunks, not dominion over the karmic energy stolen from lost souls. That's some powerful mojo.'' Neilson took a tentative sip from his cup and made a face. ''Ah, God, that's some awful stuff. Tastes like tar, you know?'' After attempting a second slug, he placed the mug gently upon the table and began to explain. ''The folks out here got a lot of rot to work with. I mean, look around. It's only natural that's what they would focus on. See, they scrape off karma from the lost soul's many incarnations, looking for that energy that's old and evil. Most people don't deal with the effect of bad karma built up over lifetimes. They try to make do without having to pay the piper for their former misdeeds. Oh, they're willing to take all the good karma they've built up over the lifetimes. Sure, that ain't no problem at all. But make a man work with the energy of retribution and repayment for doing something he knowed he shouldn't have done, then it's a different story. Anything not to suffer.''

''So, you're saying the water witches in the Coven have the means to scrape off this old past-life power and reflect it on inanimate objects?''

He nodded. ''Old karma can animate anything, but the only way you can get that kind of power is to nab a sorrowful, lost soul.''

''What is a lost soul?'' I asked.

''They're the souls who done died in this labor camp and upon the Black. Their spirits are so weighed down with bad karma that they ain't allowed on the rebirth wheel until they work out some kind of penance. I suppose it throws the cosmic unity out of whack or something. That's when Davy Jones gets 'em and puts 'em down in the locker. Here they can think about their misdeeds in past lives and the mistakes made in their most recent one. They get a chance to review the reasons they got sent to the penal colony. That don't just go for the prisoners, either. It goes for everybody, including you two.''

''If these souls are caught in Davy Jones's locker, how

do the witches steal this energy for their putrefying spell?"
LaRue said.

"I ain't sure how the Coven does it, but I got my sus-
picions. Davy Jones uses this karmic power to enliven the
creatures of this waterway. He's in charge of such things
as mermaids and leviathans. I've heard the witches know
how to shave away any extra strength these beings might
possess. One thing is for sure, though. A putrefying spell
needs some dark energy to work."

"So, what did you notice after the curse was laid on?"
LaRue asked.

"Little things, at first. I noticed how the barnacles started
building up on the hull. That's real odd in itself. It shouldn't
be like that. To make matters worse, these babies were
huge. Big as my fist. A barnacle ain't supposed to be that
monstrous."

"What else happened?"

"Happened?" Neilson said. "It ain't stopped happening.
You got rust, you got slime, you got mold. Hell, there's a
hole in the aft section that I keep patching. A week will go
by and I'll find that damn patch nearly eaten through." He
shook his head and blew a breath through his nose. "It's
frustrating, because I can't keep up with the chores. We've
got the protection charms, the energy revitalizers, and I've
sprayed a marine compound stabilized with a strengthening
spell, and still, the crud keeps coming."

"Can't that be some effect of pollution?" I asked.

"Sure, but don't you see? That's why they're called water witches. They mix the karmic energy with the water and
the air molecules."

"Excuse me?"

"What with the mist and all, things stay pretty soggy. It
gets into the mechanicals—in fact the engine keeps splitting
rings and the generator acts up all the time. The water and
air mix with the curse. This magic even affects the food.
The cook can't put two things together that taste right anymore. Add that to everyone's jangled nerves and you've
got the makings for an unhappy state of affairs."

I could see it was time to manipulate this man's beliefs

in the supernatural. "Tell me, Neilson. Did you expect the deaths of your crewmen?"

He stared at me and I noticed that the pleasant-faced young man who'd sat down with us was no longer present. He'd been replaced by a person who was obviously more resigned to his fate than his age would have suggested. His answer proved the point. "I expect we're all going to die on the *Delora*. Ain't none of the ways going to be pleasant, neither."

We sat in silence for a couple of heartbeats before I tossed Neilson's superstitions behind me. "You have the run of the boat, then."

He snared me with a frown. "What's that supposed to mean?"

"It doesn't mean anything. We're trying to establish some background here."

"Oh." With that, he visibly relaxed. "I thought for a second you were blaming me for all these awful things, despite what I told you about the curse."

"We wouldn't think of it," I soothed. "We know you're not responsible. We're just trying to find a track in the wilderness. Tell me, do you work alone, or do you have an assistant?"

"I have two rivermen apprentices—Hogan and Curran."

"Do they have the run of the boat, too?"

"Yes. They're good kids. Younger than me. Real young. Like Lily was."

"Did you know Lilith Chamberlin well?" LaRue asked.

"No. She was a new pollywog. I was introduced to her when she came aboard, but I've been busy and really hadn't had a chance to talk to her."

"Did you see or hear anything unusual prior to the murders of your mates?"

"No. I was asleep. Honest I was."

"We understand you found the bodies."

"Yes, ma'am. I came onto deck at the turn of the watch and was greeted with the massacre." He glanced down at the table and shivered. Dragging his chin back up, he apologized. "It's just so hard to lose your buddies. I knew some

of those folks, since we shipped out together the first time.
I suppose as far as karma goes, I might have been on the
killing side of the scenario in an old incarnation. You know,
maybe I ordered a bunch of folks slaughtered and this go-
round I had to make retribution by being the one to discover
my dead mates. If there is one thing I understand, it's the
sorrow I might have caused others.''

Reincarnation dealt in fantasies loaded with guilt. It had
pat answers for life's inequities, judged only on two sides
of the coin—good and evil—but in my mind, there were
no good reasons for suffering a violent death. "Did the
Delora have any prior trouble with the prisoner population?''

"We always have trouble. A day before the massacre,
they hit us with hewie-lewies.''

Hewie-lewies? I took a stab at it. "You're talking about
hand grenades?''

"No, ma'am. I'm talking about blow-dart guns. The bastards take old copper pipes and make shooters with them.
They use any kind of junk that's got a sharp point to it.
When we hit the Vivian Narrows, the stuff rained down on
us. Lost a man. McPheeters.''

"We've seen his name listed as an accidental death.''

"Well, that it was. He accidentally got in the way of one
of those flying barbs. Got one straight through the neck.''
He sighed and slurped his jo. "We should have known
something was going to happen that night.''

"Why?''

"Because of the sky.''

"What does the sky have to do with it?'' I asked.

"There's an old saying,'' he answered. "Red sky at
morning, sailor take warning. Red sky at night, sailor's
delight.''

"Yes, so?''

He sighed into an explanation. "Seafarers gauge the circumstances of the sea by the light of the rising and setting
suns. If it's a bright red morning, it'll be a stormy day; if
a bright red evening, then the storm will pass before the
next launch. If the sailor doesn't heed the warning, he and

his crew are in for trouble. Over the years the saying has been applied to all kinds of predicaments that can befall people working the water.''

''And the sky on the day of the murders was red?'' I asked.

He sighed again before answering. ''It wasn't just red, Marshal. It was bloodred.''

FIVE

At dawn, the *Delora* shoved off and the noise and vibration of the diesel engines kicked me right out of bed. Seeing that LaRue and Gibson were already up and gone, I slipped into my shoulder holster, and then decided to pour a cup of thick, black coffee from the ever-perking pot in the boat's mess before going topside.

If the sailor had been right, then there would be trouble. The sun rose slowly over the mountains of junk and the thick line of trees, coloring the sky cinnamon. Mist swirled about the boat, creating an eerie effect. This strange landscape was punctuated by the shrill calls of birds and the noise of unfortunate homesteaders waking for the thousandth time in their metal nests designed with poverty and despair in mind.

I don't know why it bothered me, but it did. I have my own problems with prosperity—specifically, the lack of it. The world is a poor place all over, and this fact is further exaggerated by the addition of sickness, corruption, and betrayal. Our society was supposed to smote these problems. Instead, they have aggrandized them, stressing equality in experience. What a load of shark shit.

Poverty spoke for the vast majority of the people, yet the

folks who served a life sentence in a labor camp were far more pitiful. Destiny had placed them in a zone of no regard. They were considered not much better than animals and used accordingly.

I slugged at my breakfast and found a seat on an overturned lifeboat. Letting my gaze pass along the edges of the cutter, I looked for places where it would be easy for someone to board. If the killer were carrying a couple of gel-cell packs with him, he would need to be a strong person. Add the rifle and you had better be able to heft forty pounds and control the kick produced by the electricity and water as it combined for firing.

As I sat there, thinking about murder, I found myself lulled by the drone of cicadas in the trees edging the banks. It was not a spectacular festival of nature's music, but my lycanthropy increased my appreciation of the melodic sound.

You see, this strange malady of mine manifests as a series of seizures during the lunar month. I call them "stretches," because my body and mind expand to fill out my supernatural disposition. During this gradual transformation, my bones stretch, my strength increases, and my vision enhances. A thousand and one subtle changes mark my path from human to wolf. I'd had a stretch just before coming aboard the *Delora* and it had affected my hearing, so my ears picked up the sound, but my brain processed it at a one-second delay. The high-pitched whistle of the insects was brighter and stranger than it should have been.

My morning symphony was soon interrupted by Dacey. She wore a crisply ironed blue jumpsuit, a wide-billed cap, and a bright smile. Sliding next to me, she immediately opened a conversation by talking about Davy Jones's locker.

"It's these kinds of mornings when the lost souls of the deep are said to lurk in the mists," she announced.

"I don't believe in ghosts. Besides, doesn't the deep refer to the ocean?"

"Out here, Davy Jones is the Lost Mariner, King of Wayward Souls," she answered. "The stories don't differentiate between what kind of watery grave he rules. They just talk about the full moons and the sorrowful spirits of those who have died in this hellhole.''

I stared at her, worried I was about to take a deep dive into a shallow pond of bullshit, but this insanity could be the connection that inspired the killer. ''What else do you know?''

''Well, probably not as much as I should, but in some of the myths you'll hear on the river, Davy Jones is also the keeper of nymphs, water spunkies, and the purveyor of bad weather.'' Pausing to remove her hat, she let the moment fade into silence by glancing around. ''Do you hear that noise?''

''Yeah, the bugs. You don't hear this kind of song back in the district. Not many trees.''

''Most of the rivermen say that sound is the call of the naiads or water nymphs.''

''A colorful story, but a little bit to the leeside of the truth, I'd say.''

''It's said that the naiads will lure a pilot into a whirlpool of destruction if he's not vigilant. It's why the RP has at least one female pilot aboard.''

''How does that solve anything?''

''Women are unaffected by their supernatural sound.''

''That's ridiculous.''

''Ridiculous or not, the naiads' song has played havoc with more than one boat on the river.''

''How so?''

''Drunken sailors will steer toward anything. After half a bottle of rum or vodka, they get the idea the naiads are calling to them and then they lose the keel from running aground.''

''Sounds like the alcoholism is worse than the naiad problem.''

She nodded. ''It's true. The women pilots tend to be of a more sober disposition.''

''Why doesn't the RP just prohibit drinking?''

''They have, but out here? Even the captain stays drunk. No one is going to squeal.''

We sat in silence for a minute, each listening to the enchanting noise of the cicadas. "You weren't aboard the *Delora* when it was hit," I said abruptly.

"That's right."

"What do you think happened?"

She snorted, but paused to scout down the river once more before answering. "Greed happened, Marshal Merrick. Pure and simple."

I was about to ask her what she meant, but was rudely interrupted by a hailstorm of rocks.

SIX

A rock the size of my fist came flying over the boat's transom and banged Dacey right on the noggin. She dropped like ten pounds of shit in a five-pound sack. I was caught ducking and running for cover under a flimsy rain awning flapping in the breeze of the *Delora*'s port side. The bombs kept coming—stones, shells, glass bottles, tin cans. I heard a shout, but in the mist and shadows of the early morning, it was hard to tell if the voice came from a crew member or a prisoner on shore.

It looked like somebody was up for a fight and damned if I was going to let a good battle get away. As a district marshal, I'm authorized to use lethal force if the situation demands it. Having a rock slung up my nose qualified as a good reason to discharge my sidearm and I didn't hesitate. Drawing my gun and leveling my aim with both hands, I targeted the enemy.

The inmates had built a motorized catapult out of assorted junk. A noisy diesel generator pumped juice to the contraption and in no more than thirty seconds they had the thing loaded, primed, and ready to fire.

I found the unfortunate guy who was operating the winch and pulled the trigger. The bank was at least a hundred

yards away and pretty crapped up with garbage, but my
bullet found its mark and the mechanic went down. I waited
for a fellow adventurer to assume his position at the battery,
suddenly pissed when the cowards turned and ran.

Someone on board the *Delora* followed my lead by popping one of the beggars. The force of the blast flung the
man forward and he slammed into his evil compatriot. My
ears throbbed with the echo from that rifle, and for a minute
I had to wage the good war against a wave of dizziness.
As I stood there trying to blink my world into stillness,
LaRue and Gibson rolled up to me.

"Are you all right?" Gibson demanded.

"Yes. See to Dacey. She got whopped by a rock."

Gibson moved to attend her, leaving LaRue behind.
"What the hell happened, Ty?"

"We were attacked, Andy. Those bastards have fuel and
electricity. That makes me wonder what else they've got."

He stared at me and then nodded. "A backdoor market?
They're trading for supplies."

At least this was something we knew about. District One
has a huge illegal market. Since most of the government-
run stores have empty shelves, the people make ends meet
by selling anything and everything—including invisible
magic. You can buy spells and potions while shopping for
your daily bread. If magic chairs and psychic healing are
more to your liking, you can always get a reading as you
wait in line for your propane allocation. LaRue and I
worked these haunts with proficiency, but here in this jumble of trash, metal, and overgrown foliage, what kinds of
things bought information and who did you approach about
it?

"What could these people be trading with?" I asked.

He shook his head. "There's no telling. This colony goes
on for miles in all directions and I suspect has some very
dark crannies."

"Dacey mentioned corruption in the ranks," I said.

"Ritter mentioned river rats," he answered.

"And that would be?"

"A whole subpopulation of who lives on the Black

River. He said we'll start seeing their dinghies and punts
pretty soon. The river rats could be bringing in and out all
kinds of supplies.''

Gibson cursed, interrupting our dialogue. We returned to
Dacey's side, found her out cold, and already turning black-
and-blue along her forehead. When he tipped her face toward us, I saw blood and exposed bone. Silently, we waited
for the good doctor's diagnosis, but instead of announcing
a hard fact that even I could guess, he asked LaRue to help
him carry the woman to sick bay.

I followed them, pausing to glance around before entering the main companionway hatch. The cicadas had stopped
their naiad song and the only sound came from the boat's
chugging engine.

I lingered a moment to make sure our backs were safe
and that's when I saw the sun reflect off of a shimmering
object lying on the deck. My lycanthropy makes me partial
to shiny things and this time was no different. I couldn't
dismiss it as a piece of trash until I checked it for certain,
so I walked over and picked it up.

To my amazement, I held a black pearl the size of a
plum.

SEVEN

Well, scoop my poop deck. Could it really be a pearl, and if so, how could it be possible? My head started filling with all kinds of questions, but the fantasies suddenly began to outweigh logical considerations. A pearl this big could buy food for a lifetime with a few vittles left over for the next one. My roommate, Baba, would know where to take this prize on the backdoor market. No longer would we live at the edge of poverty, reliant upon her pension check and her efforts to earn extra money by weaving trash blankets—throws that were filled out with plastic, aluminum, cardboard, and creativity. Suddenly, like a gift from Davy Jones, we were flush with the wealth of the deep.

I stared at the pearl for several minutes and let my visions run wild, but finally, I pulled myself together and took it along to sick bay, where I found Gibson dabbing at the blood from Dacey's contusion. He didn't pay me any mind as I entered. Stopping in the hatchway, I watched him shower the exec with concern and tenderness. I marveled at the intensity with which he portrayed the compassionate physician, and yes, I know it sounds petty. Dacey was ready to step off the wheel of life, while I'd just been gifted with fortune that had literally fallen out of the sky. Yet, truth be known, I would have gladly given away the pearl if it meant I could get such attention from Gibson whenever I desired it.

Baba would have called me ungrateful and she would have been right. I pushed away my adolescent yearnings and pocketed the gem to leave my hands free. "What can I do?"

"You can find the *Delora*'s doctor," Gibson snapped.

I took a step toward the nearby bulkhead and punched the intercom button. "Dr. Stirling, your presence is requested in sick bay. We've got a crew member down." I released the switch, expecting a reply, but there was none.

Gibson stopped swabbing Dacey's head and became abruptly animated. He laid his ear against her chest, shook his head, and sitting back, he immediately began CPR. LaRue and I stood back, watching him pound on the breast of a dying woman. After five minutes of sweat, effort, and cursing the Grim Reaper, Dacey went the way of her comrades and became one of the lost souls of Davy Jones's locker.

Her death brought several seconds of silence. As tacky as it may sound, I was more interested in finding a good moment in which to gracefully segue into a conversation about the pearl than I was about mourning the passing of a woman I didn't know.

"Well, that was a useless waste of life," Gibson muttered as he pulled a sheet over Dacey's head. "Where the hell is Stirling?"

The quiet that followed his question wasn't the ideal opportunity to launch my announcement, but I couldn't contain my excitement any longer. I dug back into my pocket, glanced at my partner, and said: "Look what I found."

LaRue's mouth fell open, and no matter what he tried, he couldn't force any words beyond his lips. He stood there shaking his head like a fool, and with each twist of his neck, he tried to snag Gibson's attention. I finally helped him out.

"Doc," I said.

"What?" he answered, smoothing the sheet.

"A second of your time, please."

He grunted and lifted his gaze toward me. His expression contained a buildup of aggravation until he saw the pearl. After that, he quickly left thoughts of healing and Hippocratic oaths far behind. A minute passed before he spoke.

"Where did you find it?"

"Lying on the deck. It came over in one of the rock volleys."

LaRue finally found his voice. "How would prisoners get something like this?"

"I don't know," I answered.

"Well, it can't be real," Gibson said, plucking it from my grasp. He studied it like a gem merchant. "This is incredible," he muttered.

"It's also mine," I said. "Let's not forget that."

He frowned, but then let the expression retreat into his wild-eyed squint. "Why don't we make sure it's real before you start spending the money?"

Hell, in my mind, I'd already bought every T-bone steak in the district. "Do you have some way to find out?"

Gibson stepped over to an instrument table and opened the lid on an analyzer. "This machine wasn't designed for this, but it should give us a breakdown of components." After flipping the switch, he moved to a nearby computer monitor and pulled up an electronic graph to watch the readout as the machine supplied the data.

LaRue and I gathered to either side of him.

"What do you see?" LaRue demanded.

Gibson grunted, but instead of answering immediately, he raised his hand to swipe a couple of fingers across his lips while he studied the screen. Then, whispering, he said: "It is a pearl."

I leaned forward, wanting to be sure with my future fortune. "How can you tell?"

"Pearls start out as a bit of foreign matter lodged in the fleshy part of a mollusk. The inside of the oyster shell is lined with a substance known as nacre. It coats the debris, building it up, layer by layer. Nacre is composed of arag-

onite and conchiolin and all elements are present." He
paused to toss me a scowling expression.

"What's the problem?" I asked.

Gibson popped the pearl from the machine and stared at
it before answering. "There's a mathematical law that gov-
erns the way size affects a living organism." We both
looked at him like a couple of class dummies and he was
forced to make the explanation simple. "The bigger the
organism, the slower the metabolism, and the longer the
life. A shrew has a heart rate seven times as fast as a human." He halted his discourse to study me. "Take a moment to consider how your lycanthropy affects you. After
a stretch that leaves you with a body larger in size, shape,
and mass, your metabolism gets faster. That's the odd thing.
You grow in inches, but instead of your furnace slowing
down, it speeds up. You defy the scaling laws that make
evolution predictable."

"So?" I said. "What does that have to do with a pearl?"

"I'm talking about the oyster that made it, Merrick. It
can take anywhere from ten months to five years to grow
a normal pearl, but this thing is enormous. It would require
inordinate amounts of nacre and decades to calcify. That
means the mollusk that made this would have to be the
diameter of this room and a hundred years old."

EIGHT

Since coming down with lycanthropy, I've run up against a variety of oddities and freaks of nature. It's like I'm some kind of supernatural magnet or something. I've faced everything from demons to angels and now Gibson was asking me to believe in giant clams.

"How could that be possible?" I asked.

He shrugged. "I don't know."

"What about all the water pollution?" LaRue said. "Chemical runoff, maybe?"

"It could be. We really don't understand the long-term effects of these things and the Black has had its share of ecological challenges. I noticed an abandoned sluice about ten miles back. I have an idea they were panning for gold on a good-sized scale."

"And they used mercury to separate the ore," I said.

"Yes. Mercury can cause chronic or acute problems in humans, but it won't grow an enormous mollusk."

Gibson was about to continue when my hearing picked up quiet footsteps coming toward the sick bay. I snatched the pearl from the good doctor's hand and stowed it in the top pocket of my cammies, making sure I secured the Velcro closing. The hatch swung open and Dr. Stephen Stir-

ling, the *Delora*'s physician, climbed into the room. He cast
an eye toward Dacey, but instead of going to her, he looked
at Gibson.

"What happened?" he asked.

"She was clobbered with a rock," I said. "Where the
hell were you when we were attacked by the inmates?"

"Down below in the engine room," he answered sheepishly. "I didn't know she was injured until a minute ago."

Stirling stared at me for a second, and I got the impression that he could tap both sides of the medical can—sym-
pathetic physician or mad doctor. It was nothing in his
mannerism to betray him, but I've been an investigator long
enough to know when a hunch hits me square in the sails.

He addressed us in a quiet voice. "I've had two other
crewmen die on me under similar circumstances."

"There were no mentions of these deaths in the reports
sent over to the Marshals Office," I said.

He shrugged. "Bureaucrats and paperwork. Everything
was filed according to regulation."

Gibson snorted and refused to let go of his indignant act,
so LaRue and I filled in his mutters and grunts with actual
questions.

"How long have you been with the RP, Dr. Stirling?"
LaRue asked.

He tactfully avoided the question by staring at the corpse,
but it wasn't enough for him to shake me off. "How
long?" I growled.

"Thirty-two years," he snapped. "I should have retired
four years ago, but I can't afford to."

"You hide your age well."

He sighed. "What does the length of my career have to
do with anything?"

"Have you always been assigned to river duty?"

"Yes."

"Then you know how the inmates think," LaRue said.

"No, I don't. I will never understand this insane concoction of reincarnation and magic."

"It's a pervasive trend among the prison population, so
we understand."

Stirling sneered. "Funny, isn't it? They believe in the
laws of karma, where the world is divided into universal
energies of cause and effect. Yet they never fail to amaze
me. A normal man would worry about heaping on additional karma. He would worry about how further indiscre-
tions would affect him in his next incarnation. But the
prisoners don't. They know their accumulated karma has
brought them to this place and they know their actions and
bad decisions have caused them to forfeit their souls to
Davy Jones. So, I ask you: why not cause trouble?"

I stepped over to the chair by the bed and sat down.
Speaking in a low voice, I said: "There's an old saying,
Dr. Stirling, that talks about biting the hand that feeds
you."

"What are you talking about?"

"I'm talking about this labor camp. I'm talking about
something besides the supernatural. The people firing rocks
at us were using a diesel generator. They've got to be getting the fuel from somewhere, despite regulations against
provisioning the penal colony unless authorized."

"The river rats will trade their souls for supplies. I'm
sure they bargain for all kinds of things."

"And that brings up a serious question."

"Which is?"

"What do the prisoners have that anyone would want?"

Stirling stared at me for thirty seconds before answering.
"All they have are their miserable lives."

"Are the guards operating a backdoor market out here?"

"I don't know," he said. "It may be hard to believe, but
I stay out of the way. Period."

I was going to have to drag the confession out of him.
"You've been here your whole adult life, Stirling." When
he didn't reply, I lost the hold on my patience. "It may be
that we should be looking closely at you."

That got his attention. "Why?"

I pushed his anxiety level to see if I could get anything
to break on the surface besides sweat. "For starters, I'm
wondering about this sick bay. The rest of the boat is ready
for the scrap yard, but you've got a nice little setup here.

That tells me you know people and can pull strings. Either that, or you've got something on someone. Which is it?"

"You're tacking down the wrong river," he said flatly. "Why?"

"Because I had nothing to do with the refitting of this sick bay. Check with the dock. They'll tell you."

Gibson entered the conversation by stepping to the sink to wash his hands. "Why don't you tell us about an inmate named Derek Wheeler."

Stirling loaded up a frown, but instead of delivering it into a scowl, he looked at the floor. "How did you find out about that?"

"I don't leave home without knowing something about the people I'll be working with. Especially doctors."

"What happened?" LaRue demanded.

"Derek Wheeler was a water witch with considerable influence in cell block two. He was dying and neither the prefect warden nor the inmates wanted that to happen."

"So, I take it the guards sent for you to try to avert a possible riot."

"The warden was worried his death might cause some trouble. Being that we're woefully understaffed out here, any kind of altercation can become serious."

"What was wrong with Wheeler?"

"When I looked at the guy I knew right away it was some form of Hansen's disease. He was missing fingers and his ears and nose had started rotting away. He also suffered from pneumonia."

"Did you help him?" LaRue asked.

"I gave him what I had in my medical bag, but there wasn't much I could do. The boats just don't carry that kind of medicine. I told the guards they would have to request an emergency airlift."

"Not likely for one prisoner, huh?"

"No. Sometimes the bastards running the show should pull their heads out of their asses. It wouldn't have hurt to help Wheeler."

"What happened after Wheeler died?" I asked.

Stirling walked to the hatch, signaling an end to his co-operation. "What happened after Wheeler died? My guess is the inmates buried him."

NINE

LaRue, Gibson, and I left Ritter the problem of disposing of Dacey's body and found a secluded spot at the portside railing. I glanced at Gibson and noticed he was pale. "What's the matter?"

He shook his head. "Death is the matter, Merrick. I'd forgotten how bad these penal colonies can be. It's like trying to stay ahead of the law of the jungle."

"I thought it was the law of karma we were up against," I answered.

"Okay, smart-ass. Whatever you say." He took a couple of breaths before continuing. "I have my reservations about Stirling. His records appear to be on the up-and-up, but there may be more to him than meets the eye."

"Records can be doctored," LaRue said. "Most government agencies do it as a matter of course anymore. I doubt there are very many honest bureaucrats who let the truth lie open for all to see."

"Do you believe he's incompetent?" I asked.

"Yes," Gibson answered. "He's got degrees from the university, postgrad work, and an internship spent at the hospital in District One. In fact, one of the records indicates he headed a joint study with the Planetary Health Organization and the River Patrol on exotic diseases that infect penal colonies." He paused to toss a baleful look across the river. "Still, his lack of enthusiasm during a medical emergency gives me further qualms."

I nodded and shifted my gaze toward the bank. It was overgrown and run-down and the smokestacks of abandoned, crumbling factories punched up through the tall, thick trees. Going into this maze of old appliances and junk cars was bad enough, but the vegetation choked the land, complicating matters by making travel difficult. It also provided good cover for criminals and a good deal of danger for us. "Tell me, Gibson," I said. "What experience do you have with labor camps?"

"I worked with a team of scientists during my humanitarian service duty." He grunted and leaned on the railing. "I was a kid, armed with nothing more than misplaced values and a year of premed school under my belt. Damn, I was stupid. It was probably a good thing, though."

"Why?"

"Because it kept me from being frightened."

"What happened?" LaRue asked.

"It was a labor camp in District Thirty-eight; one a lot like this. They had an outbreak of a disease that resembled smallpox."

"Resembled?"

"Yes, Andy. It was a bad situation. This disease was the result of an unknown strain. It affected those people who'd never been inoculated with the original smallpox virus and spared those who had been, even though the vaccine was not intended to handle the mutated form."

"Did a lot of people die?"

He nodded. "After the Duvalier came to power, the vaccination program was suspended for almost two decades, so, theoretically, that left millions of folks who had never been inoculated. It was a hell of scare for us. Over three-quarters of the prison population succumbed to the disease. The guards were spared, because government service required the usual vaccine series be given to the employee." Gibson braked the moment of his explanation by falling silent and staring at the shoreline, but I could tell his line of sight was focused on the past. "We had piles of corpses," he whispered. "They were everywhere." He let his words fade once more and swallowed hard against invading memories. Finally, he grunted, a signal that he was about to add the kicker. "Do you know what the worst part of the whole affair was?"

"No," I murmured.

"The Planetary Health Organization denied this disease ever existed."

TEN

Gibson returned to the sick bay, and after he stomped off, LaRue and I decided to see Riverman Stan Russo.

We found him oiling the dredge motor. He was a large, sturdy man who wore a hangdog face while he smoked an illegal cigarette. Between puffs, he hacked so hard I thought he was going to spit up a lung.

"Russo, we'd like a few minutes with you," I said.

He shot me a sad expression. I couldn't tell if it was just his basset-hound look, or whether he was genuinely upset over something. It turned out to be the latter.

"Slimy bastards," he muttered. "I heard they smacked Wil with a rock."

LaRue momentarily checked out of the interview to study the dredge, so I carried the load. "Yes, they did. Unfortunately, it was a mortal wound."

"So, she's dead, huh?"

I nodded.

He sighed, dropped the oil can, and sat down on the deck to face me. "That is a real shame. Wil was a great gal. Weren't nothing she wouldn't try to do for a folk. Good-hearted. Always made me wonder why she was wasting her time floating up and down this evil river."

"Maybe you can help us clear up a few of the more troubling aspects of this investigation," I said.

"I don't know anything. Honest."

"You were aboard the *Delora* the night Lilith Chamberlin was murdered."

"Yes. But I was asleep. Too much vodka, I'm afraid. It's the only way I can get any sack time anymore."

"Why? Because you're frightened traveling through the penal colony?"

He chuckled, but it turned into a cough. "I stopped being frightened a long time ago, Marshal. No, I get drunk for the same reason everybody else does—so my view of this hell is blurry. It's better that way."

I steered the subject away from alcoholism. "What are your duties aboard the *Delora*, Mr. Russo?"

"I make sure the dredge operates while we're on our tour of duty."

"Is that all you do?"

"Sometimes I monkey for other cutters. If they have minor problems with their dredges, I help the crew out. When we're in dock, I service and refit machinery."

"It must be a sizable operation under way in the delta," I said.

"Oh, yeah. It's big. Takes a lot of manpower, too."

"That manpower would be in the form of forced labor for the prisoners."

He frowned. "Something wrong with that? I mean they are in a labor camp."

"I'm not stepping on the soapbox," I answered. "We're just trying to get the feel for the figures."

"Oh. Well, the figures are up there. Lots of inmates."

"Do you ever talk to the prisoners?"

"Have a conversation? Are you crazy? I don't even want to be near them."

"Then it might be a long jump to think the crew trades goods with the prisoners."

"It might be a hell of a long jump, Marshal. No one aboard this boat does any trading."

"No one?"

He took a drag on his cigarette, blew a smoke ring, and considered my question. "Not that I know about. Most everybody feels the same way I do. The inmates are useful for one thing—hard work. They don't have much else worth bothering about. Besides, it's against the regulations to fraternize with the prisoners. It'll earn you a demerit on your labor manifest if you get caught. Too many of them and you give the government just one more excuse to blow away any hope of a pension. Nope. It would be crazy to diddle over the trash the inmates could offer."

"Is Captain Ritter the type of guy who would cut you some slack for trading with the prisoners?"

He shrugged. "I don't know Ritter real well. He's only gone down the Black a few times with me aboard. Of course, the brass is all the same, you know. What's good for the Class-A designations ain't necessarily good for anybody else."

"Do you recall hearing stories about a prisoner named Derek Wheeler?"

Russo nodded and flicked his cigarette butt into the water. "What about him?"

"Who was he?"

"I heard he was a water witch."

"What else did you hear?"

"That after he died, his spirit got to be a walk-in."

The mention of supernatural possibilities drew LaRue from the dredge. "He got to be a walk-in?"

"Yeah. That's right. I don't know the particulars, though. Afraid I can't be much help there. You can never tell what's the truth and what ain't when you listen to scuttlebutt." He chuckled again. "And I love my scuttlebutt."

Our world is an exaggerated place of myth and legend, the worst part being that fifty miles down the road, a concept so familiar suddenly becomes alien. In the district, a walk-in spirit takes over the body of a dying man, intent upon fulfilling the old soul's destiny as well as its own agenda. A walk-in spirit manages to avoid a future round of rebirth and can also blow off the trials and tribulations of childhood before resuming the course of its incarnate mission. Just by taking a casual look around the backdoor market, you can find all kinds of charms intended to send the souls of dead relatives on to another body so they can complete their tasks. Still, I was operating from an urban perspective, so it was better to let LaRue pound Russo with the metaphysical questions.

"Why would Wheeler rate becoming a walk-in?" he asked. "I thought that was a karmic state of grace, intended to help those souls who are advancing the welfare of others on the material plane."

The riverman studied us for a few moments. "I heard that Derek Wheeler stole his soul from someone else. Someone who had power and fate all wrapped up together inside them. He used it for evil and I don't have to tell you—evil begets evil. But then, karma will trip you up every time."

"What do you mean?"

"I mean, Marshal, that you can't take the eggs without paying the price of the hen. He couldn't change the destiny of the soul he stole. Fate is fate. Can't diddle with that."

"So, you're saying the soul had an obligation to complete its prebirth choices and fulfill its earthly mission, no matter how much Wheeler tried to steer the outcome in another direction."

"Yep, so I hear."

LaRue didn't bat an eyelash at this insane idea. "How could Wheeler have stolen the soul?"

"Witches can do anything they want," Russo answered. "He probably had help from the Coven."

"Tell us about the Coven."

"They're a group of water witches drawn from the ranks of the trustees. The scuttlebutt says they side with the screws." Russo rose and I heard his bones crack as he did. He fished in his jumpsuit pocket for a cigarette before continuing. "Derek Wheeler was no friend to the prisoners," he said flatly. "Like I said, the inmates got one thing going for them—hard work—but getting them to cooperate is the trick."

ELEVEN

Later that day we passed a death barge called, of all things: the *Flying Dutchman*. If there was any chance for a ghost ship to exist beyond the imagination, this rusty flat-bottom tender was a good candidate. Its cargo consisted of corpses her crew had picked up along the edges of the river camp. A bold red-and-gold awning protected the dead from the sun, but could do nothing to stop the humidity and the flies. In the heat and the sweat, the sickly-sweet smell of decay attached itself to the pathetic breeze and tried to enter the living upon every breath.

The rivermen who worked the *Flying Dutchman* didn't seem to notice the rankness of the atmosphere. As the *Delora* pulled alongside, the garbage scow's foreman trudged across the bodies like he was hiking across rough terrain. He leaned casually upon the railing while he dug a boot heel into someone's old, used head. There he stood, calmly conferring with the captain, oblivious to the death beneath his feet. LaRue and I moved closer to watch this meeting. Gibson joined us to take advantage of a captive audience and to bellyache about the senseless loss of life.

Ritter's words drifted over to us as he spoke to the fore-man. "My exec was killed in an attack on the boat," he said. "I can't keep the body on board the *Delora*. No fridge."

"We've got a ferry fee, Captain," the foreman answered. "Fifty credits for the time, trouble, and danger incurred."

Ritter's rubber face contorted at the price. "It was death by accident. There aren't any diseases present."

"Disintegration is a disease producer, Captain. Fifty credits. No more, no less."

Like the ancient Greek myth of Charon, the boatman who ferried the dead to Hades, the foreman was intent on receiving payment up front for services rendered. Ritter didn't even try to bargain with him. He simply nodded, pulled out his wallet, and paid in paper credits.

"I have to say, Merrick," Gibson whispered, "I'm glad it was Dacey and not you."

I glanced at him to see if he wore a genuine expression. It was always hard to tell about him because of the intensity flowing through his features and mannerisms. When I couldn't confirm my question, I put him on the spot. "Whose miserable life are you glad about not losing? Mine or the wolf's?"

He studied me, but in the end, he shook his head slightly and let his attention waft away across the river. I wished right then and there I could follow his thoughts and see where his feelings went.

Gibson and I rub ourselves raw from grating on each other, and since meeting him, I've discovered new definitions of integrity. We've waded through rivers of distrust, lies, and unbridled passions. No matter what we do to find a smoother course, we keep tripping over jagged rocks and nearly drown in our own discord.

I suppose that's why LaRue sees us engaged in some cosmic fugue down through the centuries. Yet the truth of the matter is far more simple. Gibson and I are nothing more than pure expressions of karma. We are cause and effect and our relationship is merely the vehicle to continue the pain.

Rather than dwell on an imperfect destiny, I mustered every ounce of mental strength I had and pushed this old

problem away by watching the barge's crane swing the litter over to the *Delora*.

Stirling and Neilson brought the body bag topside and
fitted Dacey into the carrier while the other members of the
crew gathered on the poop deck to bid their comrade a quiet
farewell. The moment the body was lifted from the *Delora*'s deck, the bos'n mate began piping a sorrowful tune
on a homemade pennywhistle. I never heard the whole
song, because those sad strains contained enough power to
unleash the wolf and launch me into a lycanthropic stretch.

The pain exploded in my solar plexus and then went
supernova. I screamed and collapsed on the deck, writhing
against the blast of heat tracing down my nerve endings.
LaRue and Gibson rushed to me and my ever-thoughtful
partner did his best to block the view of the *Delora*'s crew
while the good doctor kept me from doing harm to myself
by sitting on me.

Gibson has taught me biofeedback and self-hypnosis,
studied my gray matter for misfiring neurons, and measured
my crippled psyche, hoping for some answers to my lycanthropy. He's found some short-term fixes, but nothing that
survives the violence of the lunar transformation. Though
he's not discovered the source of the cord that links me to
the wolf, he has managed to do one thing with all his dink-
ing around: he's freed this demon by giving him the run of
my brain. In the years before I started letting Gibson experiment on me, I had painful, but consistent stretches. The
shape of my eyes would change; my bones would lengthen;
my stamina would increase. All these things I expected and
lived with it, but interference from psychiatrists, doctors,
and nuclear scans have left me with new neurological dysfunction.

Recently I spent two weeks totally cut off from everyone
and everything, because a stretch slung me into global
aphasia, a cerebral disturbance that affects language and the
ability to process it. This storm in my brain made it impossible for me to speak and write. When people talked to
me, my brain turned their words into a jumble of meaningless sounds. When they tried to make their intentions

known by writing me notes, I couldn't read them. Conversely, the things I tried to relate were as nonsensical to others as their communications were to me.

Strangely, though, in those tense weeks separated from humanity, I learned to use the range of my paranormal gifts, because with the aphasia came a condition known as synesthesia or blended senses. I couldn't make words come together, but my comprehension expanded when I started associating smells to the bright patterns and colors they left on my optic nerve. Yet five minutes into the stretch, I clung to Gibson with apprehension in my heart, because the odor wafting off the death barge was no longer sickly sweet. My nose and my eyes had linked and now death smelled like soft, saffron rectangles.

TWELVE

The seconds ticked down and I was sure I was in for some big aggravation. Stirling had hurried over at the first sign of trouble, but didn't raise a finger to offer any assistance. Even in my labored state, I knew he watched me intently, studying my twitching, and, I am sure, with the scrutiny of a scientist, he noticed the little changes that overcame me.

Finally, the pain stopped. By that time Ritter had joined us to see what the problem was and the crew peeked at me from guarded positions along the cutter. Normally, this amount of curiosity would piss me off and I would lash out like the animal I had come to be, but this time I found that I didn't have energy enough to care.

Gibson murmured in my ear. "Merrick, can you understand me?"

It took me a moment before I realized his words made sense. "Yes," I whispered. "Can you understand me?"

He didn't keep me in suspense any longer than necessary. "You're as crystal clear as ever."

I heard LaRue sigh. He patted me on the shoulder and then left me to the tender efforts of the good doctor. Stirling and Ritter, though, wanted explanations.

"What's the matter with you?" the captain demanded.

"She has a form of temporal-lobe epilepsy," Gibson answered. He paused to run his knuckle lightly across my cheeks. Then: "She's not contagious."

Stirling wasn't buying it. "I've seen temporal-lobe epilepsy. That woman has something else wrong with her."

"Why would the Marshals' Office send us someone who is sick?" Ritter asked. "Do they think this is some kind of joke?"

Gibson grunted, but didn't reply immediately. Instead, he rose and helped me to stand before facing Stirling. When he finally answered, his voice was gruff. "Marshal Merrick has had this condition for several years. It hasn't impeded her efficiency."

What a way to twist the scuttlebutt. I couldn't help smiling.

"How can she help us catch a murderer if she has such violent seizures? How unpredictable is her condition?"

The bastard was talking about me like I wasn't there. Just as Gibson opened his mouth to respond LaRue stepped into the conversation by speaking first.

"Captain Ritter, Marshal Merrick's condition is very unpredictable," he said in a hard voice. "It's also her condition that makes her so valuable to the Marshals' Office. You can believe Dr. Gibson when he tells you that she's not contagious."

The man sighted past LaRue to stare at me. This new stretch had lengthened my bones and put some ripple into my muscles. My cammies were now too short for my frame and the tops of my boots showed. At the end of this inspection, it was not Ritter who made mention of my small transformations; it was Stirling.

"Your face is different," he said. "Explain to me how temporal-lobe epilepsy can change the shape, tilt, and color of her eyes?"

According to the tests Gibson had performed on me, my eyeballs completely alter during the lunar month. Gone is the diurnal shape of a human eye and in its place is the arrhythmic eye commonly found in lions, bears, and wolves. My sight grows sharper as well, and glancing around, I saw that the world had taken on that familiar "Van Gogh glow," where all things gleamed like the painter's vision of a *Starry Night*.

I don't like to admit it, but these changes, subtle though they are, betray the fact that I walk between dimensions. It doesn't matter whether the planes are accessed on an astral level or simply caught inside my malfunctioning brain. Thought manifests reality again and again, and in my universe, lycanthropy is a fact of life. Still, sitting there suffering under conspicuous examination, I took the insanity a step farther by wondering if I endured this malady to fulfill a karmic lesson I'd chosen to undertake between incarnations.

I shook my head and tried to find my resistance to easy metaphysical solutions, but the action only dislodged a hot flash. It branded my nerve endings and made me feel flush; so much so that I groped for the railing in case my knees gave out.

Thankfully, the show ended quickly when Riverman Harvey interrupted us. He appeared on the deck, stopping to rub his chin and squint at me.

"What is it?" LaRue said.

"Dr. Wilson has established radio contact with us," he reported. "He wishes for you to return his call immediately."

LaRue pointed with his hand. "Lead on, Mr. Harvey."

As soon as the riverman turned around and marched off, my partner leaned over to speak in my ear. "Way to go, Ty. Alienate them up front, I always say."

I nodded and took a tentative step, glad to find I had my balance. As I followed, the heat slowly evaporated.

LaRue is one to talk about alienation. He gives the impression that he's a good-natured slob, but his firm beliefs in the metaphysical, his ability to run his mouth for hours on subjects no one cares about, and his tendency toward short bouts of explosive lethality tends to put most people off. Consequently, I'm the only marshal who willingly works with him, a situation that suits me just fine.

Gathering around the radio equipment, we spent several

minutes listening to Harvey raise static. He apologized several times.

"The *Delora* is starting to move out of the district's array," he explained.

"We need to talk to him, Harvey," I growled.

He nodded furiously and fiddled with the computer connection. "Hailing District One dock operator," he called to the microphone. "This is the River Cutter *Delora*. Come in, Debbie. Over."

Static escaped to whiz around the room. Then; "Go ahead, *Delora*."

"Please patch us through to Dr. Frank Wilson, over."

The voice faded for a moment, but grew strong again. "He's holding on the land line now, Harvey. Linking communications."

A minute passed and I thought we'd lost our medical examiner for good, but just as I was about to head for the hatch, the radio came to life. "Go ahead, *Delora*."

I stepped forward for the group and picked up the mike. "What's the word, Frank?"

The delay placed his answer thirty seconds into the future. "Not good, Merrick. I got the specialist to hustle on this one and he actually made a fast report. The leprosy bacteria is an unknown strain. There isn't anything comparable to it on the books."

Gibson swore under his breath, but I spoke for him. "What about that AB-negative blood type?"

"I've gone through the records of all inmates at the labor camp. There's only twenty prisoners listed with the AB combination and some of them are listed as deceased."

Gibson took his turn by grabbing the mike from me. "That's impossible in a population this dense."

"I know it," Wilson answered. "There was no one aboard the *Delora* at the time of the murder who typed AB, either."

"The same goes for this crew," Gibson said.

I could almost see Wilson shaking his head. After thirty seconds charged with radio noise, we heard him once more.

"I have no indication that the data has been tampered with, but you know how that is."

"Frank, do you have the information with you?" I asked.

"Yeah."

"Look up the name Derek Wheeler. You might have a toe tag on him."

"Hold on." Then; "Merrick, are you there?"

"Yes, Frank. What do you have?"

"Derek Wheeler is listed as deceased." His report was stomped on by more static.

I keyed the mike frantically. "Come on, Wilson. Where are you?"

We must have hit a clear spot for the signal, because suddenly his voice boomed across the radio. "When Wheeler entered the penal colony, he was listed as AB negative. At the time of death he was listed as O positive."

THIRTEEN

After a dinner of chicken stew and greasy sausages, LaRue and I decided to take a look at the river from the perch of the bridge, so just after sunset, we made our way there to find Riverman Pilot Amos Kleege the only one manning the boat.

He was a tall, lanky man who took long sips of warm vodka from a bottle he didn't bother trying to hide. A cigarette, having long since burned down to a snake of ash, rested between his dirty fingers, and as I approached him I realized he smelled like his liquor. My synesthesia made me sensitive to his odor by splashing my optic nerve with red splotches. I shut my eyes against the colors, but short of not breathing, there was nothing I could do except move to the other side of the room until my sniffer sensitized to the smell. I stared out the observation portal and watched the floodlights skim across the darkening shapes on the far shore. As I waited for my nose to stop interfering with my eyes, LaRue decided on an impromptu interview.

"I thought the captain threw out the anchor at night," he said.

"Not this time of year," Kleege answered. He paused to take a sip. Then; "It's spring you worry about sandbars and such. This time of year the Black has a good, strong current. If we stay to the shipping channel and the god-damned river rats get out of our way, we can keep running until we get to Three Sisters' Slip. We'll lay over nights while navigating the channel.''

"Why? Lots of river rats?''

Kleege shrugged. "Them bastards are everywhere. Get damned thick starting in cell block two, but they ain't half the problem.''

"What is, then?''

"The water witches. They got karma spells cast all over the place. It's like trying to push through a magical fishing net. They snare all kinds of shit right there.''

"What are you talking about?'' I snapped.

Kleege swigged at his vodka before answering. "Karmic spells dink with the quality of harmony in the world. The witches weave this energy so that cause and effect is warped.''

"For every action, there is a reaction,'' LaRue said. "The witches know how to control the normal physical vibration.''

"So, what's new about that?'' I asked. "Everyone you talk to claims to be able to manipulate the natural frequen-cies. What's so different about karmic spells?''

"The chaos caused by these drubs sticks to you. You carry along the inconsistencies caused by the changes in the energy patterns. If you don't get a clearing, then you risk taking this shit into your next life. I always get cleared before my tour of duty is over.''

LaRue pestered him for more insight. "What kinds of things happen when you push through this karmic net?''

"Well, the biggest purpose of such vile spells is to wreck the boat and send the sailors off for an eternity to lick the bottom of Davy Jones's boots. Aside from that, the witches open doors in the fabric of time and space. This lets through the goddamned lost souls.'' He checked a computer screen, took a suck of booze, and rambled on. "The bad part of this is the rotten karma the ghosts bring with them. Crap hangs on to a person even after death, and if you die on the water, it's most likely a traumatic experience full of negativity. So long as the souls are safe in the briny deep, this energy can't escape, but let a witch fiddle-faddle and there is hell to pay. This nastiness mixes up with the regular karma all normal people have.''

LaRue pursued this absurd line of reasoning. ''I suspect you've seen your share of lost souls during your years as a river pilot, huh?''

''Well, I do got the sight.''

I turned back from my review of the river. ''You can see ghosts?''

''I can see lots of supernatural things,'' he answered. ''And don't go blaming it on the vodka.''

''What kinds of supernatural things do you see?''

He glanced at me and then lazily shifted his gaze once more to the glowing monitor. ''I've seen mermaids several times. They mostly appear during the full moons, all naked and glistening.''

''I thought mermaids lived in the sea,'' LaRue said.

''For a fact, they do. But there are those who mind the river, too.''

''What do you mean, 'mind the river'?''

''They eat the sludge and the filth we humans dump into her. They're the skimmers that keep the river's soul clean.'' He lifted his attention to study me for a moment. ''Of course, with all the chemicals we push into the water, I'm sure the river could use a few more such stewards.'' Kleege paused again to wet his whistle with liquor. ''Things are just plumb out of control on the Black.''

''Like what?'' I asked.

''We had a tidal bore last year.''

Our naive, landlubber expressions made Kleege laugh, and from the sound underlying his guffaws, I was sure he was going to hack out his lung in the meantime. Then, sniffing at the snot threatening to escape the end of his long nose, he explained. ''A tidal bore is a breaking wave that moves upriver with three to four times the speed and momentum of the normal tide.''

''I take it that's not a common occurrence?''

"No, Miss Marshal, it isn't. Most often it occurs because of the narrowing of the tributary."

"Is there narrowing along the Black River?" LaRue said.

"How do you think the Vivian Narrows got its name?" he asked. "It's like trying to navigate through the neck of a bottle." He sipped his vodka again and then explained further. "The wave is highest along the banks and last year's bore rolled through here and washed down the camp. Swamped a whole hell of a lot of boats. The only reason the *Delora* didn't go down was because I was at the wheel."

"Do you have any idea what caused it?"

He shrugged and then offered his own metaphysical theory. "I think it was an energy vortex formed up by karmic spells that collected in the time pockets downriver. You can't keep polluting the world and think that it won't fight back." Reaching into his shirt, he displayed a charm shaped like a half-moon and decorated in delicate scrimshaw designs. "That's why I got me this."

"What is that?"

"A charm to ward off all the bad vibes. Since I've had it, I've been protected." Holding it toward the overhead fluorescent bulb, he drew us in to study it by letting the light reflect off the piece. "It's a beauty, don't you think?"

I leaned toward him but not close enough to encounter his stink. It was lovely, artfully carved with mystical symbols. Upon seeing it, I decided it was time to play with him. "Does it protect you from the giant water moccasins and slime lizards?"

Kleege squinted at me. "It protects me from everything. I haven't been dinner for a big, old alligator, if that's what you mean."

"Are there giant creatures living here in the river?" I demanded.

He was quick to answer. "There are some big bastards, yes. It's all the crap they pour in from the waste-disposal plants upriver. Where do you think the shit goes in all those toilets in the district?"

"Do you think it keeps you safe from the attacks on the *Delora*?" LaRue asked.

"Yes, indeed," he said.

"Why do you think the prisoners are hitting the River Patrol?" I said.

He stared at me for a minute before replying in a quiet voice. "I figure they're chucking rocks at us because they don't want us to find their hidden treasure."

I glanced at LaRue just as a frown enfolded his face. "What treasure?"

"Well, I ain't for sure about it. You'll have to ask the captain, but knowing him, it would probably be a waste of time. He's closemouthed about the whole subject. Top secret, hush-hush. Only his exec knew about it and Wil is dead." He stopped again to soak his palate in vodka. Then: "It must be something spectacular, though. Why else would the government have us looking for it?"

FOURTEEN

It was only a few minutes after our interview on the bridge that Gibson invited me down to sick bay so he could torture me with some more neurological tests. I tried to beg off, but he wouldn't let me. He kept going on about the opportunity to use free equipment and then he reminded me that like it or not, he owned me for as long as he wanted. Once his custody period was up for review, he would report my condition as deteriorating. Do you want to know the worse part of this ploy? Such a report would be the truth.

I reluctantly gave in and followed him to sick bay. Once there, he turned on a series of blue-filtered lights, which, combined with the gray bulkheads, gave the room a restful feeling. It also helped the sensitivity in my eyes.

Gibson pointed to the bunk where Dacey had died. When I threw him a questioning look, he nodded knowingly. "Don't worry, it's been disinfected and the linens changed. I helped Stirling wash it up this afternoon."

I sighed and sat down on the edge. "What is it you'll be looking at this time?"

He slid into the chair beside the bunk before answering. "I'm trying to figure out why you're getting synesthesia."

He only had to ask me. Interference in my brain, pure and simple. "What are you going to do?"

"I'm going to create a full metabolic portrait of you," he said. "By tracking certain compounds in your system, such as your glucose levels, I can measure how they're metabolized by your brain and other organs."

"What will that prove?"

"It will give me a baseline, as of this date, regarding your brain's pathology as well as corroborating data about the changes that occur in your body. You see, Merrick, I can't find a satisfying neurological connection for this symptom. Our metabolisms react in different ways to stress by interacting with the body's endocrine functions, and if anything can be said of your condition, it's that it is stressful."

"Is this test going to hurt?" I asked.

He didn't answer right away; instead, he studied me with his characteristic intensity. Then, standing, he held out his hand. I rose, and before I had a chance to brush him away, he took my wrist and ran his fingers down my palm until he interlaced them with mine. Silently, he led me into the sick bay's testing room.

Gibson paused to bathe the area in more blue light and yet he never released my hand. He pointed to a large, circular opening in the bulkhead. "That is called a hydrotomography unit. State-of-the-art. Why it's on board a Patrol Cutter is beyond me. It should be at a main facility in District One, where a lot of people can benefit from it."

I pulled free of him to inspect it. He followed and, flicking on a switch, illuminated the interior. It was smooth and white inside and was fitted with a sliding examining table.

"It works similar to a PET scanner. It's surrounded with particle-charged water which makes mapping of the entire body possible—everything from chemicals to cellular alterations. Like I said—this is a new concept." He punched a button on a nearby computer and the table rolled outward. "You lie on this and ride it back inside. The machine does the rest."

I stared at him. "You didn't answer my question. Will it hurt?"

He sighed through his nose. "The test won't hurt, Merrick."

"But?"

"I may have to push you into a lycanthropic seizure to measure the changes."

In the past Gibson has forced me into a stretch by first inducing a hypnogogic state in me and then giving me a series of words that seem to spark the wolf to life. The one and only time he did it, I had all the agony of the lycanthropic seizure without the benefits. There were no changes—no increased stamina, no growth, no extra strength. Not only did it not produce more evidence of my supernatural state, but it had royally pissed me off that he'd done it without my permission. It tore the fabric of my trust and it had been a long time returning in proper measure. Gibson was acutely aware of this breach and continually tried to repair it, and this time he kept to his campaign by being up-front with me. He even tried to coax me into doing his bidding by adding in a bit of sexual arousal to the stew of decision-making juices.

Reaching over, he flicked a lock of hair from my face, and before I knew what was happening, we were belly to belly, necking like two teenagers.

Bastard. Gibson knew I turned traitor to my own feelings when he turned on his tenderness. He'd been using my weaknesses for him to slick advantage ever since he betrayed me with his dishonesty. My desire for him continued to grow, and like my ability to control my lycanthropy, my ability to spurn his affections was equally lost to me.

Thankfully, the boat's klaxon sounded to prevent me from jumping into lycanthropic pain on a promised return of intimate companionship. The screaming of the siren knocked us both out of a fierce lip lock and sent us running topside. Once we climbed onto the deck, we saw that LaRue was the cause of all the commotion. He hung from the hatch of the bridge waving at us.

"What is it, Andy?" I called.

"It's Kleege, Ty. I found him murdered."

Gibson and I climbed like baboons up the ladder, followed close on the heels by Captain Ritter and Riverman Russo.

I entered the bridge and stopped short to stare at Kleege's bleeding body. His throat had been slit, he'd been shot through the heart by what looked like a water rifle, and his left ear and right hand were missing. Gibson knelt beside him and double-checked his vital signs, shaking his head when he didn't find any.

"What happened?" Ritter demanded.

"I don't know," LaRue said. "I returned to ask him a couple more questions and I found him like this." He glanced at me. "It wasn't more than an hour."

Russo hunkered down beside the pilot. "Ah, Kleege, you old son of a bitch. Why'd you have to go and get yourself killed like this?"

"Did you see anything unusual, Andy?" I asked.

"No. I passed the evening watch and nothing seemed out of the ordinary."

"Hey, his scrimshaw is gone," Russo announced.

LaRue and I turned our attention in unison and settled it upon the dead man's neck. He was right—the good-luck charm was missing.

I took a step toward the body. The odor of Kleege's blood settled heavily into my nostrils and bricked up my sight with saffron rectangles. I stepped away from the stink and walked over to the porthole, searching for a breath of air that didn't cause my senses to blend, but once there, I was accosted by a new smell, one that produced stacks of golden squares in my vision.

I may have been reading more into it than was there, yet something told me the scent had been left by the killer.

FIFTEEN

It didn't take long to order the evening watch to the bridge. There were two of the unfortunates: Riverman Recruit Brian Hogan and Riverman Third-Class Anthony Curran. As they took the deck and came to attention, I walked by them looking for that strong smell of yellow bubbles. Nothing; not even a pale yellow bubble.

The captain read them the river riot act while LaRue and I stared out the observation portal. We were at a dead stop in the middle of the shipping lane. Night had come on with a thunk of finality; the mist was as thick as coconut-cream pie; and if I squinted, I could see the flickering lights of campfires tracing up the side of the far bank.

"I didn't hear a thing," LaRue whispered. "Did you?"

I almost couldn't suppress a smile, but in the end, I forced my lips flat and shook my head. "Water rifles make noise, Andy."

"Unless it's been adapted with some sort of silencer."

"We were under way," I said.

He nodded. "But we were moving at a slow speed. Plenty of time for someone to catch up with *Delora* in a smaller skiff."

"What about a stowaway?"

"It's possible, but they'd have to hide pretty damned well."

"Not if they had friends on board." I glanced over to Gibson and wagged a finger at him. He rose from his inspection of the body to join us.

"Do you two have some ideas?"

"We're as dry as bones right now," I answered. "Can you do some forensics work for us?"

"Autopsy?"

"That and physical samples from the murder scene. Get Stirling to help you."

"I'll see what I can do. Am I looking for something in particular?"

"I don't know. Use your medical imagination." This time I unleashed a smile. "You're very good at that."

He grunted and walked back to the corpse without another word. LaRue and I suffered until the end of Ritter's enthusiastic display of anger before taking over.

"Captain, would you and Dr. Stirling please leave us for a few minutes?" I asked politely.

Ritter tossed me a sour expression that twisted his rubbery face into an odd angle. "We're not done here."

I continued to soothe him. "You can return to make your crewmen walk the plank if you see fit, but right now we'd like a word with them without the interference of an officer."

I may have been a tad less than tactful with that last part, because he squinted, obviously taking momentary offense. After a short staring match, he conceded and barked to Stirling. LaRue locked the bridge hatch behind them.

Gibson stayed with the body, making observations and writing them on a piece of paper he'd snatched from the *Delora*'s log book. LaRue began the interview by taking a moment to run his finger over a string of dried frog legs hanging near the boat's wheel. The tiny, delicate sound they made seemed to amplify the rivermen's fears.

"You know," he said, "Marshal Merrick and I have an idea one of you is responsible for this man's death."

" 'Tain't true, sir," Hogan snapped. "We would never turn on our mates. There's plenty of prisoners to do that."

LaRue crowded him and the riverman took a step back. I could tell by my partner's voice that he was going to fix his feathers with a lie. "We've been through all of *Delora*'s personnel records, but yours, Riverman Hogan, doesn't seem to be in the stack."

"What do you mean?"

"Just what I said. It's missing."

Hogan huffed and puffed and then started pleading. "Honest, Marshal. I didn't hurt nobody. And I ain't telling no lies about who I am."

LaRue badgered him some more. "You were in a perfect position to let the killer board this boat."

Hogan stared at him, his eyes wide with fear. "No," he muttered. "You've got to believe me. I don't know why my records ain't where they're supposed to be, and I wouldn't let nobody on board."

LaRue eased off of the terrified riverman to spin his attention onto Curran. This sailor looked like he'd been eating more than his share of the mashed potatoes. His gut threatened to burst the zipper on his cammies, his face hung with layers of fat, and he sweated a rainstorm. Curran swallowed, cleared his throat, and swallowed again as LaRue expertly urged on his monsoon of perspiration by studying him with a suspicious look. Finally, my partner spoke. "Assisting in a murder is an offense that will land you in this hellhole, Riverman. What do you say on the matter?"

Suddenly the sweating stopped and the tears began. "It isn't our fault. It was a kami what killed him."

"A kami?" I said. "What's that?"

He sniffed and rubbed at the tears. "An evil spirit sent by a water witch."

Well, of course. When the fire starts to burn out the truth, it's time to send in the supernatural guns.

Hogan jumped into the conversation. "It's why Kleege don't have all his body parts. The river witch will make the kami fetch back the flesh. He'll string the stubs on a magical chain and that way he has the power of the dead man's soul at his beck and call." Shaking his head sorrowfully, he watched Gibson scribble away. "Poor old Kleege.

Some say the soul chains don't allow the spirit to find his way into the other dimension. It traps 'em and some of them witches can live a right long time themselves.''

"They do?" LaRue said. "Why?"

"It's because they feed on the energy of the lost souls. That's what a soul chain lets you do. The more dead you got, the more power is available to you. We got more than our share of spirits around here."

"Why so many ghosts?" LaRue asked.

"Been all kind of boat wrecks along the Black River, especially in Neptune's Yawning Gorge of Death," Hogan answered.

"That sounds like an interesting place."

"It's not. The wind comes up as furious as if the god hisself was doing the blowing."

Before I realized it, I'd grown tired of their supernatural suggestions. "Did you see anyone board this boat?" I demanded.

Curran dried his eyes with the back of his hand and nicked a quick look at his friend. "We gotta tell them, Hogan. We gotta."

"What do you know?" LaRue barked.

Hogan answered reluctantly. "It's a note, sir. We found a note."

"Where?"

"On the deck. Tied around a rock." He reached into his pocket and produced a piece of crinkled blue paper. "We didn't tell Ritter because he would have chucked it in the trash."

"Why would he have done that?"

"He don't want this case solved, but that's my opinion. I ain't got no evidence. Just a feeling."

LaRue snapped his fingers impatiently and flipped open the note as soon as Hogan gave it to him. I swooped in for a closer look.

What I saw was a crudely drawn mandala, complete with magical writing. I snatched it from my partner and held it to my nose, satisfied and confused when I smelled golden squares all over it.

SIXTEEN

It became painfully clear that Hogan and Curran had been asleep at the switch. I tossed the boat's logbook at LaRue as he released the rivermen back into the captain's custody and left him there, busy talking Gibson's ear down to a nub. He was trying on some metaphysical ideas about karmic magic, and so to avoid a discourse on how witches might unwittingly employ a form of nuclear fission to power their flying brooms, I went aft to rummage through Kleege's personal effects.

The use of the mandala is a popular fixture on the backdoor market and is considered powerful enough to command the energies of life and death. Think of it as a supernatural passport of sorts. As a magical symbol, the mandala creates a sacred space in this plane of existence and then connects this dimension to others. I guess it's a metaphysical spin-off of the scientific theory that suggests it's possible to fold space and time and therefore travel from point to point in the vast universe.

Baba has tried mandalas on me by changing the concept to fit her needs. She hangs the symbols all over our flat, swearing that the mandalas help to lessen the agony of my stretches, because the wolf can travel with ease between the realms. My cranky, old sot of a roommate will not accept the fact that the pain is just as bad, so I go along with her efforts. At least it makes her feel like she's doing something productive.

This particular diagram was drawn with a six-pointed star. It was a familiar design known by its popular name, the Seal of St. Ophelia. When a person looks like he's going to die without fulfilling his purpose on earth, the witch evokes the power of this mandala, commanding trumped-up energy that is geared toward releasing the soul before physical death. In this way, the spirit has the choice of which dimension it wants to retire to or whether its life's mission is worth hanging around to complete.

It's all a ration of shit, but the mandala ritual is practiced with precision, fanfare, and a considerable exchange of wealth. It's an absurd bit of magical life insurance. Yet, on a more practical level, the mandala ritual gives hope to a people who constantly live under the gun by creating a safe haven, even if this sacred space is all in their minds. Unfortunately, I had no idea if the general interpretations of the symbol were the same in the labor camp.

Kleege shared a bunk room with Stan Russo. Ritter had put the entire crew on alert and the cubbyhole was empty, so it was a perfect time to check out both men.

Under right of law, the captain was required to turn over a set of master keys and so I used them to open their lockers. Russo's ten-inch-wide paddock was lined with strata of dirty clothes. Hesitantly, I pushed my hand between the soiled uniforms, hoping to find something besides a spider, lizard, or rat. Reaching deep into the interior, my hand contacted with a metal box. I pulled it out and flipped it open to find sugar treats, matches, and a dog-earred copy of the *Epistle of St. Ophelia.*

I'll admit, I'm not above abusing the system. The chanting refrain of our society's humanitarian values also fostered a counterharmony of hopelessness, and so to this end, cheating and stealing were essential skills in daily survival. Since I feel obligated to uphold this renegade standard and since I like chocolate, I swiped all three of Riverman

Russo's candy bars and then replaced the box. I paused to push the goodies into the thigh pocket of my cammies before slamming the locker shut.

Turning to Kleege's closet, I tried every key on the ring. The bastard remained steadfastly closed against my efforts, and being that I'm not one who is long on patience, I finally took a whack at it by gathering up a surge of lycanthropic strength. I kicked the metal door, bending it on the hinges, and grabbing it with both hands, I pulled on it until the flimsy lock snapped.

My efforts did not go unrewarded, for inside, much to my surprise, I found a standard-issue gel-cell battery.

SEVENTEEN

Like it or not, it was time to get some outside perspective by visiting with select members of the prison population. Ritter acted like I'd asked him to walk the plank, but after a short squabble he saw it my way and dropped anchor in a large, junk-strewn cove. Rather than waste a lifeboat on us, he sent LaRue and me topside to see one of the crewmen about swinging across the watery expanse on the arm of the dredge. We climbed aboard, balancing rifles and courage. I hung on for dear life, not so much afraid of entering this zone of depravity around us but of drowning in the river below. LaRue acted like it was some kind of day in the park, chattering about cotton candy and bullets as we rode to shore.

The dredge's arm didn't reach all the way and we were forced to jump for the bank. I ended up on my rump, sliding around in the mud and muck as I tried to keep the carbine out of the slime. LaRue grabbed me before I skidded back into the water and hauled me to a stand, pulling me with surprising strength into the reeds. It pissed me off that Ritter had refused to allow us to use the skiff and this further aggravation completely minced up my mood. By the time we found someone to talk to, I was ready for a sedative.

This whole part of the river was marshy and even LaRue shut up long enough to navigate across the mushy earth. It was not long into our trek before he pointed to an inmate sitting outside of a closet-sized, reed bungalow. The old boy busily cooked something atop a flaming tump of grass and sticks. He glanced our way, rubbed a hand across his bald head, and then waved at us.

Before entering the penal colony, each prisoner is castrated, injected with a compound that inhibits the growth of hair, and then his chin is tattooed with a scarlet number indicating his cell block. As we drew closer I saw that this fellow was bald, but it was impossible to make out his tattoo. The ravages of the leprosy had spoiled his skin, leaving his face a mess.

"Chilly morning," he said, after we took seats on a couple of rickety milk crates.

"That it is," LaRue answered. Then, studying the man's oozing, diseased countenance, he said: "What's your name?"

"They call me Stubby Tinkle."

"Well, Stubby, we need to ask some questions, and it looks like you're on the docket to give the answers."

He leaned back on his seat and stretched. As he did, his leg irons jangled. "I don't know nothing. I been here for a long time and the screws have forgot about me. Same goes for those SOBs who calls themselves water witches." Tinkle spat.

This guy was a walking goo factory. I was queasy for some strange reason, so as to not hurl into his smoking breakfast, I took a short walk around his homestead, returning to my seat only after LaRue began hammering him some more.

"You don't care for the water witches?" he asked. "Are you speaking about members of the Coven?"

"I'm talking about the lot of them. They ain't real witches. I'm a witch. In fact, I specialize. They call me a cooker."

"What's a cooker?"

"See that tin of stuff abubbling there?"

"Yes."

"That's what I cook. It's a drub made from secret unguents that I prepare ahead of time." He paused to stir the concoction, and when he did, I smelled the stinging odor of green circles. "I can tell you that this here basic recipe contains ground-up naiads. That makes it powerful."

That made it stink. I sat back and shook my head to clear it of the colors. "What is this stuff supposed to do?"

"It smooths out the rough spots in the karmic law of continuation."

"I don't understand what you're talking about."

Tinkle made a smacking sound and reached up to rub his hand across the tops of leprosy volcanoes plugging his face. "Well, it's simple, you know. Karma is divided into four principles: cause and effect, positive reward, balance, and continuation. Cause and effect is nothing more than an eye for an eye. You take a finger, you give up a finger. Positive reward is the result of acts of compassion and service. You know, do unto others and have it done unto you when it's your turn. Balance is the law that projects our current circumstances. If you live your life in extreme, then the next time around you come back to experience the opposite. So, if you were a killer in this life, you return a saint in the next. From aggressive to passive." He stopped in his explanation to stare at me. "Continuation is the toughest karmic law to beat."

"Why?" I asked.

"Continuation is the principle which holds us to our soul's true nature. We spend lifetime after lifetime trying to understand the lessons we are forced to uncover. If you spend an incarnation developing your talents in some wholesome endeavor, but always remain an apprentice, when you come back in a new body, you can draw on these skills and go from where you left off."

"Are you saying that the other laws of karma screw up this continuation principle?"

"Yeah. You gotta juggle things just right. Many folks find ways to draw on the knowledge of past lives, and just as many don't. Or if they do, they mess it up."

"So, what does your drub do?"

"It allows the person a clear view of his past lives and gives him the opportunity to use the wisdom he earned then to improve his situation now."

"That's something that's really needed around here," I said.

"Everyone needs my magic drub once in a while," he answered. "And from looking at you, I'd say you're a candidate for a karmic boost."

"You have that right," LaRue muttered.

I shot my partner a fierce look, but jumped ahead, knowing there was a parley beginning to happen. "Why do I need help?"

Tinkle studied me with runny brown eyes. "You're angry about your current life. You have many talents, I think. Skills you could employ to make your circumstances better."

"Such as?"

He shrugged. "Well, my intuition tells me one of the things you have in abundance is patience. It's a shame you don't know how to get to this wealth. It's buried deep inside of you, earned from past lives when you developed that patience, but life this time around ain't been so easy. Your anger has gotten the better of you and stomped out all access to this particular skill. That's the point of my drub. It releases this information so you can see who you were and how best to use your talents."

I snorted, chalking up his assertions as a lucky guess. Still, my biggest problem was my lack of patience and it took me a moment to press past this latest metaphysical absurdity. Whether it was a load of rebirth twaddle or not, Gibson would probably want to see what compounds made up the drub. I patted down my pockets and came up with a package of dried prunes. Flipping it on the ground between us, I opened the bargaining. Tinkle was quick to grumble.

"That's not much of an offer," he said.

"It's all we have. Take it or leave it."

"I can only give you half as much of the drub."

"I want the whole amount," I growled.

You could tell it was killing him. Tinkle wanted that food, but he also wanted to retain his trading integrity. Finally, his stomach won the battle and he nodded.

While he dished up some of his karmic paste, LaRue hit him with some more questions. "And you're saying the other water witches are fakes?"

"Not all, just some. The trustees are diddling with the screws. Every cell block has got their share, so I hear."

"Don't you know? Don't they come down here?"

"All the time." He paused to poke at the fire with a hand that was missing all its fingers. "They got their own secret society or something. Besides, onest you lose your ability to hold a shovel, the Coven just don't waste their time hauling your ass off to dig in the pits and drown in the delta. The only thing they got as far as magic is the good graces of their screw. I hear they be getting rich off'n their brethren, but I ain't sure. Scuttlebutt don't get much in the way of meat, you know."

"Why do they pretend to be water witches?" LaRue said.

"To control folks, but for the most part, it don't work. They think it does, and I suppose those who join the crowd get special privileges or something. I wouldn't know. I ain't never been in the running to join their stinking group."

"Are the screws water witches, too?"

"Naw. They just live off the fat of the land. I suppose they're wound up pretty good with the Coven, though."

"What about the folks who ply the river?"

"You mean the river rats?"

"Yes, for starters."

"Most of them are practicing water witches."

"Have you heard of anyone from the River Patrol claiming to be a witch?"

"I don't think none of them are witches."

"Do they often trade goods with the inmates?"

"Not supposed to, but how else are you going to survive in this hell? Folks like me don't ever get no food when they make the supply drops. Gotta eat somehow." He paused to pick at a sore before taking a couple fingers full of the paste and wrapping it up in a large, dusty leaf. "Here ya go. Mix it into water and drink it down. It will give you insight into your most inspired talents."

I fought down a moment of biliousness before taking the package with a curt nod of gratitude. "Have you ever heard of an inmate named Derek Wheeler?" I asked.

Tinkle studied me, and despite the splotches of disease obscuring his features, I could tell he weighed the question and his answer. Finally, he spoke. "I've heard of him. He was the Coven's high priest, or some such thing."

"What do you know about him?"

"The only thing I heard was that he got on the bad side of a spell and some witch turned him into a bogeyman."

EIGHTEEN

Tinkle feigned ignorance about the mandala drawing, but he did cooperate and took us to see a man who was a water witch of some repute. If anyone could tell us the meaning of the paper, he could. Whether he would or not was another story.

Our new friend guided us upriver and inland. The bog turned a little more toward dry land, but then the trees filled in around us and the undergrowth grew thorns that clutched at our feet and legs. Not a good place to be, especially with me. I was overly antsy, my lycanthropic sight feeding me shadows and sparkles. I might share the world with a supernatural wolf, but I hate the great outdoors. To add to my simmering mood, LaRue started a lecture about keeping the bloodsucking mosquitoes at bay and then ran his discourse into explaining the benefits of dabbing a little turpentine and vanilla under the armpits.

"You'll notice I'm not getting bitten," he said, helping me over a knee-high tree root.

"It's because you stink," I answered.

Tinkle grunted against the weight of his leg irons and lifted the chain so he could maneuver around a large boulder. "Sounds like good magic to me. You got some of that miracle mosquito stuff with you?"

"Why?" LaRue demanded.

"Because it'll be better if you go inside the witch house with trade items. Folks out here ain't gonna try to kill you unless you piss them off and then they'll whomp you with the wrong side of a karmic curse."

"Really?" I said. "Our boat was bombed with rocks sent in by a homemade catapult. Sounds like you'll turn mean and ugly to me."

He shook his head. "Not us. We're the worm diggers. I told you. We're the ones that ain't no goddamned use anymore. We're kept around for those jobs that don't have much of a future, you understand. It's good we are water witches, because calling up the karmic forces of Davy Jones's locker is a whole sight easier than trying to pick off screws with sharp sticks."

"Apparently, some of your comrades don't feel the same way."

"If you got attacked, then you were attacked by Hecate's Sickle."

"What's that?"

"They're a group that split off from the Coven."

"Why?"

He shrugged. "I don't know the answer to that one."

LaRue glanced at me and then for the next half hour he treated us to a dialogue on how witchcraft had been responsible for the dissolution of the old Soviet Union. He went on about the gulf between those creeds that claim to manifest divine power and those where the power is delivered through an intermediary, such as a priest. Witchcraft, he said, stemmed from Wicca, a Celtic, monistic nature religion, whose believers passionately supported reincarnation, as well as the ability to perform magic and call out the devic energy from bushes, rocks, and mud. My partner finally finished up his talk with a word or two about the origins of Summerland, the Elysian Fields of witches, a place where they could park their brooms between earthly incarnations.

It sounded complicated, and not like something that would go over well in the penal colony. Superstition and invisible magic had been blown into old myths of the sea, and though the trustees who were members of the Coven called themselves witches, I was getting a picture that told me they were closer to karmic criminals.

We stepped into a clearing to see a stick-built longhouse, the walls of which had been plastered with reeds and mud. Several inmates lounged around the grounds outside this structure, picking at sores and brushing away flies. I thought we would come under immediate and dangerous scrutiny, but Tinkle had been right. These folks were in no condition to undertake a physical vendetta on the RP. They could barely sit up.

Tinkle stopped at the door of the witch house and begged an audience with a prisoner named Curr Culaine. There was a minute when the watchman wanted to know if we had trade items and a minute more to convince him that we came to talk, not to conscript for a work crew. Finally, we gained admittance and found Culaine to be old, bald, and tattooed. He had been tall and broad at one time, but now his bubbly flesh hung on a lanky frame. His left ear and part of his nose were missing, and try as I might, I couldn't stop staring.

We were invited to share his braided reed mat, but before we were settled in and had finished exchanging greetings, Culaine demanded a parley.

"No business gets done unless we consecrate the circle," he said.

"They got skeeter medicine," Tinkle offered.

LaRue tossed the inmate a dark look, but remained silent.

"Sounds good," Culaine said. "Put up or get out."

"You've got to toss out the bread crumb, fellow," LaRue answered. "We aren't going to give over our loot unless we know we're not getting ripped off."

Culaine sucked on his rotten teeth and tugged at the ragged charm sack around his neck. Finally, he nodded. "Let me pull the demon out of the fire, then. You want to know who's been attacking the *Delora*."

"Hecate's Sickle," I lied. "Tell us something we don't know."

My bluff hit home and the leper frowned. "You'll want to know the why of it."

"That's right. Dish the info and we'll give up part of the mosquito spray."

"Part?"

I leaned forward to sear the old bastard with a sharp look and in the meantime almost puked when I got a good whiff of urine and an eyeful of tan triangles. Blinking off the effects of my synesthesia, I repeated the bid. "Part. As in not all."

Culaine shook his head and fessed up. "Hecate's Sickle has been on the outs with the screws and the Coven ever since Derek Wheeler and Eldon Emmet had a full-blown ta-do. Emmet took his followers and told the Coven to get bent."

"What was the falling out over?"

"Who knows?" he crowed. "Most likely the buggering was more than Emmet could manage. You know, shoving it to your fellow inmates will prey upon your conscience sooner or later. A man can dig him a hole of karma in this place. After a while the sin weighs on your soul. That, and the stones of truth left by magic ill-used."

I sighed, abruptly weary of this paranormal jazz. LaRue, seeing that the only thing being buggered was my patience, jumped in to ask the correct metaphysical question.

"What do you mean about the stones of truth left by magic ill-used?" he said.

"Don't you know how water witching works?"

"We're learning. Tell us more."

He shook his head and shoved a crusty iron cup toward him. "Put the mosquito spray on the table first."

LaRue brought out his elixir, carefully measuring half the contents into the mug. Culaine picked up the goods, sniffed them with his single remaining nostril, and then drank the mixture, hacking when the turpentine passed by his lungs en route to his craw. Once he was through this battle with his breathing, he explained.

"If you water-witch for good, then abundance and prosperity are your karmic reward. Leastwise, you get respect and you get left alone by the screws. But if you cough up spells and curses to hurt those less fortunate than yourself, then you curse your immortal soul to lugging around the truth of your actions. These stones weigh down the spirit. They make it impossible to be reborn into another body until the soul owns up to the facts and makes amends for the suffering it caused whilst fiddling around in the material plane. Magic, especially the water witching kind, ain't nothin' to fool with." I was starting to come around to his explanation when he blew it by adding: "Each stone weighs sixteen and a half pounds, by the way."

"Then you figure Eldon Emmet is making restitution by attacking the *Delora*," I said. "He's hoping to gain some karmic points by defending his fellowman from further persecution."

"Why else would he have gone off and stole the Book of Shadows?"

"What's the Book of Shadows?" LaRue asked.

"It's the Coven cipher book. All the writ-down spells, hexes, curses, drubs, and cures. He took it, so I hear, and split off from the main group."

"So, there is a deep division where the trustees are concerned?"

He nodded and let the spit fly. "Yep. Without the Book of Shadows, the water witches that stayed with the Coven are as useless as feathers on a fish."

I clawed into the breast pocket of my uniform and presented him with the mandala. "What's this?"

Instinctively, Culaine reached for the charm sack hanging around his neck, crossing his heart before answering. "That there is an evil portent. It means the bogeyman is after you."

"What exactly is a bogeyman?" I asked.

"A monster," he answered. "Not quite human; not quite spirit. It's had its soul transformed by the magic and power called up Davy Jones's locker. It lives outside the laws of divine grace. It is an evil thing that serves to bring down the agony of karmic retribution. It's the physical manifestation of the truth known as an eye for an eye."

The moment he said it was the second I had a stretch and dallied in a little karmic pain myself. I howled and tried to crawl clear of the mat, worried I would offend this witch with some impropriety that would, despite what Tinkle maintained, get us killed. LaRue stayed with his carbine and let me flop around until I was done. When I came to, the wolf hadn't blotted out my communicating ability with aphasia, but it had settled into my bones and muscles, making my cammies too short at the ankles and too tight across the boobs. It had also caused quite a stir among the inmates present in the longhouse.

"What has happened to her?" Culaine screeched.

LaRue, ever-efficient when it came to laying on the jam thickly, used his question to our benefit. "She's a kami."

NINETEEN

Culaine turned fearful that I might be some avenging demoness and ended our audience before we could ask him
about the mandala. We went on our way, following Tinkle
back to his campsite. He told us to have a nice life and
disappeared into the reeds, effectively ending all communication. It was another hour before we climbed aboard the
dredge and were safely delivered to the *Delora*. We decided
to have a talk with Ritter and found him on the bridge,
watching Neilson swab down the deck. A pilot by the name
of Janet Yarrow manned the wheel.

"Captain Ritter, what cell block are we in?" LaRue
asked.

"Two," he answered. "Why?"

"Is there a guard station nearby?"

"Yes. The Prefect Warden's Outpost, as a matter of fact.
Blue Moon Point. We should reach it by tomorrow afternoon. I'm supposed to stop and check in."

"Why?"

"I need to report any problems. He should know about
the attack."

"What can he do?"

Ritter shook his head. "Nothing. Reporting in is just part of the RP's regulations."

I decided to change the subject, and to draw Ritter's attention, I stepped to the observation porthole to look out into night. The captain did, indeed, settle his gaze upon me. "We understand there's hidden treasure in these parts."

In the reflection of the glass, I saw the kitten moving in his face. After a moment he managed a chuckle. "I suppose the inmates told you about that."

"No, actually. Kleege told us."

Ritter glanced down at the bloodstained deck, but didn't reply.

Riverman Yarrow abruptly announced what she knew. "Kleege believed in mermaids. The logbook is full of his insane observations. I think he had more nymph sightings than he had star sightings."

I glanced at her. "I take it you weren't impressed by Kleege's abilities?"

"He was from the old school; learned to pilot from his daddy, who owned a commercial fishing trawler. His methods depended upon the goodwill of the river nymphs, not any sort of navigational abilities."

"She's right," Ritter said. "I was told that when we enter the delta area, to put on a pilot who could read the scopes and the maps. He worried me. The last thing I wanted to do is get lost at sea with him behind the wheel."

It sounded to me like they were steering the conversation away from the treasure, but being bullheaded, I rowed back that direction. "So, what made Kleege believe the RP was recovering a treasure that contained pearls the size of chicken eggs?"

They both stared at me, but it was Ritter who finally offered the explanation. "Pearls the size of an egg? I'd sure like to have one of those." He shrugged and joined me at the porthole. "Kleege saw signs in everything. He fabricated his own ideas. But one thing is for certain. We're dredging the delta; we're not hunting for sunken treasure."

"What about that tidal bore that came up the river? Did he fabricate that?"

Ritter scowled and I knew instantly that I'd hit a nerve. When he answered, his tone was flat. "We are talking about a fluke of nature, not some magical spell."

"What caused it?" LaRue asked.

"I'm not sure." He turned to snap an order to the pilot and then stepped away to give Neilson an ass-chewing about how badly he'd scrubbed up Kleege's blood.

"What happened when the tidal bore came up the river?" I said, adding a little force to my voice.

"We were transporting prisoners," he answered. "Tugging a deuce."

"What's a deuce?"

"Two scows connected up like a train. We had a lot of inmates that trip. Guards, too. The bore hit us because we didn't get the word in time that it was coming our way. It was a huge wave. You would have thought we were in the middle of the ocean by the size of the thing. Kleege kept saying it was Davy Jones doing the bidding of a local witch." He sighed and shook his head. "Crazy bastard."

"How many people died?"

"One hundred and fifty-three."

"It created a lot of bad feelings between the RP and the Coven, I'll bet."

He stared at me before replying quietly. "The RP doesn't care if there are bad feelings among the population. If it did, we wouldn't be here."

TWENTY

The next morning, Gibson had more information for us. He'd worked through the night and found us as we dined on a breakfast of powdered eggs, powdered milk, and powdered cheese sauce. As he sat down I noticed the exhaustion in his face. It shaded his usual passionate demeanor and made me touch his shoulder in a compassionate effort to relieve his weariness. He acknowledged me by gently laying his hand atop mine and turning to stare into my eyes. We locked there, but the moment was dismayingly short-lived as he dropped his grasp and hunched forward at our table.

"We're in very big trouble here," he murmured.

LaRue ignored the warning to stuff in a forkful of food, so I reacted for the both of us. "What's wrong?"

"Everything." He paused, dragging out the drama by pouring a cup of coffee from the battered pot sitting between us. "Kleege was older than his physical age should permit."

"He was in good shape," LaRue said.

"No, no, you don't understand me, Andy. His records indicated that he was eighty-two years old."

This confession made us both stop eating and we stared at him until he continued.

"According to Stirling, Kleege drank like a fish and smoked cigarettes like a chimney. Yet there's no evidence of intestinal or pulmonary dysfunction. Judging from the test results and a visual analysis of his internal organs alone, I would have guessed this man was about forty years old at the time of his death."

"How can that be?" I asked.

Gibson slugged his coffee before pegging me with a squint. "The human body can be resilient. It was just a few years ago that we discovered how the metabolism constantly regenerates the system. By manipulating the brain's action, we can manipulate the amount of regeneration that occurs."

I speared a doughy pile that was supposed to be a biscuit. "So, I take it, his youthful innards were on account of a slow-burning metabolism."

"That's right," he said. "Slow like our giant oyster."

"Kleege wasn't a big man, though," LaRue said.

"His medical and labor records indicated something interesting. He had a growth spurt after he started working this river. He was sixty-seven years old and some quack diagnosed his problem as a latent genetic pattern kicking in. Kleege was measured each year and had gained several more inches in height. His weight expanded accordingly, though he reported no significant differences in his eating habits."

"What do you think was causing it?"

"It's Wilson's leprosy bug."

"But you checked everyone on board."

Gibson lowered his voice to a murmur. "Blood tests don't mean shit sometimes, Merrick. I have no idea what kind of bacteria I'm dealing with, what factors promote it, the life cycle, the resting state. If you want to know the truth—I know zip."

"What about Stirling?" I asked. "Did he tell you anything?"

"Dr. Stirling," he said flatly. Glancing around to make

sure he wasn't in earshot of interested parties, he laced his answer with an ominous tone. "There is something all wrong with that man. Don't trust him."

Gibson could have saved his warning, because I don't trust anyone—not even myself. So, to avoid a momentary lapse into self-cruelty, I hopped the subject back to the leprosy bacteria. "We're talking about a disease. Why didn't it kill Kleege instead of giving him long life and a bigger shoe size?"

"I believe it has something to do with the antigens in his body," he answered. "His immune system may have worked with it. In someone else, the results might be different."

"But doesn't leprosy affect the nerves and make your fingers fall off?"

"There are several different types of Hansen's disease, Merrick. This appears to be a mutated form." He took a swig of coffee. "Just so you know, Kleege did show signs of nerve degeneration. He suffered from the loss of feeling."

"How do you know that?" I asked.

"He had burn marks on his hands. I think they were from holding forgotten cigarettes."

"Do you have any idea how this illness is transmitted?"

"I can't say for certain, but the best bet is either airborne or waterborne. Inmates bathe in the water. They also pee and spit into the water. You've got to understand that the thing that forms the basis for most strains of leprosy is the incubation period. It takes three to five years, so there's always a portion of the labor-camp population who are infected but don't know it. I'm going to take some samples from the river, but as bad as I hate to consider it, we're going to have to grab a couple of inmates to do a comparison study."

"Andy and I are going ashore this morning to see what we can scare up."

He grunted, rubbing his eyes before he answered. "Be careful." Pausing, he poured another cup of coffee and tossed out the big one. "I can tell you something else for certain. Amos Kleege not only drank and smoked, but he used drugs, too. I found high levels of nuciferia in his blood stream.''

"What's that?'' I asked.

"A narcotic,'' he answered. "You probably know it as Blue Lotus.''

"Yes. It's a big problem for the vice marshals.''

LaRue, ever the one for collecting odd bits of useless information, nevertheless pulled a gem from his repository. "I remember in school reading the adventures of Odysseus when he came across the Lotus-Eaters. One bite of the plant made his crew forget their pasts and their families and live in blissful indolence.''

"Homer had it right about the lotus,'' Gibson answered. "If you take a good look around the junk out here, you'll see the lily pads growing in grand profusion.''

"You're suggesting the inmates collect it?'' I said.

Gibson nodded. "That karmic paste you brought back?''

"Yeah.''

"It was loaded with the stuff.''

TWENTY-ONE

About 2:00 P.M., we reached Blue Moon Point. It turned out to be a spit of land that extended into the river; set in the center of this swampy realm was a crumbling, concrete building that Ritter referred to as the meatpacking plant. From our place on the deck of the *Delora*, LaRue and I could see a snaking line of prisoners being herded inside by red-uniformed guards.

The pilot steered the boat toward a wooden pier, and after the anchor was dropped, Riverman Curran cranked out the plank. We were immediately met by two guards who escorted us with no delay to Prefect Warden Demitri Zoltana.

I carried my revolver, a carbine, and the business end of a bayonet and still felt underdressed for this party. Gibson and his goddamned rubber bullets would not stop the smallest of these giants.

Still, despite their obvious brawn, the prisoners displayed all the signs of a disease that rotted off ears and noses and turned fingers into gangrenous appendages. We were led past these men while they waited in silence for the guards to lock their leg irons into a twenty-man chain gang. I could feel their stares as we entered the building and cut down a narrow, crumbling corridor that spilled out into a large staging area.

Zoltana greeted us from behind a small, bent, metal desk segregated into one corner of this room. He was a tall, dark man with a hooked nose and cavernous nostrils that yanked whistling breaths from the filter of his thick, black mustache.

"Ah," he said, studying me, "the kami sent from Davy Jones's locker."

I tossed LaRue an annoyed glance, but he ignored me by speaking to Zoltana. "Word travels fast."

The warden answered without taking his eyes off me. "Still, I have heard it was an amazing transformation."

"You can't believe everything you hear," I snapped.

He let his gaze linger upon me, and then, apparently rejecting the claim, he got to the point. "Captain Ritter contacted me via radio this morning," he said. "I understand you want to interview two of my prisoners."

"Captain Ritter didn't make himself clear," I answered. "We want two prisoners to take back to the *Delora* for medical examinations."

Zoltana tried to hide his surprise by sitting back in his chair and rubbing a hand over his mustache. "I haven't seen any authorization for the release of prisoners into your custody."

Prefect Warden Zoltana was stalling. It aggravated me and immediately rustled up my suspicion. "As district marshals, our jurisdiction supersedes yours."

"What is the problem? I have a right to be informed."

"We suspect a possible biological threat," I answered.

Zoltana passed his gaze between us before dismissing the guards back to their sentry duties. "What kind of disease?"

I made it sound impressive. "A contagious form of leprosy."

"None of my guards are ill. We're inoculated against the diseases that sweep through this place."

"Yes. You and your guards may carry some immunity depending upon the types of inoculations you've been given. But we don't know for sure. We're trying to contain a public outbreak.''

He fingered his mustache and studied us for a moment. "I will release them into your protection, but you must assure me the *Delora* will remain at dock until your examinations are complete.''

"Agreed," LaRue said. "And since we're here, we were hoping you might be able to answer some questions for us.''

"I don't know anything about medicine or diseases. I'm afraid I won't be of any help.''

"Oh, it's not about disease. It's about water witches and the role they play in this prison community.''

"Why do you need to know this?'' he asked.

"Because we're also looking for a killer as well as a killer disease.''

"You're talking about the unfortunate deaths aboard the *Delora*?''

"Yes. We keep hearing about a man named Derek Wheeler. Have you ever heard of him?''

Zoltana pushed back his chair and rose, signaling us to follow him through a nondescript door at the far end of the room. Here, we found a well-appointed solarium overlooking the river. It was filled with flowering plants and soft, rich furniture. The warden waved to a couple of wingback chairs, and while we leaned our rifles gently against the mint-green wall, he walked to a round, mahogany table. There, he paused to run his hands lovingly over a carved humidor. "Do you care to smoke?" he asked.

"None for me," I said.

LaRue shook his head, sat down, and tested the spring in the chair pillow by squeezing it. "How did you put together a place like this?"

"I didn't," Zoltana said. "This was bequeathed to me by my predecessor as it had been bequeathed to him. You might say, it's the prefect's perk.''

"The cigars, too?"

"Well, we're all allowed an illegal indulgence once in a while." He opened the box and selected a cigar before continuing. "I suppose the rivermen have been filling your heads with tales of black magic."

"Well," I said, sitting next to LaRue, "they have mentioned curses and Davy Jones's locker."

He snorted, clipped the end off the cigar, and sniffed the stogie. "It was Derek Wheeler who came up with the idea of water witches."

"Well, then, why don't you explain the concept to us, because we're confused."

Zoltana sat down and took a moment to light his cigar. "This labor camp is based on hopelessness, Marshal. I should think you of all people should understand this. Without the hopelessness, we couldn't begin to control a prison population this size. I came here as warden a very long time ago. I discovered that things were out of control. The inmates were at each other's throats and the death toll was rising on both sides of the fence." He paused, puffed, and then again pursued his explanation. "Wheeler was an inventive man, and despite his sorrowful choices in life, he was brilliant. He was a cultural anthropologist with the university before being incarcerated for his crimes against society. Wheeler drew a hard-nosed judge on the case and he was thrown in here as a lifer."

"I take it he rose through the ranks of his cell block," LaRue said.

"Exactly. He started convincing his block mates that he was a powerful water witch. From what I understand, he had a talent for sleight of hand and that's all he needed to convince people he was, indeed, able to change their lives with karmic magic. I suppose in the beginning he did it to protect himself from the hatred and violence of the inmates."

"And then he came to you," I said.

"That's right. I told you he was smart. He saw an opportunity to control the prisoners on a large scale. He cut a deal for special rations in exchange for creating an organized social structure among the trustees. He called his group the Coven, and through implied fear, managed to bring the population under rein. It sounds bizarre, but it really works.''

"How many water witches do you have?'' LaRue asked.

"Each cell block keeps about two hundred prisoners on tap,'' he answered.

"And do they actually believe they have supernatural powers?''

Zoltana took a leisurely puff, blowing smoke rings. "I told you we deal in hopelessness. People will grasp at any straw. It's fascinating to see the transformation that occurs when you've been exploited.'' I must have let my disgust shine through, because he looked at me and then shook his head. "I don't make any excuses, Marshal Merrick. I have ten thousand people deemed criminal in the eyes of the district government. My guard units are down because they can't find new recruits. My budget is slashed every year and the airdrops of supplies have stopped. If I rule with fear, it's necessary.''

LaRue battered the subject. "When you issue an order, do the guards give the responsibility to the trustees to execute?''

"Yes. It works remarkably well.''

"What if there's a fight?''

"Well, there aren't any, but if there were, the water witches would cast a magical spell to steer the dissidents toward making a decision about continued obedience.''

I couldn't help sighing. It was ludicrous. Invisible magic had crept into the very fiber of our society, and whether you believed it or not, the status quo was enough to make you wonder. Superstition should have been aptly renamed "stuporstition.'' "Some people just don't believe in that shit,'' I said. "And you can't convince them.''

Zoltana smiled. "I don't care if they're convinced or not. So long as they do what they're told.''

"What happened to Wheeler?'' I asked.

"He died.''

"Well, you must have been in trouble then.''

"Not really. You see, I'm a smart man, too.''

"What did you do?''

"I relied on an old Buddhist custom. The Tibetans once believed that when a priest died, his soul moved into another body. They would search far and wide for the reincarnated lama, identifying him in young male children through an affinity they had to ritual objects owned by the dead monk."

LaRue nodded. "You concocted some kind of weird line of succession."

Zoltana smiled. "Exactly. There are several prisoners out there who believe they carry a portion of the walk-in soul of Derek Wheeler."

TWENTY-TWO

After a leisurely conversation, Zoltana called in his officer-on-duty and told him to let us chose our prisoners.

I must admit, I felt like I was selecting a side of beef. At such intimate proximity, I couldn't miss seeing the evidence of the strange disease as it blossomed through their flesh to explode in oozing pustules. There was a smell attached to them, too—one that blitzed my vision with intense gold sparks. It was so strong, my eyes started watering.

LaRue stopped short and I bumped into him. He glanced at me. "What about this gentleman?"

The guy was big, bald, and missing a chunk of his ear. His skin was volcanic, boiling with scabs and pus-filled fissures. "What's your name?"

He took a deep breath to reply but it came out as a coughing fit. Finally, he wheezed an answer. "Jasper Finn, sir."

I tossed a critical look toward the guard. "Would you say this man represents the average state of health among the prison population?"

The guard nodded.

"When'd your ear fall off, Finn?" I asked.

"Can't remember, sir."

"Were you sick before that?"

"Been sick for years, sir."

"How many years?"

He sucked in a tentative breath and paused to wipe mucus on his filthy trousers before answering. "I can't remember, sir."

The guard offered a quick explanation. "He's been put under a karmic spell."

"What kind?"

"He's been granted forgetfulness," the guard answered matter-of-factly. "The witch who did it gathered up the forgetfulness energy that erases our knowledge of past lives. He then douses the person in this energy and blots out sources of pain for the prisoner."

I winced when I heard this excuse. Spell of forgetfulness, my ass. More likely it was the juice of Gibson's lotus plant. "Don't tell me you believe this?"

The guard nodded. "I've seen how well it works. Once done, you can get a lot more attention and service from these bastards."

There was nothing to say that could change this ridiculous thought pattern, so I let the subject drop. "You'll do just fine," I said, and moved down the line, stopping for a fellow who looked like a pimply-faced teenager.

"What's your name?" I demanded.

"Otis McConnell, sir," he answered.

"How old are you?"

He thought a moment, glanced at the guard, swallowed, shuffled, and finally shook his head. "I can't say for sure, sir."

"Another forgetfulness spell?" LaRue asked.

McConnell reached up and gently dabbed a dirty rag at one of the bumps on his face. "I reckon so, sir."

Seeing it made me queasy and suddenly worry about Frank Wilson's warning. I choked down a spurt of bile before turning my attention to the pitted linoleum floor. "These two are okay, Andy," I husked.

My partner agreed and we escaped the dismal processing

house and delivered the inmates to the sick bay, where Gibson and Stirling waited. As we pushed the prisoners through the hatch I glanced up to see the *Delora*'s doctor cast a sharp, appraising gaze over our guests. He took a step back when Finn returned his look.

"Any trouble?" Gibson asked.

"No," I answered.

Before I could get another word out of my mouth, Stirling stomped to the hatch, pausing to address Gibson in a stern voice. "I've made myself clear. You know I think it is wrong for prisoners to be brought aboard this boat, and since my opinions mean nothing, I'm leaving this matter to you. It's your show. Don't expect me to lend a hand, because I won't. And when you're done, don't forget to scrub down the medical units." With that, he was gone, slamming the hatchway behind him.

"Do you get the feeling that we're not well liked around here?" LaRue said.

"The man is an ass," Gibson answered. "He doesn't want any part of this problem. That makes me uncomfortable." He took a deep breath and glanced around. "I can't think of a better way to use this equipment."

"All bureaucrats give me a rash," I answered. Then, flapping a hand at Finn, I asked: "Where do you want these two?"

Gibson pointed toward a stool in the corner. "You can chain one of them to the fasteners in the bulkhead."

"Fasteners?" I said. "Sure sounds like they planned on having prisoners aboard."

"Well, according to Stirling, it goes against regulations and safety procedures."

"Does it?"

"How the hell do I know?" he barked.

Admittedly, his answer ruffled the dust in my feathers. "What's wrong with you?"

One of Gibson's unconscious weapons is his fierce expression and he delivers it with a wild-eyed look that unsettles most people. He aimed it at me, but after a minute he put the safety back on and lowered his attention to a nearby table. "Sorry," he whispered. "I'm just a little wired right now." He cleared his throat and reached into his pocket to pull out my pearl. "Your fortune, milady. I kept the thieves and rogues from it."

I plucked it from his fingers and held it aloft for the prisoners to see. "Have either of you ever seen a gem so big before?"

Two pairs of eyes followed my hand.

"It's a serpent's egg," Finn said.

"It was launched into the boat along with some nice-sized rocks. Someone told us there's a sunken treasure." I placed the pearl into my pocket and took a step toward the duo. "Or did the witches cast down a forgetfulness spell on that, too?"

"A serpent's egg might be worth a lot of money, but it's also worth a lot of trouble," McConnell answered.

"Why?"

"Because they're bad-luck charms. They hold the dredges of bad karmic energy. Most times they cause problems down the line."

"Down the line?"

McConnell nodded. "Yes, they dink up future incarnations. It's pretty, but heavy with evil. I'd get rid of it if I were you."

I wasn't about to dismiss this subject. "Are they plentiful?"

"Nothing that size is plentiful."

"But you've seen them before?"

He shook his head. "No, I ain't. I've heard scuttlebutt, though."

"Such as?"

"I've heard the water witches in the Coven can take an ordinary pearl and lay a spell on it so it grows. Of course, they have to do it with leftover karma."

I glanced at LaRue. "Do I want to know where they get the spare magical energy?"

He chuckled. "I do."

Finn filled us in. "You're a kami, here to deliver retribution, they say. Don't you know how the magic works?"

"Is it so hard to believe that I'm not a kami?" I asked.

"Yes, ma'am."

"Why?"

"Because there have been people who have seen you change," he said.

Once more Stubby Tinkle's assertions about my lack of patience played out and I shoved the inmate onto the stool. I roughly locked his arms above his head by slipping the chain through the restraining bolt in the bulkhead. "I'm a marshal, Finn. A real, live, flesh-and-blood person. I haven't been inside Davy Jones's locker."

"Yes, of course," he answered quickly. "Begging your forgiveness, ma'am."

Zoltana did have one thing right—these folks had not one bit of fight left in them.

LaRue helped McConnell climb up onto the examining table. The man's leg irons and wrist cuffs made his work noisy and awkward, but with a boost from the good doctor, he settled in for a checkup.

Gibson turned to me. "Merrick, would you check the prisoner database and help establish a background for our guests?"

LaRue joined me at the keyboard and together we sifted through the files. A few minutes later we had our man complete with photo ID and a great big surprise.

McConnell's birth date was listed, and if it was right the pimply-faced teenager was fifty-seven years old.

TWENTY-THREE

Gibson soon chased us out of the sick bay so he could begin his research on the two prisoners. I was a little hesitant to leave him alone with them, but LaRue convinced me the good doctor would be all right, and then he left me to my own designs by heading off to talk to the pilot. It was just fine with me. The day had been overly long and too god-damn stressful, so I went up on deck, took a seat on the overturned lifeboat, and watched the sun set over this world of despair.

I tried to keep a measure of compassion for these people, but too many years of slapping up against criminals confounded my sympathy. Theirs was a sad display of futility, made more poignant by their captivity. One thing was true: the government had forsaken its humanitarian bond with the people, because the laws did indeed give the bureaucrats a chance to weed out the deadweight. Innocence was merely an idle claim anymore.

I know how easily this culling can be done. Before Gibson came along to save my ass, I was headed for much the same fate. It didn't matter that I was a marshal sworn to uphold the values of the society. To the Environmental Tax Office, I put a drain on the system by using more than my fair share of allocated electricity. I couldn't pay for what I consumed and it didn't matter that the reasons involved treatment for my lycanthropy. If nothing else, everyone suffered equally in their quarterly tax reviews.

I rose and strolled to the railing, pushing this thought from my mind. The dismal surroundings fostered my angst, and if I let these emotions get out of control, they would sink me. I was momentarily satisfied with this small recognition of self, but the wolf spoiled my little triumph in personal understanding by bringing me into sudden, agonizing submission.

I collapsed on the deck and pulled myself into a tight ball, using everything I had to keep from howling. I rocked from side to side, moaned, groaned, and growled. A good five minutes passed before I was able to pull myself to a stand and lean against the railing. My throat felt like the sand dunes of District 129 and the bones in my feet had changed so that now their bare impressions would appear remarkably similar to a print made by a canine. The stretch had stoked my metabolic furnace and on top of my concerns about aphasia, my stomach rumbled at its empty circumstances. These alterations did provide me with increased stamina and strength, but they also made me acutely aware of what my afflicted brain could concoct, and instead of walking immediately into questioning stares, I sat down on the lifeboat to gather my courage.

No more than a few minutes passed before Gibson came up on deck. For a moment I entertained the possibility of projected empathy, but when he spoke, I found out he hadn't sought me out with unexpected feelings of concern.

"There's something you need to see," he said quietly.

I could understand him, and answering, I tried not to show my relief. "What is it?" The second the sentence was out of my mouth, I knew I'd given away my predicament, because the stretch had roughened my voice until it sounded like I had a hopperful of stones in my throat. Gibson frowned and touched me gently on my shoulder, squeezing strength of resolve into me. I waited for him to speak.

"Are you all right?"

"Yes," I whispered. "What did you want to show me?"

"In the sick bay," he said, tucking his hand under my arm to draw me to a stand. "You know I'm here for you, Merrick. You don't have to suffer these seizures in silence."

I nodded, but didn't reply. What good would talking about it do?

When we reached the infirmary, Gibson paused to lock the hatch from the inside. The prisoners were chained to the wall, each fast asleep and snoring. The good doctor ignored them and motioned for me to follow him into the next room.

He sat down before a computer and tapped in a code to bring up images created by the sick bay's scanner. "You're looking at a picture of Jasper Finn's head. The equipment doesn't seem to be working at full power, but it's got enough juice to get some high definition into the pictures. Notice the colors in the images of his teeth?"

I squinted at the screen. "So?"

"This man shows signs of mercury poisoning."

"And it's coming from his head?"

Gibson couldn't keep a smile locked down on his lips. "Every molar in his head has been filled. Dentists used to use an amalgam made of metals such as silver and mercury to fill and cap teeth."

"You're saying this is the source of the poisoning."

"Yes, but there's something else more startling. The computer measures the chemical compositions of foreign matter lodged in the body."

"And?"

His smile transformed into a wild-eyed expression of excitement. "I found your treasure."

"In fillings?"

"No. Inside the fillings. The amalgam covers only the top layer of the cavity. Scrape away the silver stuff, and you'll find that Finn has a mouthful of gold."

TWENTY-FOUR

Upon hearing this confession, my confusion got the better of me. "Did you check out McConnell?" I demanded.

Gibson nodded. "Nothing. He's got a lot of rot, but no fillings of any kind."

"It could be an isolated case."

"It could be, but people who have gold fillings usually have gold fillings. They don't cover up the work with a separate amalgam."

I sat down heavily in the only other available chair. Scenarios ran through my mind until I suspected everyone in the RP of duplicity and everyone in the labor camp of plain old criminal greed. "You need another subject from the prison population."

"Yes," he answered.

"What about that leprosy bacteria?"

"They both show signs of leprosy, but as Wilson said, it's a mutated form. It's affected their metabolisms in odd ways."

"Such as?"

"Their systems are processing energy at an uncharacteristically slow rate and there appears to be some indication of a regenerative synthesis occurring in segregated parts of their bodies, even as the disease ravages them."

"And once the organs are regenerated, the bacteria switches gears and starts to utilize the new organs and flesh."

"Yes."

"That must hurt like hell."

"I'd say from morning to night. It's the most insidious disease I've ever had the pleasure of meeting."

"What about the presence of nuciferia?"

"They have it in substantial levels in their bodies. It would dull the pain, and if I were in that condition, I'd take it as often as I could."

He tapped a new key sequence and brought up a bar chart on the monitor. "I also found out that the mercury has displaced a molecule of oxygen in their systems."

"Is it possible the mercury fillings have added to the changes in the original bacteria?"

He shrugged. "Anything is possible."

"Do me a favor, Gibson, and don't mention any of this to Stirling."

He flapped the computer disk at me. "Deleted from the hard drive and not leaving my side pocket for any reason except my curiosity."

I rose and walked back into the other room, slapping Finn on the side of the head to wake him. He came to with a shudder and begging for his life.

"Jasper," I said, "Dr. Gibson tells me you got a boat-load of gold wedged in your teeth. Tell me about that."

"I don't know nothing about no gold," he whispered.

I reacted in a normal, violent way by shoving my hand against his windpipe and pushing with a bit of my lycan-thropic strength. It took all of thirty seconds before he choked, coughed, and swore he would tell me the truth. Still, I had to put McConnell in his place when he tried to bag the whole conversation.

"Watch what you say, Finn," he warned. "You'll draw down a karmic curse if you talk."

I shot him a lethal look, boring my gaze straight through that scarred, bubbly head until, in my mind's eye, I'd drilled him an opening from front to back. "You can think of me as a walking karmic curse," I growled. "If you don't cooperate, I'll guarantee bad fortune will shine through your next ten lives. Got it?"

McConnell nodded, and by the time I returned my attention to Finn, the inmate was ready to spill his teeth if it would save him from a pounding. "It doesn't matter," he said. "I'm already at the end of the line." After hacking out half his lung, he shifted his position on the stool and announced his true and proper disposition. "I'm a dead man's chest."

"What is a dead man's chest?"

"I carry around the wealth collected by the Coven members."

"Are you forced by the guards to do this?"

"No, Marshal. We're selected by our ability to protect the wealth. It's an honor to be chosen and I've done pretty good over the years. Big enough and mean enough to fight off most inmates, and stupid enough so that not many of the spells have affected me."

"So, when they need money, what do they do to get it? Pull your teeth?"

He shook his head. "No. They cut your head off."

I opened my mouth to speak, but the second I did, I was rudely interrupted for the second time. The klaxon sounded and the boat shuddered. What had we hit now?

Gibson and I dashed to the main deck. I immediately had to revise my question from "what had we hit" to "what had hit us," for there, repeatedly ramming the dredge, was a serpent so big that even Odysseus would have been sorely put upon to defend himself against it.

TWENTY-FIVE

In some relationships, you reach a point of commitment so strong that it's impossible for you to deny. You're trapped by this singular connection, and when something threatens to snap the link, you'll do everything in your power to prevent it. So when I saw the monster diving in to swallow LaRue, I charged forward to make sure the cord between us remained intact, and since I've got another rope of commitment tying me to Gibson, the good doctor spun along behind me, shooting rubber bullets like a madman.

From the size of the alligator-shaped head, the beast must have been as long as the cutter. It was a slimy black conglomeration of parts and pieces—flippers, scales, and a thrashing tail edged with bony barbs. The serpent roared, and the sound was so impressive it shook the boat, the vibration knocking LaRue off his feet. He lay there, flat on his back, holding a carbine in one hand and pumping round after round at the monster. The hide was so tough the bullets merely grazed it and a couple ricocheted onto the deck. We jumped around like acrobats trying to avoid being hit by flying missiles.

The beast arched its long neck and screeched again. Despite the zinging bullets, I reached LaRue, and using my lycanthropic strength, I yanked him to his feet only a moment before the serpent swooped in to gobble him up. Gibson bellowed at us and in the nick of time my partner and I dove and rolled out of the range of the hideous jaws of death. The good doctor stepped up to this abomination and leveled his gun smack at the bastard's head.

What was the silly SOB trying to do? This was not a time to find courage when ill-equipped to carry through to a satisfactory end.

I left LaRue to get himself together and rushed back toward Gibson, firing a new clip until it was gone. It was useless posturing, serving only to make the beast roar with aggravation before it snapped at the air above our heads.

"Come on!" I screamed.

Gibson ignored me by taking steady aim on the creature. He had obviously underrated himself when it came to his marksmanship, because he ended this calamity by hitting the leviathan in the right eye. The bullet exploded the pupil and splattered us in goo, but it gave us the opportunity to haul ass for the cover provided by the main companionway.

Rivermen rushed in to meet the enemy with shouts and handheld harpoons. They fired upon the serpent like trained archers, jumping clear when their bolts were cast so other men could shoot and run. It was a hysterical rendition of Moby Dick, but it was enough to drive the monster back out into the channel, where it swam away.

LaRue leaned against the bulkhead and exhaled, but the proximity of being a snack got the better of him and he tossed the rifle onto the deck, mumbling: "Oh shit, oh shit, oh shit."

Gibson had his wits about him and gave LaRue a quick once-over. When he touched my partner's shoulder, he received a reaction. LaRue winced, but instead of whining, he apologized. "Sorry, Doc. I'm okay. Just bruised my arm from the kick action on the carbine."

"Let's get you to sick bay and make sure," Gibson said.

"What about the glop all over you?" LaRue asked.

Gibson glanced at me. "We'll need to scrape some of it

for samples. I want to see what that thing is made of."
With that, he hauled LaRue away.

I trudged behind them, feeling like a two-legged speci-
men bank for the supernatural. Not only did I have my
lycanthropy to deal with, but now I was additionally coated
in the fluids of a monster that should never have existed.

Stirling was nowhere to be found, so we made ourselves
at home with the two prisoners while LaRue climbed up
on the table and Gibson did his thing. Finn glanced at me
as I stood there soggy and dripping, waiting to be told what
to do.

"So, you done met one of Davy Jones's prized pets,"
the inmate said.

"You've seen these beasts before?" I asked.

"Yes, for years. Please don't ask me how many years,
'cause I can't remember exactly."

"All right, what are they, then?"

They both shrugged and McConnell answered. "Demons
called up from the locker by the water witches. Most likely
Hecate's Sickle is behind it. They got a lot of real water
witches amongst that group—folks who won't ever get a
chance to join the Coven like they should."

I shook my head, feeling the monster's goo starting to
solidify on my neck. "I don't believe in magic. What other
excuses do you boys have?"

"None," Finn said. "The leviathan was drubbed up with
magic. Probably shaped from bad karmic energy. It's the
only explanation."

My attention was drawn off from this discussion of the
occult as LaRue unzipped his cammies so Gibson could
have a look at his arm. His fingers probed gently along my
partner's collarbone, toward his elbow, and across his back.
LaRue allowed a frown to perch upon his face, the weight
of which pressed down on any expression of pain.

"I thought I was going to be counting the teeth inside
that mouth," LaRue murmured. "Thank you for coming to
my rescue."

Gibson grunted and I smiled before changing the subject

all the way. "Do you have something I can scrape the slime into? This stuff is hardening."

He pointed to a counter. "There should be something in the cabinets." Then, turning back to his patient, Gibson pronounced him to still be in one piece. "You're going to be sore for the next few days."

I waltzed to the equipment case and found a beaker. God, I was covered with eyeball juice, and though it was a smear of pus and blood, my blended senses smelled it as saffron rectangles. Scraping the goo from my cammies, I ladled it into the jar with my hand, filling the container after only a few strokes.

"You should not be concerned about washing off the leviathan's life force," Finn said.

"Why?" I asked.

"Because it carries the power of the river. Since it didn't kill you, it'll give you strength."

"Great," I muttered. Then, as an afterthought, I said: "Why would Hecate's Sickle want to attack us?"

Finn glanced at McConnell before speaking. "Water witches don't get karmic power without paying for it. Who knows what bargain Eldon Emmet made with Davy Jones."

TWENTY-SIX

I left the sick bay after filling the beaker and hurried away to wash off the serpent's life force and to change into a clean uniform. The water pressure gave me more of a sprinkle than a shower, but as I tried to rinse the pus out of my hair, it afforded me time to sort through the confusion and weird expectations that apparently served as the supernatural glue holding the penal colony together.

From the point of view of the prisoners, life served as a vessel for karmic influences, and without the cosmic credit-and-debits file, there was no reason to incarnate. The trick to a successful incarnation was learning to manipulate the power of the four laws. I could understand using karma to gain spiritual growth and search for lofty ideals that might indeed make a future life more palatable. If there was a wheel of rebirth, then the only thing to see you to a better existence in the next go-round was hard work and adherence to long-held principles. Unfortunately, the travesty here in the labor camp proved that superstition could turn anything into magic—even the concept of redemption.

I'd just stepped out of the bathroom when I met LaRue and Gibson in the companionway. Ritter had called an impromptu meeting in the boat's mess and he wanted us there.

I changed directions and followed them, entering as Ritter announced new ground rules.

"If we lose any more people, we're going to be down to a skeleton crew and I'll have to abort the tour," he said. "We have come to a point of no return, with only Yarrow left as our pilot. If something should happen to her, I'm the only one left who's qualified to steer this boat. Curran, I want you to guard Yarrow twenty-four hours a day. Sleep in her bunk room, and be nearby at all times. Understand? I don't want to lose another pilot."

The riverman nodded. "Aye, sir."

"Good," Ritter said. "For the rest of you, I want everyone to carry a rifle even belowdecks or when we're plying the channel. Got that?"

There was a mutter of assent before LaRue broke the consortium apart to ask a perfectly reasonable question. "What was that thing that attacked us, Captain?"

Ritter scowled. "I don't know. There are some biological atrocities out on the water, I'll admit. I've never seen anything like that in my life."

"But you were ready with harpoons."

"Yes. We've met other large creatures and have found the harpoons more effective than bullets."

"Is the RP aware of these dangers?"

"Yes, Marshal. I've made every effort to keep my superiors informed." He lifted his attention from LaRue to continue giving orders to his crew, and finally, he ended with a further stipulation. "All hatches will be secured from sunset to sunrise. No one is to go on deck." He stopped again to scan the room, ending with a salute and a dismissal.

The captain spent no time retreating to his quarters. We paused long enough to dip up our dinners from the mess pots being set out by the cook and then carried the food back to our bunk room.

It was a tight, little place by any standards. The bunks were stacked in twos and hinged to the bulkhead. Our accommodations came with a bent metal dresser, a chamber

pot for emergencies, and a propane lantern that did little to
chase the shadows from the room.

I settled into the single chair as Gibson swung into the
upper bunk and carefully balanced the plastic bowl containing his food. LaRue, who was still busy thanking Davy
Jones for saving his butt, forgot about vittles and instead
snapped open the small porthole to stick his face into the
circular opening.

My lycanthropic furnace was boiling and I cleaned out
my cup of stew to the continued noise of my growling
belly. Gibson heard this concert and tossed me a package
of salt crackers. I chewed them down, but they weren't
enough. In these times when my body "superconvects," I
must endure a nagging stomach. It's as if I can't eat enough
to keep the fire going through me, and comparing it with
the monsters around me, I just had to wonder if I fit into
their category.

What defined a monster? Was it bad karmic influences
or was it the DNA? Did the very molecules that made up
the creature determine whether it was a beast, or was it
merely the profound sense of dread and confusion it inspired?

My considerations were shot through with presump-
tions—among which was the reality of the soul. I had a
hard time believing in its existence, whether in man or
beast. Reincarnation had too many pat answers. Easy come
was never easy for me to accept.

We were silent for several minutes before LaRue pulled
his head back into the room and turned to speak to us. "I
had a chance to go through the beginning of the *Delora*'s
log. It goes back several months."

"Did you find out anything we could use?" Gibson
asked.

He slid into the lower bunk and picked up the book. "It's
such a jumble of science and superstition, it's hard to tell
what is real and what isn't. There's a whole section on the
tidal bore."

"What does it say?"

He flipped to the middle of the thick log and ran his

finger down the page. "Kleege was on duty the night before and he reports that two mermaids 'jumped out of the water like flying fish' over the bow."

"Mermaids?"

"Kleege entered a note of record, declaring the event to be an evil portent. He went straightaway to the captain, who told him to log his observations."

"Ritter doesn't seem the type to believe in imaginary beings," I said.

"There was nothing imaginary about that serpent," LaRue said quietly. He flipped a page. "Kleege also reported seeing a UFO hovering over the abandoned remains of an ore refinery and a sulfuric wind containing a group of mist people. He also confirms that there was a red sky at morning."

"What about the other pilot?"

"That would have been Riverman Yarrow and her observations were pretty much by the book." He shook his head. "Still, this stuff gives me the creeps."

"You? Andy, you're right at home with the supernatural."

"Yeah, but it's not every day I've got to deal with a serpent about to eat me." He paused to run his finger down the page. "On the day the tidal bore hit, they were, indeed, transporting prisoners to the delta. According to Kleege, Ritter had fair warning the trouble was coming up the river. He received the report by radio from a river rat who advised him to heave to and seek safe harbor. Ritter didn't listen."

"He said he didn't trust Kleege," I interrupted. "Did he put on another pilot?"

LaRue shook his head. "Rather than cruising out of harm's way, he told Kleege to steer the *Delora* directly into the wave."

TWENTY-SEVEN

The next morning, I rose early to find Gibson gone but LaRue still passed out. I left him to snore some more, stopped by the chow hall to grab a cup of coffee, and then headed to the radio room to send a message to Prefect Warden Zoltana.

Riverman Harvey was on duty. He was a young fellow, or so he seemed, with a head full of shiny, black hair. He greeted me by evacuating his chair to offer me a seat. I asked him to dial up the guard station, and while he did that I decided to ask him a few questions.

"I'll bet you've seen some stuff happen out on these waters," I said.

He paused to lock in the signal and choke down a bite of his breakfast sandwich before replying. "I've never seen a beast like the one yesterday."

"How long have you been with the RP?"

"Eighteen years. Normally, I'm part of the dock dispatch crew. The only time I hit the water is when I need to be recertified. Damn bad time for my chits to run out."

"So, you spend most of your time in the district?"

"Yes, ma'am."

"Have you ever shipped out with this crew before?"

"A couple of the folks. Stirling and Yarrow. I don't know Ritter well at all. This is my first tour with him."

I watched him fiddle with the radio's dials and asked another question. "Why do you think the prisoners are attacking this boat?"

He shrugged. "Are you so sure it's the prisoners?"

"Who else would it be?"

"What about the guards?" he whispered.

"Now, why would they do that?"

"That's a real good question, Marshal, and I don't know the answer. Still, I've been around long enough to know that something is sour in Summerland."

I squinted at him. "Summerland?"

"Aye. That place of the great beyond, where every man hopes to walk after death."

More metaphysical garbage. "Are you suggesting there's some bureaucratic double-dealing going on?"

"Isn't there always?"

"That's true. But, tell me, what do you suspect?"

Harvey forgot the radio's knob. He straightened and stared at me. "With the help of Derek Wheeler, Zoltana organized this labor camp by using some bizarre parameters. They say the experiment worked. I guess so, but for the love of Davy Jones, it's hard to swallow, you know? Hell, my grandmother believes in magic spells and stink charms. I have to put up with the potions and drubs from her. I shouldn't have to depend on my government to fill in the spaces with hexes and curses. Aren't there any reasonable people left?" He paused to point toward an amulet dangling from the light fixture. "Do you believe this boat? That shit is hanging everywhere. You can't even move around on the bridge and not run into any of them."

I let Harvey vent for a few minutes before gently bringing him back to the question. "Do you believe Zoltana is responsible for the attacks on this boat?"

He shook his head. "I don't know for sure. I do know that you shouldn't trust him."

"What about Hecate's Sickle?" I asked.

"They're prisoners who refuse to play the game."

"Malcontents?"

"Yeah."

"Who's their leader?"

"I'm not sure," he answered. "I've seen radio traffic talking about a man named Eldon Emmet."

"What about Derek Wheeler?"

"Wheeler is dead."

"Did you see radio traffic on this?"

"Yes." He leaned close to me and spoke in a soft voice. "There was a riot after he died. I think that's when Hecate's Sickle broke away."

"How did they quell the riot?" I asked.

He shrugged. "I suppose they did it with bullets and black magic. Info on the problem was labeled 'need to know,' and I was taken out of the loop." With that, he finished tuning in the radio to the proper frequency and hailed the guard station.

Zoltana came to the horn after several minutes, immediately beginning his transmission with: "It's too goddamned early in the A.M., Marshal Merrick."

I experienced a moment of pleasure at his discomfort and then, before he had time to complain further, I made my request. "Prefect, we need another prisoner. This time I want one of your trustees, specifically a man who carries around the walk-in soul of Derek Wheeler."

TWENTY-EIGHT

Zoltana balked at the request, but in the end said he would contact us when he had the prisoner in direct custody. After this conversation, I thanked Harvey and headed back to the mess to stuff my face with vittles, and since I was there, I decided it was as good a time as any to interview the cook, a guy named Whitechapel.

The mess was empty of crewmen, but I selected a table close to the galley and away from sensitive ears. Whitechapel limped over, bringing a hot pot of coffee and two cups. He served up the steaming liquid and settled in heavily. Whitechapel wore a filthy apron; his hands were tarnished from handling raw meat; and with my blended senses operating at full tilt, he smelled like greasy, brown slivers.

"How'd you get that limp?" I asked.

"Years ago I had a run-in with a beast like that monster that attacked us."

"Was it the same kind of serpent?"

He shook his head. "No, it was more like a giant squid. And yes, I know, they don't live in fresh water, but hell, there isn't anything fresh about the water anyway. It crawled up onto the boat and I just happened to be with my back against the railing. The thing had suckers and a beak. It was the beak that got me. Snapped my leg off at the knee afore my mates could pull me clear.'' He rapped his prosthesis, smiling when he was rewarded with a hollow sound. ''It's titanium. Imagine that? The RP had to pay for it because it was an injury sustained on duty. They fired the medic who kept me alive until we reached dock.''

''Why?''

''Because he cost them money.'' Whitechapel leaned toward me and spoke in a whisper. ''Why do you think Stirling didn't go out of his way to help Dacey?'' He sat back. ''Overpopulation has made the human being an expendable commodity. Surely you know that, Marshal.''

Yes, I did. The government's idea was a simple one: three or four million people would never be missed. Instead of answering him, I asked a question. ''What about Ritter?''

''That peckerwood? The brass put him on this bucket to do their spying.''

''Why do you say that?''

''Because he doesn't know what he's doing. He runs the boat like he's fresh out of the academy, and he waits too long to make a decision.'' He paused to study me. ''I think he's right stupid, too. I can't say for sure, but from the scuttlebutt, I'd say he's all twined up with Zoltana, and that can never be a good thing.''

I leaned toward him and spoke in a low voice. ''Has Zoltana demonstrated a nefarious side?''

Whitechapel snorted. ''He's the baddest thing to ever come down the river.''

''Why do you say that?''

''Because he ain't got a conscience.''

''It's not a prerequisite for the job.''

''Well, then, they got their man.''

''What has he done?''

''What ain't he done?'' he answered. He stalled his reply by pouring sugar into his coffee cup. Then, shaking his head, he changed the subject. ''Ritter was a desk jockey.

Harvey told me he pushed papers back at the dock for the
Humanitarian Section of the RP. He was supposed to be
checking up on prisoner abuse.''

This confession meant Harvey had dicked me out of the
whole story. ''That might make Ritter one of the good
guys,'' I said.

''Does it matter? Good guy or not—he's incompetent.
Ritter plowed this boat straight into a tidal bore. Did he tell
you about that?''

''We know of it.''

''It pissed off a lot of people.''

I saw his direction. ''And still, he commands the *Delora*.
Why?''

''Because he didn't do too much damage to the boat.
That, and he knew what bureaucrat could pull his ass out
of the shark tank.''

''What about all the prisoners who drowned?'' I asked.
''Didn't that get somebody's attention?''

Whitechapel sighed. ''They were just prisoners. Like I
told you—expendable.''

''What happened to the bodies?''

''They were fished out of the water and placed aboard
an RP river scow.'' He hesitated, opened his mouth, and
then shut it.

I urged him on after sucking up an oily, fried egg.
''Something about it was not kosher, I take it.''

''Well, I'm not sure of anything, so maybe I ought to
not even mention it.''

''I think you better. You don't want to get yourself and
that nice titanium leg into a sinkhole of trouble.''

He squinted at me. ''What do you mean? I haven't done
anything wrong.''

''Tell me what you know, Whitey.'' I calmly tore off a
chunk of bread and dipped it into my coffee while I waited
for him to respond.

Finally, he decided that confessing was better than a possible stay in the district lockup for impeding an investiga-

tion. "It was my job to count the stiffs as they were put on the transport barge," he said. "There were a hundred and fifty-three bodies, but according to Harvey, only a hundred twenty-nine made it to dock for disposal."

TWENTY-NINE

I left Whitechapel with more questions than I had when I started, but I pushed them all into a pocket in my brain for later investigation and set about my duties of feeding and watering the prisoners. The cook had provided the usual ration of bread and water, but he'd also tossed in some sausages and fried onions. They could not believe their good fortune and ate like men possessed, grunting, slobbering, and breathing hard between bites.

Gibson worked at the computer in the sick bay's auxiliary room, and after chow was under way, I visited him. He glanced around when I stepped in and I could tell by his face that he was not a happy man.

"How's the serpent goo?" I said. "Get any startling answers?"

He scowled, shook his head, and turned back to the screen. "I'm still waiting on the workup."

I stepped over to the chair and slid into it. "So, why the furrowed brow?"

"It's this hydrotomography unit," he said. "I keep getting an error message that it's functioning on secondary power."

"What about the scans?"

"It didn't have enough juice to perform a tracing command I gave it while I was using it on the prisoners. It was at ninety-five percent then. Now it tells me it's at sixty-five percent."

"Maybe there's something wrong with the generator."

"I checked out a couple of pieces of equipment and they seem to be functioning normally." He spun in the chair to squint at me. "Since you're here, why don't you help me test the unit out."

I tried to come up with an excuse to worm out of it, but I was a little slow with my customary brilliance.

"Please?" he said.

"Oh, all right," I finally answered. To show him I wasn't happy about the idea, I grumbled. "This thing better not nuke my brain."

He chuckled. "I don't think it has enough power to pop those little neurons of yours. I'm not even sure I can get anything useful. Damn. It was one of the reasons I came along on this tour of insanity."

I abruptly changed the subject when I remembered his plans for me. "Gibson, you have to promise not to dink around with my lycanthropy. Don't initiate any stretches."

He stood and stepped to me, placing his hands gently on my arms. "I promise. No pain." With that, he kissed me full on the lips as if he were sealing a contract. Then, backing away, I saw there was medical curiosity behind his passion. "What do I smell like in the heat of the moment?" he asked softly.

The stinking bastard. "You smell like bright red bundles of shit."

Gibson's expression exploded into a grin and he patted the table. "Hop up here."

"Do I have to get undressed or anything?" I asked.

"If you did that, you might find yourself being rubbed all over by those bright red bundles."

"Well, then, I shall not encourage you," I said, rubbing my butt around on the table.

Sex is the one thing in our relationship I can control. Perhaps it's a karmic skill I developed over previous lifetimes spent with Gibson. Whatever it is, my body holds a mystique that is so powerful, it sways him, however momentarily, from his quest for wealth. Still, I don't do myself any favors by promoting his passion, because I worry in the end my fears will be borne out and he'll walk away from me after getting the information he wants. Worse than the fact that my world is inextricably tied to his is the idea that long after the physical relationship is over, the mental entanglement will still be there. Like the wolf, Gibson has become part of my psyche. They are both walk-ins who have sent their spirits ahead to claim the empty places in my soul.

Before I realized what was happening, he kissed me again, and like the addict I am, I dropped into that familiar comfort zone. Unfortunately, he scrapped the embrace by pulling away and asking me the same stupid question about how he smelled.

I took a deep breath and studied him. "Why do you want to know that?"

"You have functional synesthesia, Merrick. You're segregating incoming stimuli at different levels and in different ways. If you paid attention, you might be able to sort out other connections your senses have made. You've been blessed with such an interesting gift and you don't even know."

"Gift? Are you out of your mind?"

"Yes, gift. Synesthesia is a rare neurological occurrence. Researchers have done studies on the phenomenon and found that those people who have blended senses tend to be highly creative and extremely focused—two talents you possess." He stopped explaining to fit a strap around my head and under my chin.

"What's this for?" I asked.

"To keep your noggin still. If you move, you'll screw up the scan. That is if I can get one." Finishing, he returned to our conversation about my synesthesia. "Sensory input affects the body's systems, especially metabolic reactions. Fear makes us burn the calories because we breathe deeply and maintain a certain stress level. On the other hand, making love causes stress, but instead of initiating the flight-or-fight impulses, it triggers sexual excitement. Since you're probably aware at several different levels in several different ways, I'm hoping to create a baseline that will reflect your state with blended senses. Maybe it will give us some clues."

It was another long grab for a fly ball, but I didn't mention it. Gibson already knew he was paddling upstream.

"So, what did I smell like?" he asked again.

"Like a rainbow," I answered.

He smiled and asked me to lie back as he punched the electronic pad on the wall next to the unit. The table delivered my head deep inside the scanner's hole. Once the carriage stopped and locked, the lights went out. I could see the blue glow of the infirmary, but I had to practically roll my eyes down into my cheekbones to get a glimpse of it.

"How long will this take?" I called out.

"About an hour," he said. "Everything okay in there?"

"I don't like the dark."

"Pretend you have a gun."

"I do have a gun, and my nose itches. Can I scratch it?"

He yelled at me to be still and after a moment I did as he asked. Seconds later the machine vibrated beneath my head and I heard a clicking noise.

Closing my eyes, I intended to use the darkness to take a nap. I dozed off, and had a short dream about a fanciful past life spent as a winsome serving girl in some filthy dockside tavern. It was one of those visions that feel grounded in reality, as though the brain is sending some signal to the body to experience the images through the nerve endings. I could sense the rough, wooden tables and smell spilled rum, urine, and puke. My synesthesia kicked in to brand my inner eye with the odor of golden squares.

Gibson appeared in the dream, a powerful pirate for the crown. What crown, what country, what century were all questions my fantasy could not answer, but it seemed unimportant because the tactile nature of the dream fed me volumes of information. I felt Gibson's touch and knew he meant to save me from the squalor of a soul drafted into an incarnation full of hardships.

In the dream, we were lovers. I was just getting to the good part when the real doctor appeared at the opening of the hydrotomography unit to wake me from an imaginary romantic interlude. He flicked the switch and the lights came on in the electronic cave.

"Tell me my snoring didn't upset the scanner," I said sleepily, reluctantly leaving the dream behind.

"It's not you," he answered. "There is something drastically wrong with this equipment. I can't seem to get the resolution out of it that I need and the computer keeps sending a dump message. This thing has its own backup power system. An access hatch ought to be inside the unit. Do you see anything?"

I yawned, glanced around, and noticed a metal clasp holding a hinged door in place. "There's something in the back of the unit. Wait a minute." I unsnapped the head harness and rolled over to have a better look. Taking the clasp, I pulled the closet open to find quite a surprise.

The scanner certainly did have its own power source. In fact, it was run from the electricity provided by a bank of gel-cell batteries, of which two were missing. This observation was then compounded by my next discovery: Amos Kleege's scrimshaw good-luck charm.

THIRTY

LaRue would say this kind of discovery fell into the realm of synchronicity, but the minute I saw what was going on, I fell into the realm of paranoia. It made me realize that the dangerous part of the job was still to come, that of separating the good guys from the bad guys while taking a slow boat down a polluted river. Whoever was behind this had been around after Kleege was dead, because a bloody fingerprint had dried on the scrimshaw.

I carefully unwound the charm's chain from the prongs of the battery housing and snapped the lid shut, calling to Gibson as I did. "Reel me out."

He extended the table and poked his head inside when I was clear. "What is it?"

"You're missing a couple of batteries," I answered, sitting up. "Gel cells."

Gibson ducked out of the metal cave and squinted at me. "Oh, damn."

"You're in luck, sort of. I found one of those babies buried in Amos Kleege's locker. I'll go get it for you."

He nodded, pointing to the scrimshaw. "What's that?"

"Kleege's good-luck charm. He wore it around his neck. I noticed it was missing when we examined the body."

Gibson frowned and held out his hand. "May I see that?"

I handed it to him and watched as he spent a moment studying it. Then, turning it over, he said: "This isn't a good-luck charm. Kleege was feeding you a line of Class-A tuna fish."

Not being well versed in magical designs, I played my ignorance like a trump card. "What kind of charm would it be, then?"

He glanced at me. "Back in the district it's called an uukerat, a supernatural vessel that carries the bounty of the Moon Goddess, Soma. That's why it's shaped like a sickle moon." Gibson gave it a good shake, releasing the cascading sound of small stones. "Soma represents the mirror self, the part of our nature which is cast in reflection."

I stared at him and then shook my head, not happy about showing my stupidity, but unable to get around it. "I don't understand what you mean."

"Soma is the dark side of our souls," he answered patiently. "She expresses our intuitive, imaginative self. People use them as a token of Soma's karmic grace by filling the uukerats with seeds or spices. Sometimes you'll even find scented bits of fabric or gravel from the river."

"What makes it different from any other charm?"

"According to legend, Soma's uukerat has the power to change future lives."

If that were so, I needed ten or twelve of the things. "So, more than likely, Kleege got this charm off of a water witch?"

He nodded.

I paced around the room and then stopped, caught profoundly in the moment. Since coming down with lycanthropy, I often experience odd minutes when time becomes so distilled that it seems to slow down. My sense of touch is launched by a heightened nervous system and turns into a sensory array so sensitive, I get goose bumps just running my fingers down my pants. Not only does this sensitivity extend to my body, but also my thoughts. For a few seconds the world slides in with stark clarity.

I spun on my heel to face Gibson. "How much do you know about this form of invisible magic?"

"If you're asking me about how witchcraft works in the penal colony, then don't bother. I haven't got a clue."

"How do you know about the uukerats in the first place?"

"I have a few patients who dabble in spells and a couple of them are so poor they pay me with charms. The story goes that before Duvalier tore down the world in favor of his great dream, he would give these vessels to those who were loyal to his cause."

Upon hearing his statement, I suddenly realized where my moment of clarity was leading to. "Can you open it to see what is inside?"

He paused in his explanation to gently tug on one of the silver caps connecting the chain at both ends. With very little pressure, it pulled away. Gibson then motioned with his chin. "Would you bring me that med tray on the counter?"

I did as he asked and watched as he spilled the contents into it. Much to our amazement, karmic grace did, indeed, pour from the uukerat—in the form of tiny rubies and emeralds.

THIRTY-ONE

If the curse of the *Delora* meant people would throw gems at me, I should have stepped aboard ages ago.

"Looks like you've stumbled into a money pit," Gibson said.

I picked up one of the gems and held it toward the light, my lycanthropic fascination for glittering things overtaking my attention. It was only when Gibson moved that I snapped back into the moment. "You keep them," I said.

He glanced at me, but instead of a smiling visage, I saw a squint of suspicion. "Why?"

This trip had turned into a treasure trove of good fortune as well as atrocities. Some might call what we did stealing, but in our world of misfortune, the watchwords were: finders keepers—losers weepers. Since we didn't have any brass breathing down our necks, there was no reason to pitch prosperity back to the pack so the big dogs could pick over it. "I'm not going to turn the gems over as evidence, if that's what you mean."

"No," he answered softly. "That's not what I mean. You found them. Why aren't you keeping them?"

Why didn't my integrity and generosity count for something with him? After all, he'd lived the lie in our relation-

ship more than I had. I stood there staring at him, my
serenity forced to parry thrusts of anger. Finally, in a voice
made more gravelly by the wolf, I explained myself. "I'm
not a greedy person, Gibson. And not everything I do has
an ulterior motive. Maybe you should look for that quality
in yourself before you seek it in others."

That said, I dropped the ruby back in the pan and
stomped into the other room to unlock Finn from the wall.
It took me a minute to unchain the bolt, plenty of time for
Gibson to come up with some fiery comment, but in the
end there was silence from him.

I pushed Finn topside and waited for him to take a leisurely leak over the side. When he was done, I let go of
the steam that my conversation with Gibson had provoked.
I pulled my side arm, grabbed the man by the neck, and
shoved the end of the gun into his right nostril. Finn
breathed hard against this intrusion as he tried to talk
around the barrel.

"Why?" he asked. "I—I been cooperative."

"And there's no reason to stop now," I answered lacon-
ically. "I want to know the truth. Is Wheeler dead?"

He gagged and squawked but I had to really apply the
vise grips to get him to answer. "I ain't sure, and that's
for a fact."

I eased back on the force to let him speak, and when he
didn't push any more words through the hole I gave him,
I choked him again. He finally convinced me to let him
have extra air by begging for mercy. I disconnected from
him and demanded the truth. "Did you see Wheeler die?"

"No. I couldn't visit with him. I wasn't high enough in
the pecking order. If he is alive, I wish to hell I could get
to him."

I replaced the pistol in my holster and leaned on the
railing. "What happened to you after Wheeler came up
missing?"

"According to the Coven rules as they were set down, I
was supposed to become part of Eldon Emmet's treasure."

"But that didn't work out."

"No, Marshal, it didn't. Emmet had some kind of bad

argument with Zoltana. If you ask me, ol' Zol wasn't going to give Emmet anything that was rightfully his. The witch got pissy and decided he was going to stick the prefect every chance he got.''

"Who was Eldon Emmet in the first place?"

"He was Wheeler's son."

I turned to stare at him full in his bubbly face. "His son? By blood?"

"Can't say that for sure. I do know Wheeler raised Emmet up."

"What does that mean?"

"You know. Took him under his wing when Emmet arrived. Kept him from getting buggered by folks." He scanned the bank before continuing. "Emmet got to be real powerful. Soon he became the Keeper of the Book of Shadows."

"Tell me exactly what this book is."

He shrugged. "It's just a recipe book on how to turn up spells. Hell, my granny had one. Didn't yours?"

I didn't know my granny, much less her library. "I take it Emmet walked off with the magic."

"That's right. Zoltana made one big mistake. At least as far as I can see."

"And that would be?"

"He didn't give the water witches any true powers of their own. All the head honchos had one job to do and that was that. Emmet controlled the Book of Shadows; Wheeler was the High Priest. The other bigwigs did other stuff."

"Are you saying they can't perform magic unless all of them join in a cooperative effort?" I asked.

"As far as the Coven is concerned, they are like a cow with no udders. Everyone knows it, too."

"Still, you're frightened. Of whom?"

Finn sighed. "It's not the who I'm afraid of, Marshal. It's the what. My neck is right valuable and the spells can get right strong. Emmet wants me and so does Zoltana. Dead I'll be, either way."

A noise behind us made me spin on my heel to see LaRue watching me. "Morning exercises?" he said.

I was about to answer him when I noticed a guard marching one of the prison trustees toward the boat. LaRue latched onto my gaze and turned to see what I was staring at.

The inmate they brought to us was none other than Monty Philips—con artist, pimp, and murderer. LaRue and I had literally sent this criminal up the river.

THIRTY-TWO

When Philips saw who waited for him on the boat, he stopped walking, and then indignantly pegged us with a wall-eyed stare. The guard tugged on his handcuffs and was eventually forced to jump-start the prisoner with a shove.

Philips had been wanted by the Marshals' Office for engaging in a backdoor version of the adult peepshow. It was a common scam—vice was always breaking up these prostitution rings specializing in erotic enticements to draw the customer right off the street. Philips had twenty girls, all of them underage. He never billed sex as his inducement, but instead, he played up the paranormal bullshit. According to his sales pitch, his ladies were back-alley oracles who could channel the discarnate entities of such famous, sensual women as Cleopatra, Queen Nefertiti, and even Helen of Troy. The fact that these prostitutes did the channeling through their hot, pulsing loins never came up.

Rather than keeping his stable of oracles loyal with threats, Philips used drugs and brainwashing to convince his ladies that they were indeed mystical sorceresses with the power to transmit thought and emotion through their bodies. Things were going damned smooth for this bastard until the day one of his girls managed to break away from his control. She ran home to mama and daddy with Philips in hot pursuit. When she reached the house, he had one of his thugs waiting to bring her back, but the prostitute dumped his butt by shooting him with a Smith & Wesson. We were called in and the poor girl did everything she could to assuage her guilt by confessing all.

It wasn't long before we had a sting strung together with vice. I played the prostitute's replacement, putting on a performance that, admittedly, stretched my acting abilities a bit, but was enough to convince Philips that I could channel anyone from Eleanor Roosevelt to Duvalier's number-five mistress, Margo Peal, if he so desired. The moment he went for my crotch in anticipation was the moment we brought the big guns in and worked him over, finally securing the truth and arresting him on flesh peddling, statutory rape, and intent to murder. We managed to get the counts bumped up from one to sixteen, and that figure is what put his ass in the penal colony, where from the looks of him, he wasn't doing too badly.

As Philips stepped on board the *Delora* he glanced at Finn and hissed. Finn fell to his knees and groveled before I yanked him to a stand.

"What the hell is this all about?" I growled.

"He's the Baculum," Finn whispered, keeping his eyes firmly focused toward the deck.

"Big deal," I said. "He's a pimp, too."

"No, you don't understand," he murmured.

"No, she doesn't," Philips barked. "Someone needs to tell her."

"He's the wand of the witches," Finn said.

LaRue joined the fray just as I was ready to unload my opinion about profound bullshit. Addressing Philips, he asked: "What does he mean by the wand?"

"I am the vessel of magic, Marshal LaRue. I am the being that touches the netherworld and brings the dimensions together. Without me, there is no witchcraft here."

I sauntered over to this man. "Well, you look to me like someone beat you with that wand."

"Don't fuck with me, screw," Philips said. "I'm a

power to be reckoned with now and I'll lay a karmic curse
on you that will never end.''

"About that curse? You're already too late." I paused,
and then hit him in his metaphysical third eye. "Don't play
hardball with me, you piece of shit. I don't believe in witchcraft, magic, or demons. I also know that without the Book
of Shadows, your life is as forfeit as the rest of them."

After I was done with that, I ripped his ragged shirt to
reveal a clutch of charm sacks and amulets. Slowly, and
with sheer delight, I wrapped my fingers around his invisible magic and gave it one good supernatural tug. The
strings broke and the sacks came free in my hand. I nodded
curtly to the guard, who pushed Philips toward LaRue.
They headed off to sick bay, and once they were gone, I
turned to Finn, who by this time, had melted into cowering
submission.

"What the hell are you afraid of?" I demanded. "He
doesn't have a lick more power than I do."

"Oh, by Davy Jones, I'll get a birching for seeing you
cut out his magic like that."

"A birching?"

"They'll beat me with the flat of a tree until I bleed to
death," he whined. Pausing, he wiped at a glob of snot
running from his nose. Then, in a sad voice, he added: "At
least before, my death was going to be one quick chop to
the neck." He looked at me beseechingly. "I can't go back
to that cell block. I'm as good as dead if you take me back.
I won't last out the morning."

"As I recall, you weren't going to last out the morning
when we picked you up," I said. "What do you have to
offer that will keep me from handing you over?"

He wiped his nose goo on his pants, answering in a whisper. "I can take you to Eldon Emmet."

THIRTY-THREE

I deposited both Finn and McConnell in the *Delora*'s dungeon, an eight-foot-square hold in the aft of the boat that reeked of paint thinner and sulfur. By the time I stepped into the sick bay again, Gibson was drawing a pint of blood from Philips while LaRue dispassionately viewed the proceedings. The inmate tossed me a sour expression and the dreaded evil eye, but smiling darkly, I countered his curse by crossing my fingers. It was all bogus crap, yet it let the SOB know I wasn't going to play his invisible-magic games. To stress my point, I took a stool by the counter and began to unwrap his charm sacks. Philips complained immediately, trying out his prison power on me.

"I'll curse you, I swear," he bellowed. "Open those and you'll find yourself up to your ears in sea monsters. I guarantee it."

"Been there, done that," I answered.

Philips cut me such a look of hatred that I thought he was trying to use it like a magic arrow to pierce my heart. "You're unclean," he snapped. "Touching the sacred objects will only show you the soil on your own soul."

That did it. Talk about my dirt, will you? With a flourish, I unloaded one of his sacks onto the counter. He moaned as the contents of the first packet revealed its secret—three polished river stones, three bleached bones, three pieces of charcoal, and three bird beaks. "What an interesting assortment of goodies," I said.

"You don't know what power you are fooling with," he growled.

"Then perhaps you'll tell me. What power is lying here in the midst of this trash?"

Philips hesitated, but after I started to untwine the second bag, he hurried to answer. "Water, flesh, fire, and air," he said cryptically.

"And I should be impressed by this?"

"Those objects contain the karmic energies that form the world. The elements converged to make earth."

"Why are there three of everything?"

"Because water witches believe in the threefold way— that whatever you put into the world comes back threefold."

"I imagine you've suffered in your travels down this mystical path."

He snorted, but didn't enlighten us on his own spiritual development. My hunch was that he hadn't evolved an iota.

Ignoring his protests, I proceeded to open the next bag, finding it to contain a couple of oversized teeth. I held up a molar for Philips to see and then glanced at LaRue. "What is this supposed to signify?"

"My resurrection," he answered.

LaRue rose from the only available chair to take the tooth for a quick examination. "Why do you carry them?"

Philips winced as Gibson removed the blood-siphoning needle, but again he was slow to respond. LaRue turned toward me and tossed the tooth onto the counter. "They look like they came out of a horse."

"Not a horse," Philips said. "A man."

"Oh, come on," I said. "No one has teeth that big." The moment I said it I thought of retracting it. "Wait a minute. Are you suggesting that there was a human being big enough to have a mouthful of these things?"

"He was almost twelve feet tall," Philips answered. "We called him Goliath."

Gibson came around to the conversation. "What happened to him?"

"I extinguished his soul for all eternity by using the ancient powers afforded to me as the Baculum."

It was the good doctor's turn to snort. "Impossible."

"Would you deny what your eyes show you?" Philips asked. "Karmic power flows through my body. It has transformed me. Since being put down by our friendly law-enforcement officers over there, I've grown seven inches and put on twenty-five pounds."

"You must be eating real well," I said.

"No. The usual rations."

I turned back to the counter. Philips could scam with the best of them, and from Finn's desperate demonstration, I got the feeling that every inmate out there paid some sort of tribute to the "wand."

Opening the last of the pouches, I was in for a nice surprise. It contained dehydrated body parts—fingertips, an ear, and an eyeball with a blue iris. I picked up one of the grisly objects and promptly received a shock, because I smelled golden squares. It took me a minute to recover my equilibrium and the direction of my thoughts, but finally, I managed to speak. "What would these be?"

"Well, they aren't dried apple slices," LaRue said.

"Been counting coup, Philips?" I asked.

"No." The inmate abruptly dropped any attempt at belligerence by lowering his gaze toward the deck.

"Who did they belong to?"

He continued to avoid me with his eyes, remaining silent as he did. Since I had a soiled soul already, I decided to play the game dirty. Glancing at Gibson, I said: "The sick bay has a garbage disposer, doesn't it?"

The good doctor caught on quickly. "In the corner. Watch it, though, it's so powerful it will pulverize bone."

"Please," he begged. "Don't do that to me."

"Why? What will happen if I do?"

THE RED SKY FILE

He hesitated, and picking up the parts, I headed off in the direction of his destiny once more.

"All right," he yelled. "Please don't destroy them."

"Then tell me who they belonged to."

Philips's strange surrender seemed to circulate throughout his entire being. "They belonged to Derek Wheeler."

"You believe that you carry his walk-in soul, don't you?" LaRue asked.

He nodded. "Without those ritual objects, Wheeler's influence will flee me." Leaning forward, he added a sorrowful kicker. "I can't live without him. My karma and his are intertwined. Destroy those objects and you'll destroy me."

THIRTY-FOUR

The thing about having lycanthropic synesthesia is this: sometimes things get blurry. My memory will play tricks on me because I unconsciously ascribe the sensation to the image. Rather than remembering a name and attaching it to a person, I will remember his smell and color. When I work through the full moon and come back fully into my vulnerable human phase, I can't clearly recall names, people, smells, or colors. It's as if my normal comprehension has been squashed flat by my supernatural interloper. This inability to define my surroundings pisses me off, and right at that moment, staring at those body parts and smelling those golden squares, I was lost in annoyance and confusion. It was just a good thing that LaRue was doing the talking while I tried to get myself together.

"So, tell us about your good friend Zoltana," he said to Philips.

"He's not my good friend," the inmate answered.

"I thought the Coven worked with the screws."

"Sure, we do, but that doesn't mean we have to like the bastards."

"What does Zoltana have you do?"

"Anything he wants."

"Do you organize the work details?"

"No. We make sure the inmates do what they're told."

"Through threats of karmic curses and spells that affect future lives."

Philips stared at the floor again. "Whatever works."

"What do you get out of this?" LaRue demanded.

"Power."

"Do you own any dead man's chests?" I asked.

The question got his attention and he turned his wall-eyed stare onto me, adding a small frown of feigned indignation. "What would I do with wealth? Where the hell am I going to spend it?"

"Wheeler had his locker full of treasure," I said. "What was he going to do with it?"

"I don't know. He never spoke of it."

"But you do know that treasure was the reason Eldon Emmet broke off with Zoltana."

"I don't know anything," he answered.

Gibson interrupted our interrogation by shining a light at Philips's right eye. The prisoner winced.

"What's wrong?" I growled.

"I've been sensitive to the light for a long time," he said.

"When did it start?" Gibson asked.

"Soon after I arrived. A few days, in fact."

"What kind of work detail had you been on?"

He shrugged and then seemed to make an earnest attempt at remembering. Then, as if he'd been smacked in the chin with the answer, he spoke. "We were bilging a waste conduit of a chemical plant near the delta. I don't know which one, but I do know that the water and the slime and the filth were waist-deep."

LaRue drove the conversation in a different direction. "Tell us what happened when you supposedly assumed the walk-in spirit of Derek Wheeler."

"I didn't assume anything, Marshal. It really happened. That pouch there makes it all legal."

"It's impossible," I said. "You're letting your fantasies affect your logic."

"Am I? Derek Wheeler was so powerful a water witch that it was only moments after the ritual that I began to lose the feeling of singularity. It was like becoming a twin joined at the soul. The old Philips, the one you sent up? He's gone. I'm dealing from Wheeler's energy now."

"Then I'd say Mr. Wheeler was an angry person," LaRue said. "Judging by your attitude at the moment."

"Do you think it's a picnic?" Philips snapped. "We don't have anything else but anger. It's the way the world works in a humanitarian labor camp, or didn't you know that?"

"Was Mr. Wheeler an angry man?"

"He knew the value of fear."

Gibson hushed us as he listened to the inmate's heart and I turned back to the body parts. When he was done, I drilled him. "Why did you get these particular pieces of Wheeler?"

"Because I'm the wand," he answered. "Those relics represent the synthesis of thought, intuition, emotion, and sensation."

"There are only three things here."

"That's right. I am the sensation, the outward experience of karmic magic."

"And what kind of karmic magic do you do? Spells? Hexes? Transform mud to gold?"

"All that and more."

I grunted. Everyone was busy growing their own lily pads in the pond, doing what they could to collect the manure from a society that was splintering to pieces. "This scam is so hot, it burns."

"Not a scam," Philips said. "A way of life."

"Do the trustees trade with the river rats?" I asked.

Philips glanced down before answering. "Occasionally."

"What do you trade?"

He swallowed, but did not reply.

"What do you trade?" I barked. "Gems? Pearls, maybe? What about rubies and emeralds?"

When he didn't answer again, I stalked over to him and got into his face. It was then that I realized my blended senses were trying to tell me something. Standing there, I smelled yellow blobs floating inside golden squares.

Could it be true? Could I be sensing some confabulation of karma? Was I picking up the essence of Derek Wheeler trapped within the body of a pimp named Philips? I'm not prone to these sorts of metaphysical ideas and the fact that I entertained the possibility made me feel creepy. ''What did you do with Wheeler's body?'' I said.

Philips stared at me and delivered the evidence I was having a futile time comprehending. ''Wheeler's body? We ate it, of course.''

THIRTY-FIVE

As fate would have it, his confession and my confusion drove me right into a stretch. I howled and dropped to the deck, flopping around like a fish out of polluted water. LaRue was on me, using his weight to hold me still while he spoke comforting words that didn't do a damned thing to ease the agony. It was like I was being turned inside out and my flesh was being scraped away by painful inches.

Finally, the world spun back into place and I discovered that I'd gained new respect from Philips. After finding out the aphasia hadn't taken hold, my partner tenderly helped me to a stand, where I wobbled for a moment.

"What happened to her?" I heard Philips ask Gibson. "She looks different."

Indeed, I did. My muscles were buff and my hair had thickened, giving me that unkempt appearance the good doctor was so fond of. Little things had changed as well— my fingernails were longer and my gums hurt. Running my tongue along my front teeth, I satisfied myself that I hadn't grown fangs. Unfortunately, the symptoms of gingivitis were more annoying than useful. At least with sharp canines, I could do some damage. It was probably better that way, because my mood was so dirty that I would have gladly chewed holes in another human.

LaRue didn't miss an opportunity. "If you want to see the result of real water witching, then you should take a tip from Merrick."

"I've never seen anything like that," Philips said. "I heard scuttlebutt this morning about a marshal who had some sort of odd power, but I didn't believe it. How can you transform?"

Again I was saddled with hot flashes and tingling nerve endings and it was about all I could do to stagger over to the chair and flop down heavily. "I've got a walk-in of my own, Philips, and it's a damned sight more powerful than your Derek Wheeler will ever be."

Gibson paused in his medical examination to pour me a glass of tap water. "Why don't you hit the bunk room?" he said. "I'll call you when I'm done."

I nodded and gulped the gritty drink. "In a minute. I want to know something first. Just who received slices of Wheeler?"

"The senior Coven members. One from each cell block."

"Do you think Zoltana passed out pieces to other people?"

"I'm sure he did. I don't know who got them, though."

"What about Eldon Emmet?"

Upon hearing the name of his nemesis, he growled and nodded. "Zoltana promoted him. Before becoming the Keeper of the Book of Shadows, he was Wheeler's bootlicker and bugger partner." He paused to stare at me, shaking his head slightly. "What kind of magic did you run afoul of?"

"Didn't you hear all of that scuttlebutt this morning?" I asked. "I'm a kami, sent from Davy Jones's locker."

He gasped. I glanced his way to see his expression filling up with horror and knew immediately that Philips believed his own crap. As I watched he began to shiver.

"What's wrong with you?" Gibson asked.

Philips replied only after taking a hard swallow. "This is no joke, is it?"

"That's right," LaRue said flatly.

He swallowed again and rubbed at the gooseflesh rising on his filthy arms. "Davy Jones doesn't rap the stick he uses to meet out retribution." Slowly, his face leaked from horror into sorrow. "It's all lost now," he muttered. "The Sickle has found a key to the locker and got there before us. You're the karmic manifestation of the Lost Mariner's power."

I just couldn't stand it. At times I think there are more supernatural beings than there are human beings. LaRue saw my patience starting to fizz away and he took over the interview before I could swipe at Philips.

"Let's get back to Wheeler's demise," he said. "Are you sure he was dead?"

The prisoner took several deep breaths before turning his attention to my partner. "I saw him lying there on the funeral pyre."

"So, Zoltana destroyed the body rather than sending it back to dock aboard a river scow."

"Well, it would have caused quite a stir if he'd done that. The Coven had a right to his karmic energy."

"How bad did Wheeler have the rot?"

"Bad. It's what killed him."

"Was his face recognizable?"

Philips almost answered immediately, but then he frowned and shook his head. "The body was pretty far gone by the time any of us got to see it."

"Was anybody in attendance from the *Delora*?"

The prisoner hemmed and hawed, but finally gave up the info. "Yeah. The doctor. Stirling."

"What did he do during this farfetched service?"

"He was the one who cut Wheeler up and passed his parts around."

THIRTY-SIX

Though I made every attempt to stick to the interrogation, this current moment of lycanthropic illumination pummeled me. I finally stepped out of the interview to rush up on deck for a hardy gulp of polluted air and a few minutes of quiet reflection.

It was a confusing scenario, indeed, one that my innate skepticism prevented me from accepting. I had smelled golden squares at Amos Kleege's crime scene and I smelled them again, this time fumbled up with the odor of yellow blobs. It had to be the proximity of Wheeler's bits and pieces to Philips's body. There could be no crazy metaphysical explanation for this.

I leaned on the portside railing and let the breeze blow across me. It stank like sulfur, but surprisingly, the smell did not fine-tune my vision with strong colors and patterns. For that minor reprieve, I was grateful.

During the night a prisoner barge had come along side the *Delora* and now the guards herded a chain gang down to it. They were a pitiful, buggered-up group, riddled with disease and hopelessness. Seeing them, I could understand how simple it would be to surrender to mystical powers and invisible magic. I'd given in to the same crap at some point in my quest to be free of my lycanthropy. This tentative association with the supernatural made my skin crawl sometimes, and I knew that sooner or later the wolf would manage to eclipse me and I would be forced to accept my own paranormal situation. It was a galling thing to deal with. Through no desire of my own, I was transforming into a being who had part of her soul trapped in the unknown.

Gibson's voice pierced my reverie. "Are you all right?"

I twisted around and nodded. "I didn't hear you come up."

He joined me at the railing and touched my arm. "You looked like you had a bad moment back there."

"I did." Pausing, I took another big, stinky breath and then blew my words out with it. "Oh, Gibson. I'm so frustrated."

He stepped in so close that our bodies touched hip to hip. "What happened?"

The best I could do was ask a question of my own. "Do you believe in the possibility of walk-ins?"

"Science hasn't proved or disapproved the existence of the soul."

"I didn't ask you that, Gibson."

"I know." He leaned his elbows on the railing and took a moment to study the dark, swirling waters. "Do I believe in the existence of walk-ins? The answer would have to be yes."

I'll be damned. "Are you serious, or are you caught up in this witchcraft stuff?"

"I'm serious," he said quietly. "From a neurological standpoint, the idea of awareness transferring from one person to the next is entirely possible. It's nothing more than electrical energy and biochemical combinations. In fact, in the middle of last century, scientists proved that one brain and its inherent set of thoughts are not trapped to a single body."

"How did they do that?"

"It was a crude demonstration, but they surgically decapitated two monkeys and switched around their heads."

"And they lived?"

"Yes. About a week. The brains and mental processes drove the bodies with a fair amount of efficiency. If the evangelical collective hadn't put up a fit about morality, they could have kept those monkeys alive for a long time."

"People were worried it might become a trend?"

"They were worried that the scientists were wearing bigger pants than God."

"Well, that was surgery. How could a walk-in just happen?"

He shrugged. "Early this century, scientists decided that the soul may be physically found in the interstitial cells of the gonads."

I stared at him. "Huh?"

"The gonads are the sex glands," he explained. "When you tell someone you're going to rip off his gonads, you're really talking about pulling out his soul. Nests of interstitial or connective cells are found within the coils of the testes' seminiferous tubules. This is where the sperm is formed and these connective cells secrete testosterone."

"And the soul would be found here among all this male virility?"

"That's right."

"But what if you're female?"

"These interstitial cells can be found in the ovarian structure of a female. Don't worry, men and women are even when it comes to the 'seat of the soul.' "

"What you're saying, then, is the soul has nothing at all to do with our thoughts and desires."

"It's the spark of life, but found within the conscious mind? No, I doubt it."

"Would you say the soul controls the subconscious mind?"

"It's been theorized that it doesn't control the mind at all. It's the life force, the power behind incarnation, but nothing more."

"In other words, you wouldn't know if another soul encroached on you."

Gibson frowned. ''Where do you get these ideas, Merrick?''

''I'm trying to figure out how the water witches see these possibilities,'' I answered.

He leaned forward and spoke softly. ''That's not the only reason, is it? What happened back there?''

I shook off his question by inserting one of my own. ''Ultimately, wouldn't a new soul have new direction for the flesh it infuses?''

''In other words, would you see a change?''

''Yeah. Would the life force manifest with obvious differences?''

''Are we coming around to your lycanthropy?''

I sighed and scanned the bank for trouble. ''What if walk-ins are something that happens all the time, but we just don't realize it? Maybe we come in as one life force to deal with the traumas of childhood and adolescence, and when we're done with that, we abandon ship, so to speak. A new soul imparts its energy to take us through our twenties and thirties. Marriage, kids, career. Once done, this life force departs and makes room for another to guide us into retirement, old age, and death.'' I couldn't keep another sigh from bubbling up. As much as I hated to admit it, I had a feeling that truth lurked behind my words. ''I've heard the body completely changes at the cellular level every seven years. Why, then, would the interstitial cells remain untouched?''

I must have surprised Gibson at my depth of thought, because he stood there and studied me with that wild-eyed squint of his. When he didn't answer, I decided to push on. ''Do you think eating someone's flesh would produce changes in the body and install a new soul?''

He seemed grateful for a more medical slant on the subject. ''That's an old wives' tale that spans centuries, Merrick. Still, you can get some very real and deadly diseases from consuming human flesh.''

A frown escaped me and so I let it go. ''What kind of diseases?''

''Everything from worms to rickets, to degenerative

brain disease.'' He stopped and turned slightly so he could face me. ''That's not what's bothering you, is it?''

I stalled as long as I could by reaching into my pocket and pulling out one of the chocolate bars. Snapping it in half, I offered him a piece. He took it with a smile.

''Been holding out on me, huh?''

''Yeah,'' I grunted. ''Treasure.''

Again he gently towed me back into the conversation and a possible confession. ''Do you suspect someone is trying to pull the sharkskin over our eyes?''

''Well, I'm starting to come to one conclusion.''

''And that is?''

''I think Derek Wheeler is still alive.''

THIRTY-SEVEN

I never did tell Gibson about the synesthesia shock I'd had when I sniffed Philips. Instead, I begged off from our conversation by blaming a headache. It wasn't all a lie; I had a skullbanger that was threatening to become the mother of all migraines. I went down to the bunk room and hit the sack, falling into a congested dreamspace filled with witches, curses, and ghosts. There, in this strange landscape of twisted theology and superstition, I met LaRue, who stood by delivering a constant discourse on the states of subjective reality as they related to Davy Jones's locker and the possibility of walk-in souls. I came around a couple of times, stewed in my own juices, light-headed, and unable to escape my own inertia. Each time I fell back into the boiling cauldron and was forced to swim through these activities again and again.

LaRue woke me up at evening mess call. I must have been sleeping at the edge of oblivion because it took me several minutes to get up, and the first time I tried, I had a little difficulty finding my sea legs. Of course, after I found my balance, I realized I was starving. When I arrived at the chow hall, I powered down two plates of rice, oily tofu, and stir-fried turnips before turning my attention on the huge pot of green beans swimming in pork fat. Gibson entered the room, dished up a dinner tray, but instead of sitting down at our table, he joined Janet Yarrow and Ensign Curran.

LaRue filled me in on the day while I tried not to be obvious about watching them. My lycanthropic hearing caught the aria of their whispered conversation, but the boat's engineer abruptly turned on the twin diesels to air them out or something, and I lost most of it in the drone.

"I sent Philips and McConnell back to Zoltana this afternoon," LaRue reported.

"Are we still graced with dear old Jasper?"

"Yes. The nice part is he's had a shower since you last saw him and someone gave up an old pair of cammies in his behalf."

"He was really spooked by Philips," he said. "And Philips was really spooked by you. This has got to work in our favor somehow."

I spooned up a glob of mushy bacon and beans, and took a moment to relish the feel of food packing my gut. "Finn plays the fool, Andy, but he's not; you can bet on it. How long has he been here?"

"Twenty-four years. He was sent up the river on an armed-robbery charge. He tried to steal a car and ended up bagging an old woman. He also mortally wounded her husband, grandson, daughter-in-law, and the family dog. I think he got their picnic basket, too."

"So, his mental condition is beyond reproach."

LaRue chuckled as he picked at his turnip casserole. "Given the conditions in this place, I would think that mental stability would be the first thing to take the plunge." He leaned toward me and spoke in a soft voice. "We're surrounded by loonies, Ty; here on the boat and out there in the bushes."

"Not to mention the monsters in the river."

The fact was these bastards got exactly what they deserved and here we were, riding through the middle of all this suffering on a boat whose name meant "pain."

I cast my gaze by him to see Riverman Pilot Yarrow

giving Gibson her full attention. She'd laid her fork aside
and stared at him with wide, round eyes. He was giving
her the what-fors, using his hands for emphasis. I couldn't
see his face, but I knew he would be adding to her discomfort by shooting her with that wild-assed squint of his.

His stabbing motions disrupted my thoughts of the investigation and led me down an alleyway of emotion and
desire. It was a hard minute to fight back upstream toward
my partner and my plate of swill, but I managed it, punc-
tuating the truncation of my fantasy with a snort. "What
did you say, Andy?"

"I said Finn told Gibson his blood type changed after
arriving at the penal colony."

His answer made me pull my concentration completely
into his arena. "That's impossible, isn't it?"

"Gibson doesn't seem to think so," he said. "In fact,
he didn't even seem surprised. I can't say that I am either,
given the scuttlebutt."

"Has Finn participated in any experiments?"

"Not to his knowledge."

"Are we dealing with a case of karmic forgetfulness?"

He shrugged. "He swears he was type A and now he's
an O."

"Did you check his records?"

"Yes. It says he's type O, but then it could be a mistake
on either side of the equation."

But what if it wasn't? LaRue and I had been up against
this kind of base manipulation before. Hell, the reason I
had such a hard time trusting Gibson was because of his
exploitation of my ignorance. Our humanitarian society was
being subtly transformed, and these changes were always
covert, devious, and launched against the common man.
The prisoners thought that reincarnation would balance out
the score, but the truth was that rebirth only promoted more
abuses down the line. With new bodies would come new
ways of suffering.

Our conversation abruptly ended when Janet Yarrow
stood up, called Gibson a bastard, and stormed from the
mess. The crew furtively lifted their gazes to stare, but be-

fore I drew my next breath they were once more nose-deep in their chow. The good doctor picked up his tray and sat down beside me.

"I see your remarkable sensitivity and tact were at work," I said as I fought to gain control of a wiggly slice of bean curd.

He smiled. "I scored a ten on the scale, you know."

"Did you? How so?"

"I told her I knew she carried a flask of gems just like Kleege had."

"Does she?" LaRue asked.

Gibson nodded. "She has two. I noticed them while I was on the bridge, following Kleege's murder. She couldn't keep her hands off them."

THIRTY-EIGHT

We'd delayed the *Delora*'s tour of duty just long enough to make Captain Ritter nervous, so as soon as the boat's engineer gave the pilot the go-ahead, we shoved off, trying to make up for lost time.

A pounding rain accompanied our night crossing. It beat against the metal decks, striking up an echo that reminded me of a summer's downpour on the tin roof at the orphanage where I grew up. Unfortunately, I wasn't in a comfy bed, enjoying this relaxing sound. Instead, Gibson had my head strapped into the hydrotomography unit.

"What about lightning?" I called out.

"What about it?" he answered absently.

"Won't it fry me like a three-eyed fish if it hits the *Delora*?"

"Probably."

"I have a feeling my best interests aren't being considered here."

"Merrick, will you lie still?" he snapped. "It's hard enough getting this machine past minimal power. You keep moving and talking and it doesn't help."

I sighed instead of answering, and closed my eyes and

my mouth while Gibson continued to tap the keyboard and curse softly.

As I mentioned, Gibson has taught me biofeedback and self-hypnosis, and though I won't readily admit it, I practice both as often as I can. I often wear a digital pulse reader on my wrist to gauge changes I make in my heart rate and blood pressure, and when I'm without this technological wonder, I simply count backward from a hundred until I slip into an altered state governed by expanding theta waves in my brain. According to the good doctor, these are the precise mental patterns I need to control my awareness and harness the power of my lycanthropy. So, strung up like a calf waiting to become veal, I used the moments to shut out the world and to practice my breathing. Maybe it was the cold table or the uncomfortable headgear, but as I drifted I found myself floating with thoughts about the investigation.

The killer seemed to be focusing on the boat's pilots. If that were true, then it might move the motive closer to the bridge than I'd first thought. The deaths of the rivermen on watch that fateful night Lily Chamberlin was murdered may have been nothing more than a series of incidental conflicts for the killer in his course to the pilot. Still, Chamberlin was on her first tour of duty and there was no sign of a sack filled with gems. Actually, I wondered if a raw pollywog like her would have any gems. Depending on where these folks were getting them, she may have been too new to have a stash. All of which meant dear Lily may have been in the wrong place at the wrong time.

I soon fell into a light slumber, induced by my reverie, the drumming of rain, and the vibration of the engines. Unfortunately, this little nap was rudely interrupted by Gibson as he unlocked the table and rolled it back out. I yawned and glanced at him, suddenly aware that I didn't like the look on his face. "What's wrong?" I whispered.

He shook his head and squinted at me before proceeding to unhook the harness under my chin.

"I asked you a question," I said.

His nostrils flared on a hard exhale as he answered. "I need to get some blood."

My internal alarms started going off like the boat's klaxon. "Why do I have to give blood?" I asked, sitting up. "You said this wouldn't hurt."

"Merrick!" he barked. "Just give me a moment to figure this thing out." He turned away to look for the equipment he needed in a nearby drawer.

"What thing do you have to figure out?" I demanded. "Don't leave me hanging, Gibson. That's not right."

"It could be the machine," he answered as he rummaged for a hypo. "I don't like some of the readings. Your metabolism is on full alert. You're banging the meters."

"Which suggests?"

Gibson spun to face me, wearing that inscrutable mask of intensity he was so famous for. "It suggests that you may be fighting off some major infection and you don't even know it."

THIRTY-NINE

One of the blessings of my lycanthropy is my ability to heal quickly. I can take a hit harder than the average person, and given a couple of days, I'm back on my feet again. Gibson believes it's my surging metabolic rate that helps to speed my recovery, but in the process, I lose ground, because my caloric consumption never matches the caloric burn. Occasionally, I will teeter with weakness until the worst is past, yet this time I didn't feel that bad.

"It has to be the machine," I said as he attacked me with the needle.

"Let's hope so," he muttered. He poked my arm and started mining for gold. "Have you been feeling nauseous and dizzy?"

"Yeah, but I thought it was the heat and the stink. What exactly did the hydro unit show?"

He pulled back the plunger on the pigsticker before answering. "I was looking for areas of enhanced metabolic function in your brain. Your gray matter is secreting compounds that could indicate you have a blood infection."

My mind was off again, covered in the slime and goo of uncertainty. I didn't like being in this place, so I tried to gear the subject toward the investigation, hoping to lessen the impact by applying the info to the case at hand. "Have you had a chance to check out the serpent's fluid yet?"

Gibson glanced up at me and then blinked, as though it helped him to reposition his attention. A moment more spent under his stern scrutiny and I knew he realized that I was suddenly scared and needed a safety net. "Yes, I've started," he whispered. Pausing, he withdrew the spike and stuck a cotton ball on my arm. He then turned and began to prepare a slide by coating it with a couple of drops of my blood. "There was some evidence of hormonal irregularities in the creature, but this boat, for all its equipment, is not a Planetary Health Organization laboratory."

"Have you compared it to the samples taken from the prisoners?" I asked.

"Only partially; but there is something odd." Swinging back in my direction, he dropped the news. "Both species are growing."

"You mean that monster is getting bigger?"

"That's right. Both the creature's and the prisoners' tests showed growth hormone active within their systems." Gibson stopped speaking to dash his gaze against the floor, and then glancing up to me again, he added the rock that broke the bowsprit. "I did some math, Merrick. Neither the serpent nor the inmates are following the scaling laws."

"How can that be?"

Gibson returned to his work, topping his sample with another slide before explaining. "In humans, the pituitary gland controls the release of growth hormone. When there's a pituitary tumor, this gland can overexcrete the hormone. A simple blood test will reveal the presence of a tumor and the compounds produced by it. I didn't find any abnormality in the prisoners' brains, but their pituitary is releasing the appropriate chemicals."

"How fast are they growing?" I asked.

He nodded. "Slowly. Perhaps only a few millimeters a year, but they are growing."

"And you don't know why?"

"Not yet."

"Did you find the presence of mercury in the serpent's workup?"

"Yes, in high levels. Still, mercury poisons; it doesn't make animals grow." With that, he stepped to the microscope and dialed up my blood sample.

I hopped off the table and took a seat in the chair, waiting with dread for the verdict. Sitting there, I recalled all the other times I've spent my life in states of similar tribulation. Several minutes passed before Gibson did a fine imitation of LaRue by murmuring: "Oh shit, oh shit, oh shit."

My heart pounded like the *Delora*'s engines. "What?" I whispered.

He didn't answer right away and I wanted to strangle him for that. As my anxiousness turned to dismay he looked up from his blasted machine to study me. "Have you had any hot flashes?"

"Yes, this afternoon. I figured it was from all the sweating I was doing. That bunk room was like an oven."

Gibson cast a critical eye the entire length of my body before asking his next question. "Have you been fatigued?"

"No more than usual."

"What about shivers?"

I almost failed his battery of test questions because I thought about lying just to convince myself that I felt wonderful.

"Merrick?" he asked, turning to toss me one of his critical reviews. "What about it? Shivering, shaking, or quaking?"

"Shivering," I finally answered. Before I could say another word, he returned to the hypo full of my red stuff and began to load it into an analyzer. "Gibson, you better tell me what's wrong before I faint from the fright."

My statement forced him to whip his head around to check on my verticality. When he saw I was not going to fall out immediately, he took a minute to set the machine and turn it on. Then, coming over to me, he took my pulse and pulled at the bottom of my eyes before pronouncing my fate. "It looks like you have protozoal malaria," he

said. "And it looks like your body is ridding itself of the
parasite."

I stared at him and suddenly I felt creepy-crawly all over.
"Well, it's good my body is killing off the parasite, isn't
it?"

Gibson touched my face, running his fingertips gently
along my cheekbone. "Merrick," he said, "it's impossible."

FORTY

Upon discovering the parasite in my bloodstream, Gibson immediately invited LaRue down to be poked in the arm. My partner hates needles and avoids any kind of puncture wound, but when he heard he might have bugs running rampant in his body, he presented both arms for plugging. As for me, I had to clear out of the confining space of the sick bay or I really was going to be sick. I ignored Ritter's orders about keeping the hatches secure during the night and stepped outside. The upper deck formed a four-foot-wide portico that protected me from the rain, and leaning against the bulkhead, I sucked in air at a furious rate. If I'd been a smoker, I'd probably have swallowed the fire along with the tobacco.

Sometimes I'm damned grateful for my supernatural disposition. It protects me from a world pregnant with danger and staves off its attack in remarkable ways. The wolf is my shield in the material dimension, and though I deny it if someone throws it up in my face, I nonetheless rely upon it. Stupidly, I curse it for the agony it brings me, when, in fact, I should be welcoming the pain.

Standing there in the night, staring out at the twinkling firelight as it escaped through the cracks of the shacks and metal lean-tos on shore, I huddled against a stiff breeze blowing out of the north. How prosaic my human self was. It was a lackluster life not worth examining, but combined with the wolf, there was never a dull moment.

I stood in darkness for another half hour, reviewing my situation, and hoping I wouldn't become a casualty of this war with myself, when someone tried to brain me with a rock. It clanked off the bulkhead just above my noggin and fell with a thunk as it hit the deck. I ducked, and launched through the hatch, waiting just inside the companionway for more volleys. After several minutes nothing else flew over the transom and I stepped outside again to retrieve this latest missile. It was wrapped in brown paper and tied with a leather thong. I sprung a switchblade, cut through the knot, and pulling the rock free, checked it for anything unusual. It was just a river stone as far as I could tell, but I decided to keep the mailer in case it was a chunk of silver or something.

Upon glancing at the note, I found it to be another mandala; this one very similar to the other, except it included a different string of arcane symbols at the bottom. I packed the rock into my pocket and slammed the hatch shut, double-checking the lock before climbing down to the dungeon to see Finn.

The inmate sat on the hard bunk gnawing on the marrow of old, used, soup bones and looking pleased as punch as he considered his fine accommodations—a flush toilet, a ragged blanket, and an old, worn-out pillow. When he saw me, he grinned. The recessed lighting picked up the smear of grease across his face as well as the weeping wounds of his disease.

I unlatched the gate and stepped inside. "All to your satisfaction, Jasper?"

"Oh, Marshal, I ain't had this kind of luxury for many years. I appreciate you taking me down to another cell block, too."

"Not a problem," I said. "Just don't forget our bargain."

"I'll help you any way I can," he answered.

I couldn't keep a smile from creeping onto my lips. "Good. Since that's the case, I want you to tell me what you know about this." I flapped the drawing of the mandala at him.

Finn didn't react. Instead, he wiped the oil from his fingers on the blanket and reached for it. He studied it for a minute. "Yeah, so?"

"Can you read that script at the bottom?"

He shook his head and his bald pate shone in the fluorescent glow of the cell. "Sorry. I can't read any kind of script. I can tell you it's written in a magic alphabet, though. It's called 'passing the river.' The witches use it during their ceremonies to call down the power of Davy Jones's locker. It's supposed to work right good on invoking the lost souls."

I sat down on the bunk beside him. "This is the second mandala we've received since we've been floating down this godforsaken river."

"Yeah, so?" he asked, again, dipping toward his late-evening snack.

For a split second a snag of anger tangled up my patience and I almost reached out to grab him by the neck, but I managed to keep my hands to myself. If he was half-brain-dead from too many years of mercury poisoning and blue lotus addiction, it wouldn't do any good to get excited over his mental feebleness. "Back in the district, mandalas are used by practitioners to set up sacred spaces between dimensions."

"That's nice," he said politely.

"What are they used for here, Jasper?"

His brain apparently assimilated this sentence and he acted as if he finally understood the direction the interview was moving. He handed me back the paper and picked up a bone. "It doesn't do any kind of magical stuff out here."

"It doesn't?"

"No," he answered. "That there is an advertisement."

I stared at him for a second, because it simply did not register. "You mean it's like a business flyer advertising a product for trade or sale?"

He used the tip of his tongue to bore out the bone marrow before replying. "That's right."

"Can you at least tell me who sent it?"

"It didn't come from the Coven," he said. "They don't dabble in mandalas. It probably came from Hecate's Sickle."

No sooner had Finn spilled this information than a piercing scream broke the night. We looked at each other for a couple of seconds before I realized the screech belonged to a female. Janet Yarrow.

I took off for the bridge, leaving Finn to suck his bones. The companionway hatch jammed and I had to use every bit of lycanthropic muscle I had to break it free. On the breath of another scream, I put my back into it and finally swung it open. I dashed across the *Delora*'s main deck, and keeping to the shadows, I scurried up the ladder to the bridge. Once on the landing leading to the hatch, I paused, pulled my service revolver, and then stormed inside, hoping that what I'd encounter wouldn't be able to outgun me.

By Bluebeard's ghost. I faced off with a giant wearing a hood of dirty, wet rags and pointing the business end of a water rifle my direction. Yarrow cowered in the corner, shouting for help, while Riverman Curran lay on the deck trying to breathe around a bloody hole in his upper chest.

"Watch out!" she yelled.

I did as she suggested by taking a flying leap behind the wheel, using the helm equipment as a shield. The giant squirted liquid death my way, but I rolled clear, pumping the trigger on my pistol. My aim was wide and I missed the bastard. He returned the fire and I found myself suddenly on the defensive, wondering where the hell my backup was.

Again I experienced a minute of dead time when my synesthesia flicked on to give me the clue we needed, for in an effort to gulp some air, I caught a whiff of the attacker's stink and smelled golden squares.

Yarrow screamed again as if to signal the troops to our location and desperate need. Her screech was enough to bring me back into myself, and thankfully, it was enough to draw the killer's attention from me. Though he pointed the rifle on the pilot, he moved in a lumbering fashion. I used his ponderous reaction time to line him up in my sights, and firing, I plugged him in the shoulder. He bellowed at this insult, letting his hood fly back to reveal his true identity.

I can only say that what I saw was not human.

FORTY-ONE

Well, shiver me timbers, matey. I was so stunned by what I saw, I couldn't make my finger pull the trigger again. The bastard had long dark hair and fangs like a saber-toothed tiger. I stopped short when I saw these choppers, unable to tell in the flickering green glow of the instruments if our attacker wore a mask. A second later my synesthesia broke loose from its moorings and I was awash in stinking golden squares.

The monster roared, a sound that landed somewhere between a banshee and an elephant. My lycanthropic hearing dragged at the noise and the delay coming into my brain vibrated my skull and dazed me. Before I knew what had happened, I was on my knees, figuring that I was bleeding gray matter from my ears. I thought to save the day by getting a wild shot off, but by that time the attacker had fled. I heard a big splash as it dove into the water and a minute later the excited voices of the crew.

LaRue showed up, followed hot on the heels by Ritter and Gibson. I confess I hadn't moved from the spot where I'd rolled for cover, not because I was frightened of this demon, but because my brain had gone on a tangent of its own. It seemed I had no control over the thoughts issued

me. They were frightening snippets of ideas that included
monsters, metabolism, and lycanthropy. No sooner had I
measured my response to these theories than the questions
came into play and I suddenly had no clue as to what realm
I navigated in. I was swamped by my own perspective;
helpless, and confused.

Gibson rushed to me immediately, ignoring Curran, who
gushed a bilge bucket of blood. "Are you all right?" he
demanded.

I nodded, unable to clear my throat for words. He helped
me sit up before turning to the injured riverman. Moments
later Yarrow started with her histrionics, sobbing and hy-
perventilating. Her theatrics drove Ritter and LaRue to her
side.

"What was that hideous creature?" she wailed. "Oh, my
God, did you see its face?"

Everyone, including Gibson, turned to stare at me.
"Yes," I murmured. "I saw its face."

"Did you recognize him?" LaRue asked.

"No. He may have worn a mask. The light was bad in
here."

"He wasn't human!" Yarrow screamed.

"What do you mean?" Ritter said. "Of course he was
human. Don't start with the demons, Janet. You, of all people, shouldn't believe in them. There are no lost souls and
no Davy Jones's locker." He placed his hand on her arm
to calm her, but she snatched it free from him.

"It was a beast, I tell you. In all my years out here I
have never seen anything like that. Ask the marshal, she'll
back up my story."

I shook my head. "I'm not sure who he was, but I do
know he wasn't a prisoner. The guy looked like a sas-
quatch. He was the hairiest son of a bitch I've ever seen."

They froze, each one staring at me. Then Yarrow
screeched into the moment. "Tell them about the fangs."

"It looked like he had some teeth. Big ones. That's why
I think it was a mask."

LaRue walked over to me and hunkered down. "Are you
sure?"

My partner always managed to walk that fine line between science and superstition, but he usually pulled toward
the side of logic. Was everybody succumbing to the dark
rumors of this strange world? "It had to be a mask," I said
slowly.

"No, it wasn't," Yarrow said. "It was a bogeyman, if
ever I've seen one."

"Do you think you hit it?" LaRue said.

"I can't say for sure. Maybe I put a hole through it." I
crawled to a stand, feeling weaker than I normally did during this stage of my lunar cycle.

My movement drew Gibson's attention and he watched
me rise. When I was all the way up, he continued to study
me. His scrutiny made me uncomfortable and I turned away
to stare out the porthole, letting my consideration wander
into the night. Ritter called an all-stop and escorted the
quaking pilot to her quarters while LaRue helped Gibson
carry Curran back to the sick bay. I remained behind,
searching for answers that would satisfy me as to the meaning of life and its diversity.

I qualified as a freak of nature; this was something I
could not deny, but what the hell had that thing been? I
had no doubt it was the creature whose blood and mucus
had tested as human. Yet for all intents and purposes, he
looked like a kissin' cousin to the wild man of Borneo and
that was something I wasn't in any hurry to admit.

An hour rippled by while we sat stalled in the middle of
the Black. From my vantage point I could see the remaining
riverman swinging from the yardarms, hooking up halogen
lights to signal our presence in the middle of the stream. I
scouted along the nearby bank, straining to see past the
flicker of a million insects. All appeared quiet, with no
movement among the reeds and the junk.

When I finally returned to the sick bay, I paused outside
the hatch to hear LaRue telling Gibson that the Nazis of
the last century borrowed heavily from a satanic organization called the Illuminati. He explained it as a practice
erroneously compared to Wicca, the nature craft practiced
by all real witches. The fact that my partner was holding a

one-sided discourse meant that his blood test must have
showed him free of malaria, and so I charged in to save
the good doctor from having to endure a meaningless lecture on devil worship.

"Good news?" I said, stepping through the hatch.

LaRue sat on a stool near the door and glanced at me,
nodded, and smiled slightly. Gibson tossed me a look
loaded with medical curiosity and not one bit of human
compassion. Before I could react, he turned away to tend
Riverman Curran's wound. Rather than get caught up in
more ill-defined emotions, I did my best to ignore him by
presenting the mandala and the rock to my partner.

"This nearly brained me when I was topside getting a
little air."

The good doctor forgot his patient long enough to see
this latest prize. He joined LaRue to close in on the counter
and the evidence.

"This makes me think that Ritter had an ulterior motive
in ordering us down below at night," I said.

"Why?" LaRue asked.

"Because our good friend Jasper tells me this is an advertisement. Someone on this boat was invited to a yard
sale."

"An advertisement? What kind?"

"I don't know. Finn says the writing on the bottom of
the page is some kind of code used by Hecate's Sickle. Can
either of you read it?"

They shook their heads and LaRue answered. "There's
a good bet it was intended for someone aboard this tub."

It occurred to me that there might have been more to
Dacey than met the eye. Since no one was running to fess
up, I mentioned an idea to LaRue. "Dacey may have had
the code book to decipher the writing. I think it's time we
had a look through her personal effects." Before Gibson
had a chance to stop me for another test, I turned and
headed for the hatch.

LaRue came up behind me and spoke softly into my ear.
"Gibson is really worried about you, Ty."

"I feel fine," I lied. "If I hadn't laid in that machine

and let him count the demerits in my metabolic rate, no one would have been the wiser."

"Including you," he said. "I wonder where you picked it up?"

"Out here I guess. I've gotten a few mosquito bites since we shoved off."

"But Gibson told me it's at least a week to ten days before any symptoms show up."

"Well, you know how fast my furnace burns. Just watch out for yourself, partner."

"None of our guests showed any signs of malaria."

I stopped in the dimly lit companionway to study him. "And they should have."

"How could they miss?"

"According to Gibson, this place is a cauldron of dengue fever, along with malaria and sleeping sickness. They should have shown some signs of these diseases, but . . . nothing."

"Maybe they've already been affected and the diseases have run their courses."

He shrugged. "Who knows? I'm just glad I don't have it and I'm sorry you do."

It was my turn to blow kisses. "Don't worry, Andy. I'm okay."

"Yes, but will it last? This is not a good place to be ill."

"We've got the best doctor in town with us." I started toward Dacey's quarters again. "By the way, have you seen Stirling?"

"Not since he stomped off after we brought the prisoners aboard. Not even at mess call."

We dropped the subject as we found the exec's tiny cabin. LaRue and I had had the foresight to lock up her quarters after her death, but it was certain we were late in rifling through her things. Her small chest of drawers was in disarray, as though someone had searched her personal items. LaRue found the same clutter in the narrow closet.

"We're too late," he muttered.

Were we? I scanned the room, looking for any cubbyholes where Dacey might have hidden a cipher book. Under the bunk, behind the chest, under the chair—nothing. I even glanced up at the recessed lighting panel, looking for shadows that might have revealed a hiding place, but still came up empty. It must have been LaRue's day for abundance, though, because he found pay dirt taped to the underside of the hatchway's lip. He yanked it free, pulling out a small manila envelope.

"What have we here?" he said. Moving to the tiny writing desk, he unclasped the mailer and tipped it onto the ink blotter.

Well, let the crows pick my scurvy bones clean. We had diamonds. Beautiful, sparkling diamonds.

FORTY-TWO

LaRue turned as still as a statue of St. Ophelia. His long hair fell forward to hide his expression but the tone of his voice betrayed his emotion. "The curse would be if we can't get back to spend this."

It was true, but I didn't want to discuss lousy possibilities. "That should be enough for you to live on a long time, Andy. Good for you."

He finally pulled his attention from the diamonds. "I could repair the Trabi," he whispered.

The Trabi. It was an East German driving machine, a two-cylinder relic of the former Soviet Union. As autos went, it was dinged and battered and the engine was composed of parts that included metal pot scrubbers, hairpins, cardboard, and used aluminum foil. It bucked and banged like a Moscow hooker, but the Trabi was the place where LaRue kept his heart. It had been severely damaged in the line of duty, and he'd had a hell of time getting repair funds out of the Marshals' Office. Now it did indeed look like the commie car would be crossing the potholes yet another day.

Still, LaRue shook his head. "As wonderful as this is, I've got to tell you, Ty, this whole thing gives me the willies. I feel like we're aboard the *Flying Dutchman,* blessed with wealth and heading toward a bad bend in the river.''

I picked up one of the gems and held it to the light. It sparkled, catching my eye and my attention. I'd never in all my life been this close to a diamond. "I've got an idea that if we went on a little scavenger hunt, we'd find a whole hell of a lot more."

LaRue scooped up his treasure trove and I turned to drop my sample in the packet. He accepted it with a grateful smile before speaking. "What are you driving at, Ty?"

"Presumably Dacey, Kleege, and Yarrow had the gems on them from the beginning of their tours of duty. Why were they bringing the money into the labor camp?"

"That's certainly not a smart way to do your banking, is it?"

I took a slow circle around the room. "Do you think Zoltana might be doing a little investing on the nefarious side of town?"

"You're talking about blue lotus?" he asked.

"The lily pads grow in profusion," I said. "Finn admitted to crunching up his own narcotic after collecting the flowers. Why couldn't the prefect warden be working on a larger scale?"

"There has been a dramatic increase in blue lotus overdoses in the district over the last few months. I just read a tally sheet a couple of weeks ago that listed fourteen arrests in one night, all linked to the narcotic. Do you think the pilots are bringing it out?"

"Did the sheet say where the drug came from?"

He tucked his prize into his pocket before answering. "Southern districts were said to be producing the stuff, but the point of delivery was not known."

"It's an interesting scenario."

"But the attacker," he said. "Do you think it was after the loot Yarrow has around her neck?"

"No, not if Kleege is an example. I found his stash stuffed in a hidey-hole in sick bay." I stopping speaking to force the hatch open. "I think it's time to have a talk with Riverman Yarrow."

We took a turn by her bunk room but it was empty, and when we didn't find her in the mess, we figured she'd resumed her duties. Drawing our revolvers before leaving the safety of the companionway, we paused to glance around for rocks and monsters and then did our best to stay in the shadows. It was a quiet night, with nary a naiad whispering. The river had gotten narrower, the mist had come up, and the lights did nothing to penetrate this ethereal fog. They also didn't hide our movements as we climbed the ladder to the bridge. Russo answered our knock and then let us stand outside until he unbolted the hatch.

"The captain ordered restricted movement at night," Yarrow snapped. "What are you doing here?"

We paused to holster our weapons before LaRue answered. "We need to ask you some questions." Glancing at Russo, he added: "You might want a little privacy for this conversation."

Yarrow had a face with too many sharp edges and a personality to match. She glared at us for a moment and then shifted this lethal gaze toward her watchdog. "Get lost."

"But I'm not supposed to leave you, sir," he said.

"Get out!"

When she barked the order, the riverman found his sea legs and scooted off the bridge. She waited for the hatch to clang shut before addressing us in a tone scrubbed with venom. "Haven't I been through enough already this evening? What is it?"

"Yes, you have had quite a night," I answered. "That's why I don't understand your uncooperative stance."

She fiddled with a nearby computer before spitting out her displeasure. "I've got to check the systems on this wreck and get us back on line. I was nearly killed by some horrendous creature. I'm up to my ankles in Riverman Curran's spilled blood. And guess what? We have a full moon coming up, and going at this speed, we'll be caught in the current and not out in the delta, where there is at least a marginal amount of safety. Now, if that's not cooperation, I don't know what is."

I stopped to stare at her when she mentioned the high-light of the lunar month. "What happens on a full moon around here?"

She returned my critical gaze. "The water witches believe that the karmic energies are at their strongest. They think they can call up the power of past lives."

"The power of past lives? What could that be?"

"The knowledge, energy, and unused karmic choices of a person's previous incarnations."

"Stealing souls, are they?" LaRue asked.

Yarrow snorted, layering it with a sigh. "Something like that. Their full-moon ritual also draws out any unused grace left over from those lives."

"Unused grace?" I said. "What the hell is that? I thought grace was a gift of divine intervention."

"Grace follows karma," she explained. "It's two sides of the same coin. There can't be one without the other. If you grab the past-life power, then you can get your fair share of the goodies. That is really what their full-moon rituals are all about. Grace is just something to collect, bottle, and reuse. They think they can somehow add it to their tally sheets before they die."

What an ingenious way to keep folks under your thumb. "I take it the Coven pulls this crap?"

"Yes, Marshal. They all do it. Hecate's Sickle and the scabs who fancy themselves water witches, too."

"I take it they have plenty of bodies to use in their rituals," LaRue said.

She grunted, but didn't offer any explanations.

I stared at LaRue, hardly sure where he was pointing his hypothesis. He cleared up my confusion a moment later.

"Where do they get the past lives?" he asked. "Steal them from living people? What witch would be in his right mind to give up his karmic energies and his current incarnation to please someone else?"

She nodded. "You're right."

"Do they use dead bodies?"

"I understand that the energy from recently dead bodies is easier to collect, so they hold endurance tests of sorts. If you pass, that means you're still alive. If you don't, your karmic energies are up for grabs.''

"What if no one dies at these little gatherings?"

"It hasn't happened very often, but if it does, they use a dead man's chest," she said. "When the witches collect the power, they need to store the access in a spare receptacle. Not only do these vessels carry their gold, but their extra grace as well. Each witch with a chest must at one time or the other offer his wealth for the cause."

"Who determines how much energy each person receives?"

"Not who—what," she said. "The amount is figured on how much the participant has grown since the last time he took part in the full-moon ritual."

Upon hearing this confession of lunacy, LaRue and I both fell silent for a minute. I took a few steps to the observation porthole and studied the eerie reflection of the floodlights on the mist. "What about that giant serpent?" I asked. "No invisible magic made that."

She checked her consoles before replying. "You really don't know what kind of magic they wield out here, do you?"

"Suppose you be up-front and tell us what you mean," I said.

"It's all based on genetic unguents."

"And that would be?"

"You use a creature—say an alligator. Contained within the lizard, you have the basic genetic structure of the animal. You then add different magical rubs and balms, a little past-life energy, and say some spells until it starts to transform." Yarrow paused in her ridiculous explanation to suck a deep breath. Then she confessed her change of heart. "I thought that the bogeyman was just a myth. Now I wonder if he's not made of the same stuff as that serpent."

I was stuck in my imagination and scanning for mermaids, so I was glad LaRue had his wits about him.

"How do the witches make these unguents?" he demanded.

"Mud, water, and slime. If you manage to pack the concoction with gold dust, you have a powerful mixture. There are lots of tributaries where the prisoners pan for gold, but how much flake they get out of the sand is a good question.''

I pulled back from my fantasy, because suddenly we had a strange reason for the existence of a dead man's chest. ''And Davy Jones? What does he have to do with it?''

''The Lost Mariner is the keeper of karma. It's his blessing that allows the witches to do what they do. He supplies the power in the water, so it's said, but I think it's more likely a combination of the chemical runoffs from the factories in the district.''

''Supernatural pollution,'' I said. ''What a concept.''

Yarrow jockeyed the wheel before answering. ''The chemicals are something. Hell, I once saw a PCB monster. It was the most hideous thing you can imagine. The serpent who chewed on our dredge was a worm compared to it.''

''PCB?'' LaRue asked.

She nodded. ''Polychlorinated bifemals. You know, the stuff the factories dump from their electrical transformers. After seeing that monster, I'll never be convinced that the bogeyman is a myth. I just wonder if what they say is true. If it is, we all have reason to be nervous.''

''What do they say?''

''Once a bogeyman gets a whiff of you, he can taste your shape and follow you anywhere.''

The moment she mentioned the idea of synesthesia, I experienced a hot flash of paranormal insight, but this enlightenment came laced with denial. Could the chemicals, hormones, and disease have produced a mixture that provided the afflicted with monstrous proportions as well as changes in their nervous systems? Did it affect their array of sensory abilities, too?

According to Gibson's figures, synesthesia was the oddball happenstance of a brain rerouting incoming stimuli. If the bogeyman really did have this skill at hand and was able to control the nuances and the blurring, then he could be used like a paranormal bloodhound. Had this theory

been in the back of Gibson's mind the whole time he was
getting a baseline on me?

I must have flinched or something, because LaRue immediately moved the conversation in a different direction.
"Dr. Gibson came by to talk to you about your scrimshaw
good-luck charms and you blew him off," he said. "That's
not nice."

"You can stop with your condescending bullshit right
now," she answered. "There is no scrimshaw."

"Of course there is," he said, stepping next to her at the
wheel. "And do you know what, Pilot Yarrow? You're in
luck. We're not here to con you or blackmail you for your
stash. We just want some answers. Now, isn't that a nice
thing? Can't you be an eensy bit cooperative because of
that?"

She stared at him and I noticed that even her lips had
sharp points to them. "What, then?"

"Simple question to start. Why would you carry half a
pound of gems around your neck while traveling through
the wilderness?"

"I don't have any safe place to leave them in the district."

"Come on, Janet. You don't expect us to believe that."

She hemmed and hawed and then finally answered. "Oh,
all right. I keep them with me because it's the only thing
that might get me out alive if this tub sinks."

"Why?" LaRue asked. "You don't think they're magical, do you?"

"No," she answered. "Their value is only monetary.
Nothing more."

"Come clean with us and I promise we won't run you
in on a drug charge. Do you buy blue lotus with the gems?"

Yarrow shook her head. "I don't use any of that stuff. I
told you. If I need to walk out of this camp, I'll need the
gems to get through."

"You're talking about paying for your life?"

"Well, I am a woman, no matter how old I am."

"How old are you?"

She glanced at me and then back to him. "I'll be sixty-four next month."

LaRue swung around to stare at her and I did some of my own. "You don't look like you're past thirty," he said.

Instead of answering, Yarrow settled her attention onto the wheel.

"Why would gems buy off the prisoners?" I asked. "What good would it do? Where would they spend it?"

She snorted. "Marshal, I never said the gems would go to the prisoners. It's the guards you have to worry about."

FORTY-THREE

From that point on, Yarrow claimed ignorance about everything. There wasn't much we could do except threaten her with impeding an investigation, but that didn't scare her, so we left. I returned to the sick bay while LaRue went to find Stirling to ask him why he hadn't turned up to help Riverman Curran. Gibson was hard at work on the computer and squinting fiercely at the image of a blood cell on the screen when I entered. I didn't see the patient.

"Where's the crewman?" I asked.

He flashed me a sideways look and then patted the stool next to him. "He wanted the comfort of his own bunk." Before I reached him, he'd turned his attention to the microscope. "I want to take more blood from you in the morning," he said, without glancing up.

His matter-of-fact statement, the evening's events, and my thoughts of monsters, mortality, and fractured cosmic truths led me into uneasiness. "Why?" I asked hesitantly.

My question lured him from the machine and he spent a minute staring at me. "Malaria is cyclical, Merrick. The parasite lodges in the red blood cells and they rupture, spreading the parasite through the system about every six to twelve hours. In normal people, there's a high fever, chills, hot flashes, shivering, and without the proper drugs, it can be life-threatening.''

''Would it hurt for me to take the medicine?'' I whispered.

''It would be the first thing I would usually do,'' he answered. ''Unfortunately, the sick bay's pharmacy is empty of everything. I needed something today and I couldn't find Stirling for a set of keys, so I broke into the bastard. There are mouse droppings on the shelves and not much else.''

''No medicine?''

He shook his head.

''Then the major purpose of all this equipment?''

''Bureaucratic misappropriations,'' he muttered.

It was my turn to shake my head. ''Treasure hunting, maybe?''

''Looking for dead man's chests?''

''Seems logical.''

''That would implicate every one on board,'' he whispered.

I slipped off the stool without answering, taking a moment to make a cursory check of the sick bay.

''What are you looking for?''

''Do you recall your history, Gibson? The part about old South Africa and their diamond mines?''

He shrugged. ''Not really. Why?''

''The miners would often try to smuggle the gems out in the holes in their teeth.''

''You think Stirling may have had a profitable sideline of picking out dead man's chests and stripping them of the wealth. These little gifts may have been tokens of continued silence?''

''Andy just found a packet of ice in Dacey's quarters.''

''Diamonds, huh?''

I flashed a smile. ''I hear greed dripping off your syllables.''

He chuckled. ''That Andy is a lucky SOB.''

''He is lucky, but he's got a big family, too.''

He nodded, but his expression turned sad. To avoid showing it to me, he dashed his gaze against the deck.

Could it be envy that I saw? "What's wrong, Gibson?"

Raising his head, he spoke softly. "You're what's wrong. You have a serious illness and I'm worried about getting you treatment."

"Are you worried about me or the untimely loss of your meal ticket?"

A frown navigated the channels of his face. "This is an old song and dance, Merrick. I'd have thought by now that we're past all that."

"Maybe it's just old fodder from previous incarnations."

"I don't believe that crap any more than you do."

Studying him, I searched for a clue to his true feelings, but saw neither love, compassion, nor fear—only that sustained intensity that blended the display of his emotions. I returned to the stool and burned a minute of silence to gather my courage to ask a pressing question. If this illness might turn bad and kill me, I would at least know the truth as I marched into Summerland. "Gibson," I said, and then paused to rephrase myself. "Lane, tell me something. Do you love me?"

He sat so still that I had the urge to reach out, shake his shoulder, and demand to know if I'd made the question too hard. Thirty seconds slipped by, and when he finally spoke, his words rode on the wind of a gentle sigh. "I've told you before how I feel about you."

"No, you haven't," I whispered. The moment the words were out of my mouth, my brain got in on the act and supplied me with the answer he alluded to. When the full moon comes around, my lycanthropic symptoms intensify, so much so that I have blackouts and amnesia about the events during this period. The son of a bitch had hidden his feelings within the backdrop of my misery.

"I've wanted to tell you," he said. "I was afraid."

"Why?"

"Because I've used you. I guess I wanted you to trust me before I said it at a time when you would remember my confession."

"If you don't do it now, there may not be another chance," I murmured.

Gibson stood, and guided me to my feet. "I love you," he said softly. "From the moment I laid eyes on your medical chart." With that, he led me to the sick bay's anteroom, where we passionately expressed ourselves until it was time for my next blood test.

FORTY-FOUR

Red sky at morning, sailor take warning. I should have known the bottom was going to drop out and we'd be treading water, but my skepticism, or perhaps my survival instinct, prevented me from entertaining the idea. Admittedly, I'd grown more concerned with my strange illness now that I finally had an answer about my relationship with Gibson, so rather than be confronted with bad news, I slipped out of the sick bay while he hunched over my medical test.

The day was washed in scarlet colors. The cicadas sang their haunting refrain, and yes, standing there in the midst of an eerie, dangerous world, I felt strangely at home.

LaRue was on deck, too, doing a series of tai chi exercises while he regaled Harvey with metaphysical theories concerning giants, magic beans, and geese that could lay golden eggs. Upon seeing me, the riverman waved at me, and once I'd joined them, he excused himself, seeing, I'm sure, the only possibility of escaping my partner's effervescence. LaRue didn't miss a beat.

"Did you know that the ancient Greeks believed in a race of giants born from the blood of the god Uranus after his son Cronus had castrated him?"

I smiled. "Sounds like the very same problem that plagues the guests here in the Hotel Hell."

He paused, executed a graceful tai chi pose, and then responded. "The giants rebelled against the gods of Olympus, but they were crushed by Zeus and his family."

"But they were gods, too. What happened to them?"

"They were cursed to wander the dark places of the earth."

I leaned on the railing and caught a hardy whiff of saffron rectangles coming off the water. Shaking my head, I waited for my visual acuity to return. LaRue stopped his twisting to join me.

"How do you feel this morning?" he asked.

"I'm fine, Andy. I'm just a little tired, a condition Gibson thinks is caused by my raging metabolism." I stopped, reversed gears, and changed the subject. "Did you talk to Stirling?"

"No, Ty. He's not on the *Delora*."

"Any ideas what happened to him?"

"I guess we spooked him. I brought the fact to Ritter's attention and he didn't seem very concerned."

"Someone jumps ship in the middle of the Rio Grande and he's not worried?"

"He said he'll start worrying when a body shows up."

"Real nice guy, huh? Did he give you a reason for his lackadaisical attitude?"

"He told me it happens that way sometimes. Rivermen abandon their tours of duty for no reason at all. They give up all the retirement and bennies they get from working for the government."

"That's crazy," I said, glancing at him.

"Insanity seems to be an underlying current on this river," he answered. He took a moment to stretch his back by touching his toes. Then: "I need to show you something in our quarters if you have a second."

"Of course I do. Lead away."

I followed him below, and after we entered our bunk room, he explained. "I couldn't sleep last night, so I started reading the logbook and discovered something interesting."

LaRue fetched the binder and flipped to the back cover. Running his finger beneath the plastic, he pulled out a small sheet of paper. "This is the Rosetta stone for that writing we found on the bottom of the last mandala."

"So, someone was expecting it—presumably Yarrow," I said.

"She or Kleege." He patted his cammies, looking for the right pocket. "I put the translation somewhere." Finally, he came up with the goods. "Finn was wrong about this thing being an advertisement."

"What is it, then?"

"If I understand it correctly, it sets up the sacred space that protects the person from harm or injury."

"It didn't work," I said. "I opened a hole in him with a bullet."

He shrugged. "I didn't say it had any real power. It was tossed onto the boat ahead of time, thereby forming the necessary magical vibrations to allow the bogeyman to move around freely."

I stared at him, unable to hide my frown. "It sounds like all that mandala can do is manifest bullshit." When LaRue didn't answer, I was forced to ask him a stupid question. "You don't really think it was the reason we didn't hear any noise during the attacks, do you?"

"I suppose it comes down to what you believe," he answered noncommittally. "If this bogeyman is Derek Wheeler, he's obviously in a state of mind which requires this kind of ritual to make him an effective killer." He tapped the sheet with his knuckle. "We've seen what happens when a person loses his free will to madness and manipulation."

"Do you think the attacker followed us by boat?"

"Yes."

"And he may have had help."

"I think he had several people with him."

If that were true, then we could have been boarded anytime by prisoners bent on murder. It meant that our lives had been spared because of the perceived limitations of water-witching magic. "We need to have a conflab with

Ritter. There's more to him than that kitten inside his face.''

"In a moment.''

We both turned at the sound of Gibson's voice, surprised because he had entered our quarters so silently. He approached us with a smile on his face, and seeing it, I knew the critters in my blood were being eaten by the wolf.

"I can't explain any other way than that fantastic furnace of yours is doing its stuff,'' he said, coming up to me and squeezing my arm.

LaRue grinned and patted my shoulder, and for a second there I experienced a sense of camaraderie that I didn't want to end. The fact that it was focused on me made it all the better.

"The blood smear looked a lot cleaner than the last,'' Gibson explained. "How do you feel?''

"All right. Just a little tired, but I haven't gotten much rest lately.''

He nodded and winked and then settled in to scan the bank as he went on with the good news. "Thanks to you, I have an idea how the mutated leprosy disease works.''

Upon hearing his declaration, my anxiety crowded me. "Go on,'' I murmured.

"The leprosy explodes from the blood cell like the malaria protozoa each time the pituitary gland in the brain secretes a growth hormone.''

"I thought the brain stopped sending out growth hormones when a person reached adulthood,'' LaRue said.

"Normally, yes,'' Gibson answered, and holding his finger up, he stressed his next point. "But these men are given a hormonal inhibitor to stop hair growth before entry into the penal system. I think something has gone terribly wrong with the process. Whether due to a combination of outside factors or not, they are growing. It's a slow process that takes years, and during this time their symptoms get progressively worse. Instead of incubating in the normal way, the leprosy invades the system with a series of errors. Small things—nerve damage, for instance.''

"It then compounds until the prisoner has the full-blown symptoms of leprosy,'' LaRue said.

"Yeah," I answered. "And by that time he's as big as a boat."

Gibson nodded. "I think the mosquitoes are part of the problem. The crewmen show no signs of malaria or dengue, but their records indicate at one time or the other they've all been infected. They don't show any major symptoms of leprosy either, but they do exhibit a mild form of the disease. This could be due to an influence of an inoculation— that part is up for guesses. Still, I'm sure the creature, the prisoners, and the rivermen are experiencing chemical and hormonal changes through the intercession of the insects. These alterations manifest according to what compounds are already present in the body at the time of infection."

"Did you check for these irregularities in our blood?" LaRue asked.

"Yes," Gibson answered. "I don't see anything. Yet."

The last part was of little comfort, but I cut the notch low on my worry stick. I told Gibson we would see him later and abruptly hauled LaRue away to ask the captain to drop anchor so we could hunt down a few more prisoners and their polluted unguents.

Finn turned sniffer for us, and we'd barely clawed our way up the east bank when he found someone who would talk to us. The inmate he'd rooted out was a character named Shinola Bola. He was a bruiser, too, well over seven feet tall, bald, and bubbly-skinned. When we were introduced, he was busy creating a voodoo baby, using mud, slime, and sticks. As we entered his decrepit cardboard camp I noticed he worked his sculpting material with the deft touch of hands that still had all their fingers.

Bola greeted us with a grunt, unconcerned about the harassing screws, intent instead on water-witching someone into ill health or ill fortune by using the karmic energies at his beck and call. Finn solved his concentration problem with one sentence.

"This here marshal is the kami sent by Davy Jones," he announced.

Bola glanced up so fast I thought he might lose a couple of scabs from the way his head rocketed back. He stared at me, squinted, and then decided I wasn't that special. "Yeah, so?"

"She wants your help."

The prisoner didn't answer and so Finn began preaching. "Davy Jones knows what he's doing. He knows we have to help ourselves if we're going to ever have justice done. If we don't, we ain't water witches true to our calling and our karma will just get worse instead of better. You know I'm speaking the truth."

Bola studied him, even as his hands fashioned the Black River muck into a magic symbol. Then he turned to consider me again. "I don't know what I might be able to do," he said. "My specialty is binding up bad karma. How's that gonna help a demoness?"

LaRue stepped in to the rescue with ridiculous metaphysical reason number 101. "Surely, as an accomplished water witch, you understand how the supernatural energy works. You have to mold it. Davy imbues a human with karmic energy and the desire for retribution. The Lost Mariner expects the avenging demoness to harness the free will of others. Those others must surrender and link their powers with hers. If not, she can do nothing to change their circumstances. That is the law of cause and effect made manifest."

LaRue was mouthing some of the best junk I'd ever heard, and it looked like Bola was starting to latch onto my partner's magnetic, bullshit personality. The inmate continued to dab at the mud and gook of his voodoo doll, but his attention was fixed firmly upon me. I sat there wearing my best lethal look. After a minute Bola replied. "I've got some stored up karma that I collected from my clients. You can have that, if it will help." He gently placed his sculpture on the ground and rose, bones cracking, to rummage through a wooden crate. After pulling out a rag-covered container, he paused, sighed, and then turned dramatically. "I was saving these scraps of energy for a rainy day, but I suspect saving humanity is a better use for the power. I worked the scraps until I cleaned out the negative influence, so what you got is pure energy—neither good nor bad."

He stepped back to his seat and held the package out to me. "It's all I got to give, ma'am."

I accepted his tribute graciously, bowing my head a little. Unwrapping the present, I found it to be an empty glass container. "Oh," I said. "Karma in a jar. How nice."

"That represents near five hundred folks whose destiny I bound up for them," Bola said. "Of course, it's scrap energy, you understand. When I tie up the loose pieces of fate, some of the extra has to be snipped away. The spell I use takes care of all that, you see. I just scrape the bottle over the patient and collect whatever karmic nodes are sticking out. They come off real easy, too."

"Well, thank you," I said, glancing at LaRue for help. He didn't let me down.

"Marshal Merrick has the power to glean the energy she needs. She won't take all the karmic energy."

He smiled.

I did my best to put on a show by caressing the jar while LaRue got down to brass tacks and asked for answers that we needed. "What do you know about the Coven's claims of Derek Wheeler's walk-in status?"

Bola snorted. "They wish." Shaking his head, he took the roundabout way to explain. "You know why I got my first name?"

"No, why?"

"Because I was a con artist once. I could sell anybody anything, from shit to shinola. I could make up a story faster than the fastest, but that one about Wheeler? I can't believe it. Not for a second."

"Why?"

"Because Wheeler was through here not long ago."

We all stared at him. Finally, Finn spoke softly. "Wheeler died."

"No, sir, he didn't. They passed out his body parts, but that's all they did."

"I don't understand," LaRue said.

Bola picked up his doll, dabbed, and answered. "They were old parts, already having fallen off the man."

"Don't tell me you save your rotted flesh," I said.

He nodded and pointed to his charm sack hanging around his scab-covered neck. "It's not good to let go of the pieces. You can trade them for spells and cures. If you're lucky enough to find a jigger man, you got it made."

"What's a jigger man?"

"He's a water witch who takes the parts and grinds them down. He then puts them into a jigger shot glass and adds some unguents and water, along with a powerful spell. The person drinks down the drub and a few days later he's growing all new fingers, ears, and nose tips."

I tossed a look toward Finn. "Wheeler was in bad shape, wasn't he?"

The prisoner was silent for a moment. Then: "His charm bag had to be full. For a fact, it was a right, big sack, too."

FORTY-FIVE

I began to suspect more interference from Gibson's information about the leprosy's regenerative properties upon hearing this confession by Shinola Bola. Like it or not, this truth pushed the bogeyman into my lycanthropic realm. My metabolism steams shut my wounds and it occurred to me that the disease could spare a man while subtly transforming him into the perfect nutritional host.

It certainly made me think and it made me uncomfortable, too. As LaRue pulled at the taffylike concepts of labor-camp reincarnation, I followed around my thoughts until I accidentally stepped into a pile of paranoia. If the prisoners were baptized in the polluted water flowing downstream from the factories and filth of the district, what catastrophe might be happening on our very doorstep? The sanitary treatment plants were always the brunt of bad jokes about efficiency, but now it didn't seem like such a laugh.

Before I could get very far from my jolting observations, I found myself mired in a possibility that further weighted Gibson's claim that there were many physical reasons for my lycanthropic symptoms, yet no physical evidence of the cause aside from the obvious misfiring of my brain. Could it be, then, that the carbon monoxide from that faulty furnace had mixed with the chemical compounds already contained in my body to cause an irreversible change in the mytosis of each cell? Could these alterations be subtle enough to guide my lycanthropy into full bloom?

When I finally disconnected from these disquieting images and launched back into the conversation, Bola was making a case for the stark reality of Summerland. "It's here the spirit can rest between lives," he said. "But you gotta go there with the right mind-set."

"Why?" LaRue asked.

"Because the mind you die with is the mind you reincarnate with. It follows a man into the afterlife, where he can't do nothing about changing his thoughts and ideas. He's stuck with his last life until he gets the chance to clean himself up in the next one."

"Was Wheeler concerned about this?" I said.

"Yes, ma'am, he was. He done lots of bad things, but then, we all have. Hell, I would have rolled Vivian Duvalier if someone had told me I could have made a credit from it. Wheeler hacked up a bunch of folks just for starters. When he got in here, he went to the side of the screws right away. He helped ol' Zol to mess with the natural order of things. There has always been water witching in this penal colony, but what he did to confound the truth takes our honorable arts into the realm of black magic. Wheeler is a man who's got a soul filled with hatred. It don't matter if he brought some of that horror with him from the last life or not, because he's stuck with the results of his past decisions."

"He was repentant?" I asked.

"No," he answered. "He just wanted a quick fix. The way he sees it, he's run out of grace, and that's what my power tells me, too. I did a dowsing on him and his energy flux is way out of whack. To make matters worse, he's got all this galloping karma—lots and lots of past-life drivel, shit he couldn't or wouldn't work through. Derek Wheeler is a doomed man. His soul is already up for grabs."

"What's that mean?" LaRue said.

"That means when he finally does die, the energy vultures will be on him for real. His soul ain't gonna escape this labor camp. Whatever karmic power is left is going to be sucked up. He knows it. That's what's giving him the fright."

"What could you have done to help Wheeler?" I asked.

"We all got free will. It's the one thing that determines the content of our karma. Folks come to me because they are out of control. The will begins in the mind and expands to the outer world and can cause a right good amount of interference in things. I bind up this force and help the patient to recover. It's a damned sight harder than it sounds, too. I have to redirect the person's free will by collecting the bad energy and then I gotta fill in the holes in the soul with liquefied grace."

"Liquefied grace?" LaRue said.

"Yes." He leaned in, pulling on a conspiratorial tone as he did. "The goddamned Coven don't want anyone to know that the Black River flows with grace. You just have to know where to find it."

Despite a long chain of disbelief, I said: "Do you have some of this elixir?"

He bowed his head slightly. "A little. You can have it if you want."

LaRue stampeded through the conversation. "So, Wheeler was concerned about dying with his current mind-set."

"Yeah. He thought I could rub on some ointment that would solve everything without him having to work at the change."

"He had dastardly plans in the works?" I asked.

"Wheeler was on a vendetta. He was real pissed off at ol' Zol for passing out the booty in his charm bag. He had a major hatred for the screw and he was afraid he was going to the Summerland with this debilitating problem. Wheeler wanted his missing parts back and he would do everything he could to work over the prefect until he got them."

FORTY-SIX

We left Bola about midday and returned to the boat with the bottled karma and liquefied grace. No sooner had we boarded than I had a stretch and dropped the karma jar, spilling the invisible energy contained there. The odd part came after I'd expanded my lycanthropic horizons, because I could have sworn I smelled golden squares wafting from the shards of old karma. It took me a moment to interject reason into this scenario and decide that the container had actually held something more substantial than the odd bits of souls.

As the agony progressed I balled into a fetal position more to protect the container of liquid grace than to slow the rise of lycanthropic pain. Gibson was on top of me before I came completely out of the stretch, and as I relaxed he took me in his arms, cradling me gently. I'll admit, I could have stayed that way forever, because this was grace as good as it got. Still, comforted in love and tenderness, I had an oddball consideration: did this emotional euphoria have something to do with the water sloshing around in the jar I held?

The thought was enough to make me squirm from Gibson's embrace and present him with the bottle. I stood,

dusted off my cammies, realizing abruptly that I was at
least two inches taller than when I'd grown last. My uniform was so tight in the crotch, I could barely walk, and
the material cut into the bulging muscles in my upper arms.
It was then that the terror of possibilities set in.

"I'm turning into one of them," I said.

Gibson shook his head, handed the jar off to LaRue, and
took a step toward me. He stopped when I backed away.
"Calm down, Merrick."

"Calm down?" I growled. "Look at me! My bones are
stretching more than they ever have." I turned away, suddenly embarrassed about this latest transformation.

"Ty," LaRue said. "It's not that bad."

Sure it was. With this kind of change, my lycanthropic
strength would grow. I'd have to be careful about crushing
things—radio microphones, water glasses, and people's
necks. I could already feel the surge of profound power as
it consumed my humanity, blending it with the supernatural
until there was only a hint of the real Ty Merrick left. Was
this, indeed, what it meant to be a monster, something paranormal constrained by the physics of the material plane?

"Merrick, you've got malaria," Gibson said.

"So?" I whispered stupidly.

"So, it's affecting you and your seizures. It may be your
body's defense mechanism, the very energy you need to
thwart the disease. Don't look at it like a curse."

"But what if I don't shrink back down at the end of the
full moon?" Yes, the question sounded hollow and egotis-
tic even to my ears.

Gibson used the opportunity to wave LaRue and Finn
off. He cornered me by pushing me against the railing and
keeping me there with the bulk of his body. "Your lycanthropy works differently than the disease affecting the prisoners," he said firmly. "Trust me."

"You always say that," I shot back. "And it always
works against me."

Despite my lycanthropic strength, he overpowered me
simply by studying me with that fierce squint of his. "Re-

lax, Merrick. You're experiencing post-traumatic stress. Take a deep breath.''

I did as he asked, feeling like a fool for my outburst. Glancing toward the deck, I pushed back a swell of emotion, unsure where it had come from in the first place.

"What's going on?" he asked quietly. "What haven't you told me?"

How I wanted to evaporate into his soothing tone, but instead I pulled away, trying to stall the inevitable confession. I took a moment to slow my pounding pulse by shooting my gaze to the nearby bank. Our arrival on the *Delora* had signaled the crew to shove off and now we floated beneath the canopy of old oak trees swathed in streamers of Spanish moss. A tattered garland of toilet paper decorated the branches, blowing in the breeze like a Buddhist prayer pennant. I chuckled when I saw this potent symbol representing the meaning of my own karmic destiny: it's a shitty life; get used to it.

I turned back to Gibson, who stood quite close but did not touch me. "Do you think my lycanthropy has any limits?"

"Boundaries?" he said thoughtfully. "Plain old mathematics will dictate the limits of your physical transformation. I don't think you'll grow to be seven feet tall, if that's what you're asking."

"But we know the brain alters our physical and mental bodies with nothing more than a little hormone here and an enzyme there."

"So?"

My fears have never been easy for me to admit. "So, what does that make me? Human or monster?"

FORTY-SEVEN

The next morning the *Delora* squeezed through the Vivian Narrows. It was slow going, because the channel was so slender, a person could reach out and touch the concrete pilings keeping the river's shore at bay. Nonetheless, Ritter navigated the corridor with precision. Once clear, he dropped anchor and we joined the river rats gathering to do some brisk trading business among themselves.

I caught Russo's sleeve as he walked by us to crank out the plank. "Why are we stopping?"

Since I returned on board with my kami fame, the riverman had avoided looking me in the eye. He pulled clear of my grip and shuffled on, mumbling toward the deck as he did.

"What?" I growled.

"We gotta bring in supplies to the district personnel working here," he said, louder.

"How long will we be here?" I asked.

"Till we're done."

"I want you to take us to the narrows supervisor."

My sentence forced him to snap his head up. He stopped walking to stare at me like the wolf was showing, and then, perhaps afraid I would lay a karmic whammy on him, he spoke to his shoes when he answered me. "I have other duties. The captain won't be happy if I don't get them done."

"Take us to the supervisor," I growled. "Now."

Russo jumped with the inflection in my voice, nodded, and kept his gaze securely toward the center of the earth. He stumbled a few times when we made our way up a cracked concrete stair leading to the operator's shack. The word *shack* proved to be an accurate description of the building. It was a crumbling stone structure with broken windows and a dented corrugated aluminum roof, surrounded by a gooey, muddy compound. We sucked up slime to our ankles, and despite the mess we tracked inside, the supervisor, Rick Orion, greeted us in a boisterous, jovial manner.

Orion was a fat, moon-faced fellow with a headful of greasy blond hair and a mouthful of rotten teeth. He puffed against the small exertion of pushing himself out of the desk chair, but before we were done shaking hands, he offered us seats, coffee, and homemade dingleberry pie. Not knowing if a dingleberry would kill me, I accepted only the drink while LaRue decided to test out the dessert. He ate with gusto, using the spoon to scrape up every bit of crust sticking to the saucer.

"I suspect you want to know if I've seen Derek Wheeler," Orion announced, pushing another dingleberry slice toward my partner.

"My, word travels fast," I said.

"You bet it does," he answered. "In fact, I've heard some claims about you just in the last day."

"Such as?" I asked innocently.

"They say you carry the walk-in soul of Tidus Neal."

I glanced at LaRue. "I thought I was a kami?"

He shrugged, but instead of answering, he stuck to his chore of inhaling food.

Orion filled me in. "You're supposed to be a kami, too."

"Well, who was Tidus Neal?"

"Wheeler's son."

"Was he raised up in the same manner as Eldon Emmet?" I asked.

"No. Neal really was Wheeler's son, by blood. He found himself incarcerated along with his old man."

"What did he do?"

"Tried to defend him in court, so I hear. The judge had a case of the ass or something and sent the son up the river for contempt." He paused to cut a wedge of pie, slipped it onto a delicate, china plate, and then licked his fingers loudly, making sure that none of the dingleberry juice was lost. "They say Neal and Emmet were bitter enemies, each vying for the cushy spot behind the old man. Emmet was supposed to have bludgeoned Neal to death one esbat."

"Esbat?"

"It's one of the gathering days for the water witches. Kind of like getting together and doing magic on Halloween."

LaRue straightened us both out following a quick bite. "Esbat is a ceremony held during the full moon."

"We've heard about the full-moon ceremonies," I said. "Have you ever been to one?"

Orion lost a portion of his joviality. "Now, why would I go to one of those? I'm a district employee, not an inmate."

"I didn't mean to offend you, Mr. Orion. We're just trying to get information on what happens during these celebrations. It may help us catch a killer."

Orion laughed. "And tell me, what will you do with him? He's already in prison."

"We'll take him back to the district for questioning," LaRue said.

"What will happen after that? The death penalty carried out quietly, so no one knows that their rights as citizens have been violated?" He sat back and the load he placed upon his chair made the poor old thing cry out. "Maybe a nice, illegal electrocution. Yeah. With the electricity rotated so damned much back in the district, I'm sure there would be plenty of juice for the execution."

Neither of us answered, because he hadn't gotten it far

wrong. The whole truth, though, was darker. It was a good
chance the killer would become a lab rat. When the scientists finished using his body and mind, then they would
destroy him.

LaRue steered the interview out of deep water. "I take
it the Coven makes a big production of the esbat."

"Oh, sure," Orion said.

"What about Hecate's Sickle?"

"I suppose. I don't know for sure, though. Try to keep
my nose out of their affairs."

"Why?"

"Because ol' Zol doesn't control Eldon Emmet and his
followers. A person can get in trouble on both sides of the
river."

"Has Emmet ever attacked Zoltana's people?"

"I would guess so. We had a considerable riot after ol'
Zol passed out Wheeler's parts. Emmet couldn't stand it,
because he knew it was all bogus from the start. They're
at war and the prefect is losing ground like a one-legged
emperor. If he doesn't get a handle on it soon, he'll start
losing more and more of the Coven to the Sickle. Once that
happens, he's going to have to run for his life. I'm telling
you, Marshals, if they don't get the bastard out of here
before long, this whole place will explode. Knowing the
government, they won't move as fast as they should, and
the putrefied bogeymen will overrun the district. Then
what?"

I ignored his question to ask my own. "Have you seen
Wheeler?"

"No. Emmet, neither."

I rose and took a few steps around the shack. Glancing
up, I noticed the rafters were strung with bear traps. "Let
me guess," I said, pointing to them. "Old-fashioned land
mines."

Orion chuckled, popped another piece of pie into his
mouth, and spoke around his food. "I put them at the doors
and windows at night. They keep the bastards out of the
shack."

LaRue sat back and sucked his fingers before changing

the subject. "I'll bet you've seen some pretty good boat wrecks, huh?"

Orion nodded. "The narrows have sunk some of the best. If you're not careful, you can shear off part of your vessel."

"What about along the river?" I asked. "Are there many accidents?"

"More than there should be. The mist and fog, you know."

"How long have you worked here?"

"Almost thirty years," he said.

I spun my attention onto Orion and found him wearing a smug expression. I pushed on with the questioning. "So, you've been around a long time. Have you heard any stories about sunken boats loaded with treasure?"

Orion abruptly lost his pleasant, homeboy attitude. "Why would you ask such a thing?"

"We've been told about pirate ships," LaRue lied.

"Pirates?" Orion said, relaxing. "No galleons filled with doubloons, I'm sorry to say."

"Nothing that might carry pearls or diamonds?"

He frowned. "You're talking about the Boat of Wishes."

"What's that?" I asked.

"It's a district boat, always disguised, which is carrying the payroll and assorted wealth to other localities. You never know who has the sack of gold. I've heard the District Council has gone so far as to select certain people to be couriers, so the boat has a good chance of getting through without being attacked."

I tossed LaRue a quick look, satisfied, now that I had another idea about the stashes of gems we were finding on the *Delora*.

"Why do they call it the Boat of Wishes?" LaRue asked.

"Because money makes the wishes come true. Even out here."

"What does that mean?"

"That means, these inmates will skin you alive if they think you're carrying wealth of any kind. If you can pay off a guard, you can live in peace for a while. No work details, decent food, and a warm, dry cardboard box somewhere.'' He popped another dingleberry into his mouth as if to punctuate his statement.

I sat down and leaned forward, tapping the desk with my knuckle as I gently redirected Orion to the original question. "Has there ever been a big boat wreck anywhere along the Black?"

He made an earnest effort to think, concentrating a minute on his forkful of food. Then: "Twenty years ago there was a big accident in the delta. The boat was called the *Karmic Wind*. That's what happened all right—it hit a wind that delivered the crew to their destiny—two hundred feet underwater."

"Did the government try to recover the boat?" I asked.

"Oh, they made a halfhearted attempt, but then decided it wasn't worth the equipment and manpower. That's deep, you know. It would take diving suits and decompression chambers—stuff like that. At the time there was a call to hack expenses, so the bureaucrats decided to cut their losses and fed the media with the usual crap. You know, 'all wealth has been moved from the wreck and is heading to the district it was intended for.' "

"But in actuality, they just let the *Karmic Wind* lie."

"Yeah. I heard an independent contractor tried to pull it out a few years back, but he had to give up."

"Why?" I asked.

Orion shook his head sorrowfully. "Because there are just too many big, dangerous water monsters to deal with."

FORTY-EIGHT

We left Orion soon after LaRue helped him finish off his pie and coffee. As we returned to the *Delora* we decided to take a detour and visit with the river rats whose skiffs and longboats gathered like sucker fish at the bow of the river cutter. My partner pointed to an ark made of old boards, torn canvas, and plastic bleach bottles. A white-haired woman, bent and frail looking, sat on the deck weaving a fishing net. Sitting beside her was an odd companion—a stuffed dog whose paws had been tied to a small red wagon. She invited us on board after we identified ourselves.

"I'm called Dinkim Sue," she said.

"What's your friend's name over there?" I asked, nodding my chin toward the dog.

She smiled. "Scuttlebutt."

LaRue and I took seats on an old military footlocker and watched the ancient work the shuttle and knots. She reminded me of Baba at her loom, and thinking about it, I experienced a pang of homesickness. Following that, I groped around in a minute of despair, wondering if I would ever get back to my flat and my cantankerous, vodka-swilling roommate.

Thankfully, my partner put the kibosh on my worry and longing by immediately moving to the focus of our visit. "How long have you plied the Black River, Dinkim Sue?"

"All my life, young man," she answered in parchment-paper tones. "I was here before this penal colony was even thunk of. My family owned a lot of the land between here and the delta. Of course, Duvalier didn't care none about things like legal ownership. One day, his army done up and took it." She sighed as she flicked knots. "Sorrowful shame, but that's the truth of it."

I'm known for my lack of tact and I demonstrated it. "You said you were here before the labor camp? How old are you?"

She gave me a gap-toothed grin. "I am the daughter of Methuselah. I turned ninety years old this past month. Still, I reckon I'm not the oldest out here."

"There are others?"

"Why sure. There are folks who've lived on the Black since before that bastard dictator was born."

"Do you live on this boat?" I asked.

"Yes."

"Do you trade goods with the prisoners?"

"When I can. We ain't supposed to, but you've got to make a living." Dinkim Sue paused in her work to swat at a mosquito. "I'm a water witch who specializes in changing the influence of past lives. Maybe you're interested."

"I don't understand," LaRue said.

"One of the reasons we're all stuck in the cesspool of hopelessness is because we are under the influence of past incarnations," she said. "Our current choices are ruled by whatever past life happens to be in control at the time. I can tell folks what incarnation is making them miserable or joyous. Still, if folks would pay attention to their habits, they wouldn't need for me to read 'em."

"How can people tell?" I asked.

"Look to your likes and dislikes. The signs are subtle, but if you got your eyes open, you won't have no trouble seeing them."

I glanced at my partner and found him squinting just like Gibson did.

"In other words," he said, "if a person loves caviar, then he might be working off the influence of a Russian lifetime."

Dinkim Sue nodded. "That's right."

If that was the case, then LaRue's fascination with the old Soviet Union meant he was the reincarnation of Karl Marx, and with my partner's metaphysical bent, he sensed the path that this brand of magic was taking. It was a good thing, because I was mired in the mud and had no idea what question to ask next.

"So, throughout our current life, we deal with a variety of karmic lessons that need addressing," he surmised. "These past lives move like the wheel of the zodiac, each queuing up for a moment of influence before being replaced by another, whether the lesson has been learned or not."

Dinkim Sue grinned. "Now, Marshal, you're one of the smarter people I've met. You got the idea down pat, you do. The energy of these past lives floats through our sub-conscious minds. They impress us with old desire. They affect our free will. My magic tells me what trump card most folks are playing. When I figure out what's guiding you toward your current destiny, I can do a smudging and help you push that wheel ahead."

"Of course, you can't guarantee that the new past-life influences will be any easier or any better than the one previously pushing the person," he said.

"No, no guarantees. A person can paddle between hope and fear only so long before he has to make a choice. We can make the most of our current lives by relying on karmic credit. We can use the strengths we've built up over thousands of years of incarnating into this pisshole plane we live in. Still, most folks just whine about the hurts and ills instead of doing something constructive with the crap that the universe throws at them. I've seen folks so stuck by the influence of a particular past life that unless they did something, they were never going to solve the issues at hand. So, I nudge the wheel a mite. Nothing wrong with that. It gives the person new confidence. It, at least, gives him something different to look toward."

Were we discussing a broken understanding of grace? Had the hopelessness and shame turned a concept of compassionate mercy into something that could be gained by dabbing on an ointment rather than receiving an enigmatic gift of higher consciousness? This was an essential quality of humanity, and so to lose it might be the cruelest punishment of all.

"How much for a smudging?" LaRue asked.

"What do you got?" she countered.

He reached into his pocket and pulled out one of his mother's lycanthropy charms. Despite all the years her son and I had been working together, Mrs. LaRue still suspected me of complicity with the evil forces of the fourth dimension. She chose to do battle with the dark energies by making her son carry all manner of potions and sacks intended to keep him safe during a full moon spent on duty with me. My partner is a dutiful child, and to get her off his back, he did as she asked. Because of that, he always had a ready supply of invisible magic. "This is a bag of sultana raisins laced with allspice, sugar, and a laxative spell," he announced. "Use it on the full moon if you want a good cleansing."

Dinkim Sue reached out, took the charm, and sniffed it. "What else do you have? The unguents I use to make up my smudging incense cost me a bundle."

LaRue glanced at me and I pulled out a hard biscuit I'd saved from morning mess. I handed it to her. "That's it."

She squinted at me, but then nodded. "Who wants the past-life reading?"

My partner volunteered me. "See what's under Ty's subconscious skin."

The old witch stood up, and after shaking out her fishing net, she began to wrap me in it. I tried to let LaRue know of my discomfort through my expression, but he ignored me to ask Dinkim Sue a few questions while she worked. "Have you ever heard of a government boat called the *Karmic Wind*?"

"Yes. The money barge. It sank." She stopped to cackle. Then: "They should have named it the *Karmic Ill Wind*. That was a boat of lost souls right from the start."

"Why do you say that?"

"It was overloaded with silver ingots and heavy with jewels, so it's said. It was pure greed, right from the top, and because of that, it was destined to become part of Davy Jones's locker. Still, all those prisoners."

"Prisoners?" LaRue said. "There were inmates aboard?"

"Like slaves, they were. A hundred in all. Each one carrying a dead man's chest, ready to meet his fate for the gold in his teeth."

"So, are you saying that inmates have been used as dead man's chests by government employees?"

She shrugged. "Seems likely. I heard it was the way ol' Zol got his money out of town without the environmental tax collectors getting all over him. He was right pissed when it went down. I understand he's been trying to get at that cache for years. Ain't gonna do him any good."

"Why?" I asked through the fishnet.

"Because of karma, Marshal. You see, the threefold law of water witching prevents it from happening. Zoltana is just too stupid to see it. Ol' Zol got what he had coming. You put out sorrow and despair and that is what you reap in triple measure. It never fails. Never."

"How did the boat sink?" LaRue asked. "Bad storm?"

"No, hell no," she answered. "One of ol' Zol's pets took a chunk out of the *Karmic Wind*'s hull."

"You're talking about a serpent attacking the boat?" I asked.

"That's what happened. I was there and saw it. The creature had a mouth full of fangs at least a foot long apiece." Dinkim Sue demonstrated by holding her hands apart. "It had sparkling scales, the size of my ass, and a tail that looked like it was kipped from a rattlesnake. Hideous."

"You said it was one of Zoltana's pets," LaRue said. "What does that mean?"

"He raised them bastards, using unguents made from the

pools and streams. Well, he didn't do it personally. His mad scientist did it for him.''

"His mad scientist?"

"Yes," she answered. "A man named Stirling."

FORTY-NINE

Dinkim Sue admonished me to sit still, but I had the deep-down jip-jumpies and continued to fidget. We were floating into a strange mythological world, complete with all the supernatural elements firmly in place. Do you want to know the worst part? I was forced to admit my lycanthropy offered me an unparalleled entry into this paranormal fairy tale. As if to prove it, Dinkim Sue began her past-life witching ritual and I was left feeling embarrassed on top of everything else.

She touched the crown of my head and began to chant a nonsensical song. After five minutes of this magical mantra, she lifted her hand and blew on my hair. I caught a whiff of fishy-smelling blue dots, and so as not to give my blessing to this show, I shut my eyes and concentrated on the colors generated by my optic nerve. She placed her hand atop my noggin, again, and after a few more minutes her performance wound to an end. The blue dots began to burst and disappear, and I looked up to see the old woman scowling at me. She pulled her hand away and examined her palm, as though some of me had rubbed off on her.

"What's wrong?" I asked.

Dinkim Sue didn't answer immediately. Instead, she

worked to pull her fishing net free. Moving into the clap-
board cabin of her boat, she scrounged around, eventually
returning with three different bottles of invisible magic. She
carefully measured out jigger-sized portions of goo into a
crockery bowl, and setting it onto the deck, she nicked a
battered butane lighter toward the contents. The stuff
burned like Sterno and smelled faintly of bacon grease. "I
call this drub my pungent unguent," she said. "That will
help you get yourself back together. Guaranteed. Just sit in
the smoke for a while."

Again I glanced at LaRue for help, but he ignored me
masterfully. "Exactly what is your diagnosis of Marshal
Merrick's karmic problems?" he asked.

She sat down on a wobbly lawn chair, grunting as she
did, and reached out to pet her stuffed dog. "I ain't seen
her karmic condition for many a year," she said mourn-
fully. "It's good you comed to me when you did."

"Why?" LaRue growled.

Dinkim Sue didn't even blink at LaRue's impatient snarl.
"Every person alive in the material plane has got himself
a soul mate. I suspect you've heard of this."

"Yes," he answered.

"Well, every once in a while you come across somebody
who is one half of a twin soul. Twin souls work just like
having twin children does. You get two kids from one cell.
Same thing happens to our invisible selves." She paused
to cough as the wind shifted and started blowing her magical karma smudge in her direction. Glancing at LaRue, she
said: "The shit smells terrible, doesn't it? But it does do
the trick."

"What is Marshal Merrick's problem?" LaRue demanded.

"Instead of the twin souls inhabiting different bodies,
you sometimes get a situation where they are joined like a
couple of Siamese sisters. That is what has happened to this
young woman. I can feel their connection along different
points in the karmic energy. It must cause her a heap of
trouble."

I have to hand it to her, Dinkim Sue was right. The wolf

and I were stapled together and no surgeon had the ability to snap the splines linking us. "What past life supposedly influences me and this invisible entity I'm stuck with?"

"You're both working out the karmic influence of an incarnation when you were slaves," she answered matter-of-factly.

"Oh, how do you know this?"

The old woman smiled and shook her head. "You like onions, don't you?"

"Sure, most people do," I said. "But that doesn't prove I was a slave."

"Well, it don't disprove it none, neither. You were a slave in ancient Egypt and your master gave you onions and bread as your food rations." She paused to pet her dead pooch again. "Whether you believe it or not ain't none of my concern, but I can tell you it's the reason why you feel like you're chained in your choices."

A normal person would have called the old bat crazy. She was, too, loony as the loons floating on the gentle waves of the Black River. Still, her prophecy was nothing more than a difference in syntax, because like it or not, she spoke the truth about my metaphysical carpetbagger.

My chagrin must have shown in my expression, because LaRue deftly moved the subject off to another tangent. "Has an inmate named Derek Wheeler been out to see you?"

"Derek Wheeler?" she asked. "I heard he was dead from the rot." Dinkim Sue leaned forward in the rickety chair. "Now, you see, the leprosy is a good case in point. It's caused by a past-life influence, a life that was filled with decadence and focused on giving others a good deal of pain. What goes around eventually comes around, I always say. That's something you don't see much of among us river rats."

"No signs of leprosy?" I asked.

She shook her head and spoke proudly. "It's real rare. In fact, the last time the rot took hold of one of us was at least twenty years ago."

FIFTY

After our visit with Dinkim Sue, LaRue decided to visit with a few more river rats while I returned to the *Delora* smelling faintly of bacon. I found Gibson sacked out cold in our bunk room, so rather than disturb him, I went down to the sick bay to see what I could scare up on Tidus Neal. Unfortunately, the moment I stepped inside, I was met by the sorry sight of Dr. Stirling.

He was haggard and dirty, and his uniform was ripped. He also sported a gaping wound on his left cheek. When he saw me, he nearly jumped out of his skin, and snatching up something from the examining table, he tried to move past me, but I was having none of it.

I grabbed him by the collar and growled. "Where the hell have you been?"

With a force I would not have expected, Stirling yanked free of my grip and rushed through the hatch. I tore after him, but pulled up as he jumped from the gangplank into the midst of merchant boats. He hip-hopped across the vessels, leaving panic and angry shouts in his wake. I lost interest in the chase when I saw him scuttle up the far bank with LaRue on his heels. They disappeared into the thick tree line and a few minutes later my partner returned alone, waving and shaking his head.

I returned to the sick bay, sat down wearily before the computer, and opened the desk drawer looking for the labor-camp records. LaRue showed up just as I started running the disks.

"What was that all about?" he demanded breathlessly.

I shook my head. "He was here and it looked like he was in some kind of fight. I think he was getting a supply of catgut and bandages."

"Well, I can tell you, he was on the move. He was gone once he hit that tree line."

"Yeah, runs mighty fast for an old boy, doesn't he?"

LaRue pulled a chair alongside of mine, climbed onto it pony-style, and changed the subject. "Maybe Dinkim Sue is right about your lycanthropy," he said softly.

I glanced at him and smiled slightly. LaRue measured the mysteries of life from a causal standpoint. You get what you give, and yes, maybe that was how the universe worked. Certainly it was how this labor camp ran—an eye for an eye, a tooth for a tooth. "The old witch missed the point in her past-life divvying. They all have."

"What do you mean?"

I sat back, sighing, knowing that if I didn't get it out, he would hound me until I did. "Why do I need to know who I was in my last incarnation?"

"So you can learn from your mistakes," he said.

I shook my head. "But don't you see, Andy? We don't. What we did is over and done with. There is no going back again."

"What are you suggesting?"

"I'm suggesting that if what we've been told is true, then we need to break out of the restrictive patterns established by our free will. Free will is the builder. Because of free will, we rely on our intuition, our power of thought, and our sentimentality to see us through. If that's so, then the soul is merely the spark of the life force and has no determination at all."

"You make it sound insignificant."

"Maybe, it is. Without the mind-set to guide it from one physical life to another, it can't do anything by itself."

LaRue shook his head. "These people trapped here believe that they've violated the law of karma to an extreme point. Otherwise they wouldn't be suffering in a labor camp."

"That's right. And it seems everybody believes some part of the reincarnation story."

"Are you saying that in order to break the karmic patterns in our lives, we must change the way we view and relate to the world?"

"Bingo," I answered. "And that's where ol' Zol has them. That is the only point of control he has. He establishes the prisoners' view of the material plane. He's set up the rules and they must abide by them or be lost to more negative karma. The inmates, on the other hand, are trying everything they can to beat the laws of karma and put one over on the bastard."

He was silent for a minute, considering this theory. Finally, he nodded toward the computer. "What are you looking for?"

"Something on Tidus Neal."

He turned to stare at me with those deep, dark eyes of his. "Tell me you don't believe you're carrying his walk-in soul."

"His name rose to the top of the muck, Andy. It tells me that he was involved with Emmet and Wheeler and may have had something to do with the wreck of the *Karmic Wind*. If Zoltana lost big-time money, he may have wanted revenge in the worst way. His free will has him as caged as the prisoners and just as desperate."

"Greed."

"You got it. I'll bet you there's enough wealth in this place to literally sink a ship, and ol' Zol wants it all. Every last doubloon, diamond, and giant pearl."

"That's a longshot guess about Neal, Ty. What do you expect to find in the records?"

I shrugged. "I don't know."

LaRue kept me company while I fed different files into

the computer. He tip-tapped across subjects of immortality like I tip-tapped across the keyboard. I pushed his lecture into the background and before long what he said slid into my awareness without my notice. My concentration was armed and several minutes later I interrupted him in the middle of a story about lycanthropic fever in the Dark Ages to announce I'd found a file. Upon reading it, I discovered it answered many of our grisly questions with grisly facts.

It was in a twenty-year old medical document. The information pertained to a defunct study on the effects of a chemical known as teratoxin, a man-made substance which had been accidentally released in the lower delta. According to the sketchy data, teratoxin changed the DNA structure and, combined with other hormonal manipulation, caused a distortion in brain function.

I pushed away an ominous feeling as I scrolled through the file. Even LaRue shut up, amazed at what he was reading. Finally, I pulled up a digitized, black-and-white medical photo of Tidus Neal. He was shown from the back, naked, his bulk exaggerated by the long black hair that covered him from head to toe. The next picture I flipped to was taken from the front, and it was clearly evident that Tidus Neal had fangs. More surprising than that was the mention of his son, Derek Wheeler.

FIFTY-ONE

LaRue and I were sitting there with our mouths open when Gibson entered the sick bay. Upon seeing our expressions, he said: "Find the bogeyman?"

"As a matter of fact, we did," I answered, pointing to the computer screen. "That is the same creature who attacked us on the bridge. Do you know how old this picture is?"

Gibson stomped up behind us and indicated his awe with a low whistle. "Where did you find this?"

"In an outdated folder." I glanced at him. "According to this there was a chemical spilled into the Black called teratoxin. Ever hear of it?"

He frowned. "No."

"It screws up the DNA sequencing in humans."

His features slid into disbelief. He raised his hand and swiped his fingers across his chin, as if to drag away his expression. "This can't be good news. It could be the chemical that puts the shine on everything. If it does exist and the mosquitoes are the facilitating force, then I'd say everyone may have this compound in their systems." He stared at me. "Including us."

"What a mess," LaRue muttered. "Disease, pollution, mosquitoes, and chemicals capable of making a person grow and eventually turning him into a bogeyman. Oh, and let's not forget the giant water moccasins.'' He glanced at me. ''And you give me a hard time about my beliefs in the supernatural. The truth is more frightening than any demon could ever be.''

My partner was right, but I pushed past his observation by addressing Gibson. ''Did you have a chance to check our liquefied grace?''

He held up a finger and then turned toward the counter and a printout. A silent moment passed between us before he spoke. ''I have the usual compounds found in polluted water: soda ash, oils, PCBs, heavy metals. There is the presence of human fat.''

''Human fat?''

He nodded, and continued reading. ''The liquefied grace also contains gold dust, dirt, and algae. There are six unknown compounds as well. One of these might be a mutated form of teratoxin, but I don't have any breakdown information for the compound. The computer medical analyzer just can't handle it.''

I shifted my attention to the keyboard and scrolled the document until I reached the end. Just as I suspected, I found Stirling's name listed as a researcher. ''Looks like there is a dab of shared karma between Neal, Wheeler, Emmet, and the mad doctor.''

LaRue shook his head. ''How many bogeymen do you think there really are out here?''

''It could be all of them,'' Gibson said quietly. ''One day.''

Great. We were a people caught in the clinches of a corrupt government, helpless over matters of life and death, pawns in a chess match that had pitted the stupid against the egotistical.

To avoid finding further shattered illusions, I checked out of the file and stood up, firmly committed to moving beyond this latest atrocity, but my legs felt like jelly; I had a hot flash; and the next thing I knew, my butt hit the deck.

Gibson was on me, laying his hand across my forehead. ''You've got a fever, Merrick.'' With that, he picked me up and guided me to the examining table, where I became the lab rat, yet again. The good doctor was in the midst of his ministrations when he abruptly slid out of sight as I fell into a faint.

Unfortunately, my trip into this mini-coma was not to be the sweet oblivion it should have been. My brain kept up its annoying pitch and I moved from one hot, steamy dream to another. In one, I found myself in a building trying to unlock door after door. I was looking for answers while being chased by some unknown adversary. The dream was confused with colors and patterns formed by my synesthesia. Whatever Gibson used in the real world stank enough to push into my unconscious vistas and affect the outcome of these fever-induced visions.

This anxiety-driven hell seemed to go on for hours and at some point I became lucid within the dream state. I realized that I had the ability to make logical connections between images loaded with bogeymen and strings of mathematical equations that proved eloquently that karma and grace could fit easily into the physical laws of the universe. With thought alone, I could change the numbers and divine the mysteries behind life. Things were going along pretty well there for a few minutes, but it all ended when I woke up to a pounding headache. I was still in the sick bay lying on the table. LaRue was nowhere to be seen, yet Gibson was nearby, gazing intently into a microscope.

"What happened?" I croaked.

He looked up from his slide, smiled, and rose to walk to the table. "You had a malarial episode," he explained.

"Can I have some water?" I asked.

He nodded, turned slightly to hand me a beaker already prepared. I sat up, pausing a moment until a wave of dizziness crashed over me. When it rolled away, I drank greedily, coughing as the liquid dribbled down the wrong throat pipe. Gibson patted me gently on the back. Finally, I found the voice and energy to speak.

"How long have I been out?"

"Two days."

"I thought I was getting over the malaria."

"You were," he said. "Apparently, you needed some downtime so your system could finish flushing the parasites. I drew blood from you less than an hour ago and there is no sign of the malaria."

"So, I'm out of the woods?"

"You'll probably be weak for a few days." He took the empty beaker from me and set it on the counter, turning back to check my pulse. "You know, you are amazing. What has happened to you here is one for the record books. I can't explain it, but I'm grateful that you're all right."

I stared at him. It was tempting to fall back on my suspiciousness, but seeing the expression of concern on his face, I decided to keep my mouth shut and enjoy a little attention.

FIFTY-TWO

LaRue and I decided to use Finn like a bloodhound and head inland to try to get the goods on Eldon Emmet.

The place where Ritter had docked the *Delora* was a mucky peninsula leading to the biggest junkyard I have ever seen. It must have gone on for miles in both directions. As we slogged through the reeds and mud we passed temples of tires and monuments of rusty metal; dirty rags hung out like prayer flags; and an altar built of sticks and slime, attractively decorated with the bleached bones of some enormous fish.

Except for the lousy weather, I usually don't complain about my environment, but then, I'm usually on dry land. We were up to our nubs in silt and squirmy things and every step was a battle with the forces of gravity and suction. Though I knew LaRue was in a state of readiness, he nonetheless used the moment to turn on his lecture mode and escort us with a running commentary about how the ancient Egyptians had fed their captives raw horseradish and magical spells to release their free will, thereby making them compliant slaves. It all sounded like good, clean fun, but in reality, about all horseradish could do for you is give you what Baba calls the widdershins. As for free will, how much can you have when you're fighting diarrhea?

We slogged through the mud and reed monsters for another two hours. At points along our soggy trail, the trash rose up around us until I felt like I was trudging down the middle of a fairway painted by Salvador Dalí. My lycanthropic sensibilities were hyped up, and even in the morning quiet, I knew we weren't alone. People watched us and followed us. I could practically hear their breathing, and as if to bear witness to my ears, my synesthesia informed me of our stalkers' smelly colors.

According to Finn, he knew a prisoner who lived in one of the trash barrels in the dump. He was good to his word and did, indeed, bring us to a shack, the walls of which were made from old refrigerators and the roof created with strips of plastic bags. We found a gnarled, warty old gent sitting in the midst of all this splendor, wearing leg irons and a satisfied expression at seeing he had company. Finn exchanged greetings and introductions and soon we were settling in to sit by Cleaver Van Metre's hearth, where he contentedly roasted two huge, black rats.

It was evident that this man suffered from the leprosy affliction. His skin was a countryside filled with pustules, scabs, and scar tissue. Every finger on his left hand was missing and his right ear was gone.

"Why do they call you Cleaver?" LaRue asked.

The old man chuckled. "Because I done cleaved people to death, Marshal. Seventeen in all." He shook his head and smiled wistfully. "God, what a bender that was."

"Cleave," Finn said, "I need your help and so do the marshals."

Van Metre stared at us, rubbed the tattoo on his chin, and then pronounced us to be less than dog fleas. "Why do ya want to help such as them?" he asked.

"Because they got me out of cell block two," Finn answered. "The Baculum has it in for me."

"Philips? You ain't ascared at the piece of dung, are you? I keep telling folks that onest your family jewels get cut away, then so does any ability to make up a magical marvel. Cain't happen without the life force. Nope, cain't happen.''

''You don't believe in water-witch magic?'' I asked.

''I don't believe in none of it. Ain't gonna be a second chance onest I die. That's just wishful thinking.'' He turned to cast a critical gaze over me. ''I suppose you're the one they been harping on. The kami, is it?''

I shrugged. ''I've been told I'm also carrying the walk-in spirit of Tidus Neal.''

He snorted. ''Tidus Neal is a ghost, but I reckon you ain't got his soul.''

''Do you know for sure he's dead?'' LaRue asked.

''I don't know nothing for sure. Don't exactly get the daily news, you know.''

''We heard Eldon Emmet killed Neal.''

''Tidus hated that upstart. When he was younger, you'da thought he was the cock of the cell block, all high-and-mighty and stuff.''

''Why?''

''Why? Because Derek Wheeler showed him some favor and raised him up out of the slime. Gave him a place in the abomination they call the Coven.''

''Do you know what Wheeler's association was with Neal?''

''No. I do know at one time they were real tight, but they had a to-do and didn't speak to each other for years.''

''What was the to-do about?''

''I ain't sure. I heard it was because Wheeler sided with Zoltana.''

''Will you help us find and get word to Eldon Emmet that we want to meet with him on neutral ground?'' Finn asked.

''Well, now, that depends.''

''On what?'' I growled.

''On what ya gotta trade for my help. If ya done come empty-handed, ya might as well walk back to that boat right now.''

I dug into my pocket and pulled out my remaining chocolate bar. When he saw it, an expression of delight spread over his pitted face.

Van Metre took the candy bar and slid it back and forth under his rotting nose. "Come back tomorrow afternoon for your answer."

FIFTY-THREE

The next afternoon, LaRue, Finn, and I trudged back in to see Van Metre. It had rained during the night and the ground was muddy. The mosquitoes swam in the humidity around us, attacking exposed skin like bombers during a strafing run. Breathing was hard and our sweat was running red from the aerial bloodsuckers. By the time we reached Van Metre's camp, I was ready to sit down and pop open my canteen, but our host had other ideas. He led us onward another mile into this disaster until we reached a moldy cave.

I paused at the entrance to check the load in my rifle. The hole was huge, but camouflaged nicely with streamers of Spanish moss and creeping vines. Bats flitted into the sky one by one—leaving the safety of the cave to enjoy an early happy hour. LaRue pulled up beside me, did his own preliminary weapons check, and then stated the obvious.

"This is a perfect place for an ambush."

"If it turns bad, just make sure you draw and quarter a few of them."

He grinned and held out his hand to choke wrists. "If it comes to that, I'll meet you in Summerland."

I grabbed his arm, giving him my most confident smile, and off we went.

"We call this place the Head Shop," Van Metre explained.

"And what happens here?" I said.

"Here we forge souvenirs."

"Not invisible magic?"

"Bah, magic. Such crapola. Everyone talks a good line, but it's just hot air."

"What kind of souvenirs do you make?" LaRue demanded.

"You'll see. Maybe you'll buy, too."

Van Metre paused to talk to a large, swarthy fellow who was apparently on guard duty. They exchanged brief words before the sentry disappeared around a boulder. A minute later we were greeted by an inmate who wore no restraining irons of any kind. He called himself Thor and he stared at me like he could see the soul of Tidus Neal, but I soon found out that he was more interested in the kami story.

Waving us to follow him, he boldly stated what was on his mind. "They say you're here to do a number on ol' Zol. You got water magic that Philips saw firsthand. Is that right?"

I decided to do a little flag-waving. "I'm here to see that Davy Jones's justice is meted out."

"And you think by finding Eldon Emmet, this can happen?"

"Yes."

"You want the Sickle's help, too?"

"Yes."

Thor shook his head. "A covenant will be required. The Sickle don't trust no one. Even such as yourself, who comes highly recommended."

Highly recommended? "What sort of covenant?"

He shrugged. "Uriah is the only person who's got that answer."

With that, our guide shut up and led us through subterranean passages lit by torches fashioned from reeds, sticks, and rags. The place smelled kind of cheesy, but the odor didn't signal my blended senses to begin a stereoscopic symphony, and for that, I was grateful.

We soon entered a large chamber where we found, much to our morbid fascination, a shrunken-head factory. The place was hot and steamy; taking a deep breath was difficult. Several prisoners labored over individual fires, busy with the gruesome contents of large metal tubs and buckets. The smoke from these hearths rose lazily toward the ceiling, but then was swept deeper into the cavern by a vigorous current of air. We walked down the middle of this underground plaza toward an old man sitting in the corner, busily ladling sand into his cook pot. When I reached him, I caught the whiff of golden squares coming off the bubbling cauldron.

"This here is Uriah," Thor announced. He bowed slightly to the man and stalked back the way we'd come.

Uriah had leprosy so badly that he was missing his right eye and much of his face, but amazingly, he had all his fingers and toes, though these looked like they were gangrenous. He pointed to the floor and so we took a seat at his hearth.

"You know, the trick to a good shrunken head is to get the ones that ain't been spoiled by the rot," he said matter-of-factly.

I shot a look at LaRue, whose only sign of emotion was displayed in his flaring nostrils.

Finn immediately jumped into the conversation to explain away our growing horror. "Shrunken heads are good trade items with the river rats."

"Why?" I asked.

"Because we fill them with karmic energy," Uriah answered. "A mojo head can bring you good fortune in your next life. People will pay a lot for that." He rose, and I realized how tall and thin he was. After stepping to a canvas sheet draping a large reed basket, he paused to turn back in our direction. "Fixing heads is a right delicate process. Bone don't shrink none, you know. The skin has got to be sliced from the skull real carefullike. It takes a steady hand."

"And your hand is the steadiest," I said.

"It's true, despite the rot. I can do more with a stump and half a knuckle than most men can with all ten fingers." He pulled away the dirty canvas with a flourish and picked out a finished head. Uriah displayed it proudly before tossing it to me. "See how it shines in the light? We pack the heads in special sand that's got gold dust mixed in. Beautiful job, ain't it?"

I'm usually not a squeamish person, but I've got to admit that it was a big job just to keep my gut from revealing my mundane truth. LaRue leaned over to stare at the thing lying in my lap. I suppose as shrunken heads go, it was a dandy—not more than six inches long, complete with miniature tattoo, curling eyelashes, and a leather nose ring decorated with a plastic, red bead. To be rid of the monstrosity, I handed it off to Finn, who openly marveled at the craftsmanship.

Uriah studied my partner. "Maybe you want one. Maybe you need a headful of good karma. I could fix a good price for you."

LaRue took the prize from Finn and examined it, but in the end he decided against it. "As nice as this one is, it's illegal to own a shrunken head back in the district."

Uriah wasn't about to let go of a sale without a second try. "Are you going to let a little thing like the law get in the way?"

LaRue chuckled and handed the head back to its owner. "Sorry. We didn't come to buy. We came to try to find a killer or killers and we feel we need to talk to Eldon Emmet to do that."

The inmate caught the toss before replying. "Emmet is a man who believes in the power of karmic magic. He believes in Davy Jones's dominion over the water and the lost souls who inhabit the locker." Glancing at me, he said: "The trouble is, he don't believe in you."

"I beg your pardon?" I said.

"You heard me," he answered. "Are you a kami or are you carrying the walk-in soul of Tidus Neal?"

"Are you talking about this covenant of trust we keep hearing about?"

Uriah nodded, sat down, and stoked his fire by kicking embers toward the bucket with his bare feet. "Eldon Emmet will meet with you if you can prove you are what you say you are."

"What do I have to do?"

"You have to participate in the next esbat," he said. "Survive and Emmet will talk with you."

FIFTY-FOUR

Uriah directed us to a large, secluded bend on the river known as Swine Switch. While en route, Ritter never stopped complaining that the water was deep and the monsters were so bad that the river rats would throw pigs at them to keep the buggers off their fishing lines. Though giant creatures were a concern, it soon became evident from confessions of the crew that the captain didn't like this spot in the Black because it was where the tidal bore had swamped him and his boat.

When we pulled into the junk-strewn lagoon just before sunset, we realized that the esbat celebration was not confined to the water witches. Merchants crowded the area, their skiffs, punks, and water cottages crowded side by side as they surrounded a large floating platform made of logs. Dinkim Sue was among the attendees, and when she saw me hanging over the railing like I was riding a cruise ship into a beautiful harbor, she waved, calling out a question about my health and my soul.

I nodded and assured her through a smile that I was fine, but the truth of it was a bit bleaker. On the day before the full moon, I get especially cranky, mainly because I know what is ahead of me and because I get a supernatural form of rabies that prevents me from taking food or drink until after the lunar cycle is complete. This current-enforced fast had been particularly difficult for me. My stomach kept rumbling and my throat was dry from breathing the caustic, chemical-laden air, so by the day of my ultimate transformation, I was ready to chew through Ritter's leg for all his bellyaching. Gibson gave me a hypo filled with glucose to keep my brain function at an efficient level, but the sugar water did nothing to settle me down.

Ritter had the crew on red alert, fearing an attack by Hecate's Sickle. He had the floodlights on and used them to scan the area. It was a stupid thing to do, because bright light did nothing to deter an armed party; it simply gave them more glow to kill by.

I watched inmates gathering on the small, sandy beach, each carrying a large wooden torch. They placed them like fence posts while several other prisoners built the extravagant base for a bonfire.

"Red sky at night, sailor's delight," LaRue intoned as he and the good doctor came up behind me.

"I thought this esbat was a private celebration," I said by way of greeting.

"Looks like everybody knows about it," Gibson said. He leaned on the railing but turned to study me. "How are you doing?"

"The same as always. I feel like jumping right out of my skin."

"I still think this is a very bad idea," he said. "Why must you always take chances on the full moon?"

"It just works out that way," I answered. "Believe me, I would much rather be home chained to my bedpost."

In fact, it rarely worked out in my favor. As though I was indeed laboring under the weight of karmic debt, I was often called upon to perform my job on a full moon. It was in the midst of such madness that I almost finished off a murderous perp and my enforced association with Gibson was born.

LaRue honestly believes that my lunar change is driven by memories of my past lives, because I find myself tripping out of current reality into situations that, in his mind, lead me back into previous incarnations. My perspective is often dumped into otherworldly scenarios that play out like past lives, complete with strange ideas, memories, and circumstances. Gibson's explanation is more medical, but equally appalling, because he contends that these flashbacks are delivered into my awareness by a series of temporal-lobe epileptic seizures.

We waited and watched as more and more people crowded into the cove, and finally, it seemed the esbat was under way. The torches were lit one by one, and then the bonfire was set ablaze. Uriah, dressed in black rags and cape, settled into a small rowboat with Thor at the oars. They pushed their way between the river-rat barges until they reached the log platform. Thor climbed aboard the raft and helped the ancient from the boat. Like props in a pageant, several black ducks launched into the darkening sky the moment Uriah stepped aboard his stage. The audience grew silent, and except for the gentle sounds of waves knocking at the boats, there was no other noise.

Uriah took a deep breath, ready to infuse this quiet with some theatrical presentation, but I screwed up his moment by having a stretch.

FIFTY-FIVE

The wolf couldn't have timed its entrance any better, and when it opened the door, the pain walked in with the beast. Though I would never admit it out loud, I believe my full-moon transformations are twisted with agony that flows with supernatural vigor. Why do I believe this? Because normal pain doesn't make the air above your belly button sting. When I'm crossing the lunar line, the very atmosphere crackles around me, as if my normal electrostatic charge is somehow given an extra spark. The energy not only flows into my body, but I'm also blanketed by it. This night I found myself wrapped in heat, humidity, and hopelessness. There was a moment when I must have lost my bid for consciousness because I turned numb from bow to stern, but the pain of the fit brought me back again. Before I could react to this new wave of nausea and self-loathing, Gibson took me in his arms and LaRue pressed close to protect my back.

I could feel my body lengthening and thickening and I knew Gibson could, too. The lycanthropic power overwhelmed me, building within my very cells until it superseded the human by synthesizing my body. Regardless of

this building vitality, I became acutely aware of my embarrassment.

Five lousy minutes later I came around and noticed that
something was different. My symptoms were familiar, but
locked inside my skull cavity were the sounds of whispered
voices. I recognized none of them, yet they spoke to me in
strange languages that I understood. I panicked, remembering my bouts of aphasia, thinking this might be some
horrible manifestation associated with the comprehension
center of my brain, but a mumbled word from Gibson
spared me additional fear. Instead, I was forced to concede
the day to past-life Peeping Toms.

I usually flip in and out of lucidity at an annoying rate,
but this time I was caught in a state which was wholly
connected to my surroundings, both external and internal.
My synesthesia provided me with an extra dimension by
allowing me to catch the whiff of golden squares, and flush
to this sensation was the inescapable impact of déjà vu. The
esbat activities moved against the smear and sparkle of my
lycanthropic vision; the *Delora* padded the environment by
gently creaking; and from far off in my mind, someone
softly reminded me that in my lifetime spent as a pearl
diver, I was an excellent swimmer.

I know; I know. I'm sure the feeling came from stress,
combined with all the garbage I'd been listening to over
the last few days, and then further enhanced by the presence
of malaria bacteria in my system. Still, if there is one thing
that I've learned in my association with Gibson it is that
reality can only be measured against a limited perspective.
What can I say? For a kami, I was a full-moon mess.

A few minutes of complete lucidity settled in upon me,
as though the conduit linking me to my whispering past
lives was experiencing technical difficulties. In that time I
realized everyone stared at me. I saw their critical review
in the harsh glow of the *Delora*'s floodlights and suffered
a thousand more deaths, but LaRue, ever the showman,
used the moment to weave a paranormal persona around
me.

"She has been infused with the energy and power of

Davy Jones," he called out. "She reeks of karmic justice!"

Uriah answered for the crowd. "We shall see, Marshal. We shall see." Then, turning toward the audience, he spoke in a thundering voice that belied his apparent frailty. "Tonight is the Esbat of Initiation, where water witches from cell block three will gather for anointing and trial. To succeed means entry into Hecate's Sickle; to fail means death." He paused for effect, drawing down scattered applause and a couple of whistles before continuing. "Long ago ol' Zol created the Coven." Boos and shouts issued from the onlookers and Uriah was forced to calm them by holding his skinny arms wide. "Ol' Zol and his Coven corrupted the natural order of magic and water witching. They stole the physical bodies of men condemned to Hell on Earth, compounding their karma while ladling on further temptation to those who were misused. They became dead man's chests, walking bank accounts, creatures who own none of the wealth they carried. Finally, ol' Zol and his Coven got way too greedy, and while they should have been making offerings to the Lost Mariner, they tried to hoodwink Davy Jones out of his fair share of the loot." The crowd interrupted him to hoot their approval of divine retribution. Uriah spoke above them, eventually pulling in their silence and attention. "Davy got even with the Big Screw by taking away his wealth. He sent a great storm acrashing down the Black and overturned a barge of desperate men, each weighed down by the gold in their teeth. This bend in the river is a well of lost souls—a place of death over sixty feet deep. Their skeletons litter the mud, and so do their treasures. Hecate's Sickle finds purpose in recovering this loot, because with each skull comes a measure of satisfaction in knowing these men died for naught. So, to this end, Eldon Emmet, Keeper of the Book of Shadows, High Priest to the Sickle, requires each initiate to dive for the bounty. Find a skull and return to the surface and enjoy the power bestowed upon you by Emmet. Beware, though. The waters are ruled by the karmic powers of the Lost Mariner."

The initiates on the beach began chanting and the river

rats turned up the racket by tooting horns, hollering, and drumming. This insanity was further inspired by a return of the cooing in my mind. This noise pushed my fear buttons as much as it comforted me. I was caught between realities—in one, I couldn't swim; in the other, I felt the undercurrent of wisdom derived from experience. Whether it was merely the strange feat of telepathy produced by a swelled brain, or whether I accurately gauged the phenomenon, I still didn't like the intrusion into my thoughts.

Uriah spoke again, pointing at me. "This district marshal claims to have a magical background, as you have all just heard. She says she is the point of Davy Jones's stick of retribution, but for this to occur, she must speak with the Keeper of the Book of Shadows. Emmet wants to know if she is the for-sure thing. She will participate in the esbat, but to show we ain't the animals everyone says we are, I'm ordering an initiate to dive first. That way she can see how it's done."

The moment I was invited to jump into the bleak depths of the Black River was the second Gibson started trying to talk me out of it. He clung to me like letting go would be to let go of life itself.

"Please, Merrick, don't do this," he whispered. "You can go around Emmet. No investigation is worth this."

LaRue agreed with him. "You can't swim, Ty. This is a fool's game."

With my lycanthropic whispers to feed me the info, it seemed I did, indeed, know how to fish the depths. Still, admission, even in my current state was something I could not afford to do. It would just get the good doctor more upset. "I'm certain that Emmet is the one who knows where Wheeler is," I said haltingly, aware of the gravelly noise that now backed my words. I pulled from Gibson's embrace and turned toward Uriah. "Let's get this over with."

As I hustled toward the dredge to await a ride over to the log pontoon, Gibson kept up his excuse maker. "You don't have that much control, Merrick. You could drown." When I refused to stop and argue, he grabbed me roughly by the arms and spun me around to face him. "You'll die. If that happens, so will I."

I am not real clear on the full moon and the one saving grace of it all is my inability to recall details, but for some reason, I knew I would remember this confession. Placing my hands over his heart, I said: "If that's to happen, I'll see you in the next life."

FIFTY-SIX

The inmate willing to be the first to take the dive was ferried out to the platform in the rowboat while we prepared for our ride over to the festivities. He was a hulking sort who had a stump that stopped above his right elbow and a dragging left leg. After waving his appendage in triumph at the river rats and his compatriots anxiously awaiting their trials, he began to slowly disrobe, showing the crowd his hairless, ravaged body. Uriah spoke, following this presentation.

"We call down the mercy of Davy Jones," he said. "And may you find your chest of gold."

"There is no way this guy is going to make it," LaRue murmured.

Gibson shook his head in agreement, and I just kept silent, unable to get clear of the lesson I was being fed behind my thoughts—breathe deeply, expel a few bubbles of air at twenty feet, another bit at forty feet, and hold steady at the bottom while pawing in the mud. So foreign was this information that I had no idea if it was even correct, but rather than being upset by my ignorance, I accepted this obvious lycanthropic manipulation, hoping to use it to save my goddamned life. Still, my questions were many: Could

I be accessing voices of the past filtered through the seat of my soul or was I plagued with nothing more than a malfunctioning gland? Could this be evidence of life—past or present—a racial memory stuffed into some corner of the brain waiting for activation? Once pumped into sentience, did it, indeed, carry the seed of who we were and who we might yet become?

I left my thoughts behind, surprised that I had this much control over them, and watched the inmate take a final look at his world. With that, he picked up a large rock, tied to the platform. He straightened a kink in the rope, and using it like a fishing weight, he dove headfirst into oblivion.

The river rats applauded and started chanting a weird conglomeration of sounds and words while the initiates stranded on the beach banged drums and shook long rattles made from iron pipes.

Gibson glanced at his wristwatch and timed the event, pausing to lift his eyes only when the dark water began to churn. Uriah nearly lost his balance on the platform and the guy rowing the initiates to the ceremony cleared out before he was dumped out. River rats paddled away from the growing tumult, several bumping into the *Delora*'s hull, their collisions sending vibrations through the boat and through me. The water boiled, simmered, and boiled again. I leaned over the railing, drawn into the spectacle and half expecting to see a giant octopus push up from the depths to grab us all.

"He's been down three and a half minutes," Gibson reported. "Fool."

A few moments later he was the fool for doubting. The inmate launched from the river so hard that he walked on water. In his one good hand? A skull.

Uriah pumped a satisfied look my way before helping the initiate onto the platform. "Your turn, Marshal."

I drew a deep breath of my own, nodded, and heard the voice in my head command me to disrobe. Not on your past life. I was raised in an orphanage by a lady who took lessons from the Puritans, and despite knowing that my cammies would work against me, I ignored this eerie plea.

LaRue and Gibson accompanied me over to the platform, riding the dredge in such a way as to keep me wedged against the boom. I was glad for their support, because on the way, the wolf got the better of me and I phased out of current reality to step lightly into a scene where I readied myself to fetch pearls from the bottom of the ocean. This vision was so real, I could literally feel the grease slicking down my naked body. The fantasy took place at night and I saw myself standing on the stern of a small fishing boat, preparing for a dangerous midnight dive. I felt a minute of immense fear, and of course, like the idiot I am sometimes, I got entangled within the paralyzing tentacles of this emotion.

I pushed myself bodily from this scene, finding a noseful of golden squares as we touched down on the floating plank. We debarked, and our combined weights made the raft sink a couple of inches. Paranoia flooded my own locker, but I think I managed to stand there, feigning dignity. One thing was for certain: if I went through this insane test and Emmet pulled a fast one about talking to us, I would find him and shoot his ass dead.

Uriah waited for the crowd to quiet down and spent the next several minutes pulling the rock up by the rope. After he brought it on board, he turned to speak to me. "You are allowed a weapon."

LaRue, my faithful partner, had thought of everything. He reached into the calf pocket of his uniform and produced a bayonet with a nice, deep blood groove. "Don't cut yourself," he said, with a small smile.

I accepted it with shaking fingers. "Don't worry."

"Remember your biofeedback," Gibson said.

Yes. I could control my pulse, my blood pressure, and my breath with a thought. The problem was: Would I be able to think or would I be at the whim of the wolf?

I stowed the knife and took a minute to calm myself with several deep inhales, mentally willing my autonomic nervous system to come under my direct control. Gathering the steam I needed, I picked up the rock, took one last inhale, and jumped into the murky, polluted river.

The water burned my eyes instantly, but I forced them wide, searching in the blackness for any light. It came, strangely enough, from a school of bioluminescent fish. They darted around me, and the deeper I sank, the more of them there were. I dropped quickly, painfully aware of the building pressure. As it worsened, the wolf flicked in, nipping for control. Any other time I would fight this intrusion, but fifty feet underwater was no time to commence a counterattack. I let my mind go and dissolved into the energy of the full moon, remembering to blow out a small nick of air through my nose.

One of the benefits of lycanthropy is added vitality and increased efficiency of my internal organs. Gibson has measured changes in my lung capacity, and now, descending into this offensive world, I hoped it would see me through along with my biofeedback.

I did my best to slow my heartbeats with a thought, tussling for supremacy with the wolf. In the end it let me be and crawled back into the recesses of my oxygen-starved brain.

Finally, I touched down gently, but forgot to drop the rock until it caused me to lose my footing. A momentary surge of adrenaline reminded me that the minutes were ticking down, and from any angle that I looked at it, I was at least a minute away from air. I paddled toward the silty, slimy riverbed, twisting my ankle around the rope so I could stay submerged. The pressure was awful and I was sure my eyes were bleeding or popping from their sockets. I pawed at the sand, brushing it off when my fingers felt something long and narrow. It turned out to be a tree root and nothing more.

What a waste of time! I beseeched the voice in my head to tell me what I needed to know, but as fate would have it, the whisper had stopped and couldn't be coaxed again. Too deep; the water pressed my lycanthropic companion into silence even as it compressed my brain. Frantic, I swam around the rope until, with the help of the lightning fish, I saw a bulge in the mud. I dove for it and yanked a skull from its resting place. As I did I dislodged another

one. Grabbing both these prizes, I kicked off the bottom
and zoomed toward the surface.

I could see the glow from the *Delora*'s floodlights and
knew I wasn't far away from victory, but Davy Jones took
the opportunity to smack at me by sending in the leviathans.
In this case, it was a giant snake. The SOB swam right
toward me, eerily aglow with its own power source. I
swung one of the skulls, but the water did nothing for my
aim and I missed. The bastard came at me again like a
dangerous ribbon. It opened its jaws and I saw rows of
teeth. This time I did my best to remain calm and wait for
the snake to swim at me again, all the while fighting for
the need to breathe. My lungs ached; I was dizzy; and in
a vicious mood.

Rather than playing with bravery, I dropped one of the
skulls so I could pull the bayonet. I almost lost it all when
it caught on my uniform and refused to slip out of the
restraining circle of my utility belt. The beast from four
fathoms swung back one more time, and though I couldn't
hear a noise, it snarled at me as it missed latching onto my
leg. I slashed out, my aim wide of this wiggly creature. It
was then the wolf gave me the power and my past-life voice
returned. It admonished me for laziness before passing on
the crucial information I needed to defend myself from the
monster. Swing late, it said. Use an arcing slice.

As the snake came in for another strike I summoned all
my lycanthropic might and brought the blade around and
under the beast, cutting it long, deep, and continuously. The
guts spilled out and the serpent arched against its own
death, preceding this exit by cycling through a series of
dramatic rainbow colors.

My laboring lungs suddenly reminded me that my stored
oxygen was turning into carbon dioxide. I blew out some
bubbles, hoping to send the offending gas into the water. I
kicked for all I was worth and twenty seconds later I
popped out of the water, just as my air supply was done.

FIFTY-SEVEN

According to LaRue, I was a big success at the esbat, but a lot of trouble to get home. I have to admit, I don't remember anything and had to listen to the events from top to bottom. During my underwater adventure, I was down in the deep for over five minutes, returning with a dead man's chest for my time. LaRue also confessed that Gibson became so concerned for my safety that it was all he could do to keep the good doctor from diving in after me. At first, I clung to this valiant story, but as usual, my natural-born suspicion took over. Though Gibson claimed his love for me, he still had to prove it.

Uriah had proclaimed me kami of the year. Not only did he crown me with supernatural laurels, but he also named me the walk-in soul of Tidus Neal. He assured us that Eldon Emmet would speak to us at a place downriver known as the Tin Circle. Finn had sworn on the lost soul of Derek Wheeler that he could find this destination, even in the dark.

The Tin Circle was located two days up the Black in an abandoned industrial park. The weeds and undergrowth choked the decrepit, crumbling structures and the sun glinted off the sharp edges of broken glass. Inmates had moved into abandoned cars, one prisoner having actually hung ragged curtains to the rear window of a Duvalier Classic. Others had secured similar accommodations, using every chunk of metal they could find to build walls and roofs. A twisted ribbon of chain-link fence surrounded the park, trampled in places as the prisoners moved up and down the banks to trade with the river rats.

"Do you think this is Emmet's home base?" I asked.

LaRue shrugged. "Maybe. See all the magical symbols? If anything, it's probably an exclusive neighborhood."

Ah, yes. An exclusive pile of shit. Still, he was right. The enclave was decorated in hubcap hangers and bean-can bangers, prayer rags, and homemade billboards displaying crosses, circles, and strange writing.

"I think we should do what I suggested," LaRue said.

My partner has a flare for the dramatic, and since the word on Emmet mostly concerned his belief in magic and his supernatural powers, he thought it would be good to dress the part. Looking at this strange conglomeration, I sighed and nodded, knowing that from a certain perspective it would improve our odds about getting the correct information from the mystically blinded water witch.

We went below and found Gibson in the sick bay already preparing for the kami and her court to appear at the Tin Circle.

He did have some dandy outfits under construction. By procuring a few bedsheets from the linen closet, he'd made magical capes by using a can of fluorescent spray paint to color them with the skull and crossbones of the Jolly Roger.

"I take it I was outvoted for this fashion party?" I said, seeing the preparations.

LaRue gave me a sheepish grin, but didn't answer. Gibson merely grunted and put the finishing touches on his design.

We pinned these capes to our uniforms, and though I felt stupid as hell, I had to agree with them that the cloaks would hide our personal armories. LaRue presented me with one of his special, hand-sawed shotgun specials and a nice, hand-tooled thigh holster to carry it in. Packing the weapon, I took a moment to acknowledge the feeling of power it brought me. We passed around cherry bombs, sparklers, and a couple of strings of firecrackers just in case we needed a smoke screen or a couple of quick kabooms. As I ran a comb through my hair the good doctor created a cardboard tiara shaped like a sickle. He came over to the mirror and fitted it onto my head.

"You better take a real gun with you tonight, Gibson," I said.

He took a step back and pulled his cape aside to show me his own weaponry, which included a harpoon and pistol.

I nodded my approval. "Please, don't be afraid to use them. These people are already dead; they just haven't accepted it yet."

He stared at me with that wild-eyed squint before answering. "Stay out of the line of fire, then. I'm a hotshot marksman only in my imagination." Turning, he picked up a small canvas bag and clipped it to his utility belt. "Medical supplies," he explained.

Ritter dropped anchor just before sunset, fervently complaining as he did. Neilson set us on shore by the "dredge" express and Finn hurried up the sloppy, muddy bank. He found an opening in the collapsed fence, and as we cut through the dilapidated warehouses, tripped over cracked concrete, and stepped around pools of raw sewage, he told us about the Tin Circle.

"Derek Wheeler built it a number of years ago," he said.

"I know. I was here to help put it up. We scavenged metal for weeks."

"Looks like you had plenty to choose from," I answered as I glanced into the darkened hole of a doorway.

"Well, we had to get the right kind of metal."

"And what would that be?"

"The kind of metal that deflects the karmic energy. You can't leave yourself open for mischievousness, ya know."

"I take it Wheeler built it for the Coven and somehow Hecate's Sickle ended up with it."

"Emmet drubbed up a life-force spell to protect the place. He's one who knows how to use the karmic energy.

It's so powerful, they say, that he ran out the Coven and they can't return.''

"Did this event take place during the riot?"

Finn tried to look innocent, but it wasn't working. "Riot?"

"Don't waste my time, Jasper," I ordered. "We know Zoltana had a dickens of a time after Wheeler's supposed death.''

He sighed. "I suppose it ain't no big secret. Things got really dangerous for a while.''

"Sounds like they still are," LaRue said.

"What I can't figure out is why Zoltana doesn't level this place,'' Gibson said.

Finn had a pat answer. "He can't get by the water-witching magic. You've gotta be a whole lot more insight-ful than ol' Zol. All he's interested in is the wealth. Only Davy Jones knows what he's doing with it.''

Shades of Stonehenge. "Do the Coven and the Sickle fight over the Tin Circle.''

"Yeah. Sometimes.''

Suddenly I felt underdressed, ballistically speaking, but I kept my fears to myself as we trudged onward toward our next lives.

The Tin Circle turned out to be a ringed stockade created from corrugated aluminum and placed in the very heart of the industrial park. A metal bridge linked the inner and outer walls and spanned a muddy pit of sharp stakes and rocks. I shone my flashlight beam toward this moat, finding to my chagrin that not only was it punctured with instruments to impale the unlucky person who lost his balance, but it also held a family of monstrous, snapping alligators.

Once we reached the central corral, we were stopped by a hooded attendant, sans leg irons, and armed with a staff made from an iron pipe. The sentry gave us each a once-over before announcing: "Weapons aren't allowed in the inner sanctum.''

LaRue took care of this brash doorman by pulling his shot gun and leveling it at his chest. "Our invitation said this would be a 'bring your own guns' party.'' Then, lowering his tone, he pushed away all jokes and artifice. "Step aside, asshole, unless you want to see Summerland the hard way."

The inmate clenched his staff and I readied myself for the first shoot-out of the evening. He must have been a slow-witted man, because it took him a full minute before he decided to admit us, hardware and all.

We entered this corral one by one through a squeaky, metal door to find several other hooded attendants, each a giant in his own right and each bearing a knife and a long iron staff as well. LaRue did not holster his shotgun. He whispered to Gibson to pull his sidearm and make sure the safety was off. I could feel both men tense at the sight of the bodyguards.

The floor of this strange temple was made from white-washed cinder blocks and painted with a large, black pentagram. Ritual items were placed at the ends of the star— a bent sword, an overturned crate decorated with large white candles, a bucket filled with what appeared to be salt, and at the apex of the design a small black book placed atop a short stone stele.

We clung to the perimeter of the Tin Circle, and the longer we waited for recognition from the welcome wagon, the more nervous I became. Finn kept assuring us that Emmet would be along anytime, the High Priest preferring theatrical entrances. He showed up just as I was starting to lose my patience and proved to be nothing at all like what I expected.

Emmet walked in through a small door draped with a valance of woven sticks and dead flowers. He wore a torn, black robe and mud-encrusted, military-style boots, but more than that—the High Priest of Hecate's Sickle was so old, he creaked.

I have never seen so many wrinkles, pockmarks, and oozing sores as this man's face contained. He wore a pirate patch over his left eye and I had a feeling that to look underneath would expose his brain stem to the air. This Goliath also had a bad leg. He approached us slowly, dragging his foot across the blocks. He paused in the center of the pentagram to adjust his robe and wait for the attendants to bow deeply before retreating into the shadows.

I stepped forward, but remained silent. We held a pissing contest for about three minutes, but I was victorious because I made him open this meeting.

"Welcome to Hell, Marshal Merrick," he said in husky tones. Pausing, he accepted an iron staff delivered to him by one of his assistants. He leaned heavily upon it and then threw me an insane warning. "You now stand within a karmic vortex. Take care, for retribution will follow intrusion."

I decided on belligerence right away. "I carry Davy Jones's stick of retribution. Don't mess with me and you can keep yourself surrounded by your precious past-life power."

Emmet chuckled, obviously pleased with the Mexican standoff. "We understand each other well. What have you come to ask of me?"

"For starters, what's the real reason you're on the outs with Wheeler and Zoltana?" I asked.

Like some sage of Western wisdom, he clasped his hands and bowed his head. "There are many reasons, Marshal. Neglect, foolishness, anger, stupidity. Take your pick." Raising his eyes, he focused on Gibson. "Ah, the golden-boy doctor. I've heard about you. Have you brought the cure for our disease yet?"

Gibson glanced at me and swallowed hard. "There is no cure. None that I can find with the equipment I have on board the *Delora*."

Emmet nodded sadly. "I thought perhaps you would be able to dispense our saving grace."

"You talk like there is a cure."

"Well, of course there's a cure," he growled. "Zoltana has saved it for his precious few. That butcher, Stirling, was the one who came up with it—years ago." He pointed toward Finn. "You, hiding back there. Come into the light so I can see you better."

Finn hesitated, but finally moved into the glow of a torch.

Emmet scowled when he saw him. "You were one of Wheeler's chests, weren't you?"

"Yes, sir. Ol' Zol almost got me, but the marshal saved me."

"Well, then, I'm beholden to the kami." Glancing my way, he added: "I'll take him from your care now."

"No, you won't," I answered flatly.

"His treasure was deeded to me."

"I don't care if this man was deeded to Davy Jones. I saved him and he's mine. Do we argue over property, or do we get what we were promised?"

Emmet's expression lengthened and darkened. "I could take you down with the bat of an eyelash," he said. "Do not play games with me."

His attitude pissed me off and I boldly took a step toward him. "I passed your sweet little test and set you up with a dead man's chest already. Don't change the parlay now, or you'll find I'm a whole lot more magical than you might think. And a whole lot more dangerous."

He grunted. "So, Zoltana finds another way to cheat me out of what is rightfully mine. Yet again."

"You are a prisoner in a labor camp. You have no rights and no one to complain to." To prove I wasn't afraid of his hokey witchcraft, I casually strolled around the pentagram, stopping at each point to study the ritual object there. When I reached the altar containing the thin volume, I realized it was, indeed, the famed Book of Shadows. Emmet must have had a deficit in available spells, because it wasn't more than a few pages thick. I started to pick it up, but the witch stopped me.

"Please, don't touch that," he begged. "You haven't been ritually anointed. You'll harm the book's power by interfering with its pure energy field."

Well, I was dirty, but I wasn't that bad. "Then tell me about Wheeler and Neal."

"What do you want to know?" he finally asked, with a sigh.

"Are they alive?"

"Yes, they are."

"Why are you using them to attack the *Delora*?"

"I'm not," he answered.

I pegged him with a boring gaze. "Zoltana maintains that you're trying to derail his dredging of the wreck in the delta."

"Hecate's Sickle is trying to lift the spiritual values in this penal colony," he said. "I'm trying to help those who are dying."

"While being a pain in the ass to the Coven."

"Whatever I can do to improve conditions."

"What do you know about the murders on board the *Delora*?"

"Nothing. I'm not responsible."

"You're lying."

"Think what you want, Marshal. I don't control Derek Wheeler or Tidus Neal. I never have."

I tabled my opinion. "If you're not controlling them, then why are they attacking the River Patrol?"

"Because ol' Zol double-crossed Wheeler. It's revenge, pure and simple. An eye for an eye. It's the only way they can get back at the screws, or so they think. Hit them in the wallet." He sighed. "I understand their feelings and applaud their actions, but I don't have any spells drubbed up on them and I haven't talked to either one in quite a while."

"What happened between Wheeler and Zoltana?" I asked.

"Ol' Zol promised to give Wheeler the world in return for his cooperation," he answered. "Wheeler had a silver tongue and he knew how to organize the water witches. They were fluff partners for decades, but then Neal started getting in a bad way. Wheeler demanded that ol' Zol cure him, but our illustrious warden refused. He thought Neal was useless and not worth saving. So Wheeler and his father have been hitting him where it hurts by attacking the *Delora*." He shook his head. "The inmates were stupid to join with that slimy bastard. Never trust a screw. Unfortunately, none of us learned that lesson until it was too late."

"They're trying to keep the dredge from reaching the delta?"

"Ol' Zol thinks so."

"But that's not the real reason, is it?"

"I don't know."

"Don't play with me, Emmet. Why do they steal their victims' body parts? Noses and ears and hands?"

He smiled, and in the firelight, his lips looked wide and leathery. "Zoltana stripped both Neal and Wheeler of their charm sacks. It, in effect, made them powerless."

"But you've offered them a salvation of sorts, if they bring these little trophies to you."

"You're smart, Marshal, but I'm afraid I can't help them with this life or any other lives. You can't reason with a bogeyman, so I don't try."

"Why are they stealing the body parts?" I demanded.

"They are stealing these things because Wheeler thinks I can use them to help cure his father. You know, use them to renew a failing life force."

"You're getting back at Zoltana by using Wheeler indirectly. His hits on the boat delays the warden's efforts in the delta."

Emmet shrugged.

"What about the gems?"

"Gems? You're talking about the district couriers." He held a stubby hand out. "What good are gems?"

"Zoltana is getting a cut of the profits going to other localities, isn't he?"

"I'm sure he is. The captains of that vessel have always offered tribute for safe passage. Of course, ol' Zol can't control the Sickle and he can't control Wheeler and Neal and so his nice bank account is shrinking. I'd say that is karmic justice in itself."

I shook my head, but had to admit that I wasn't surprised by this audacity. The district had lost all authority in this bogeyman's land.

Emmet continued. "We have a little saying here: what goes around, comes around. Can't escape that karma, whether this incarnation or the next."

Apparently, Emmet was due for a little karmic backflash, because the moment he said it, there was a loud explosion close by. It rocked the walls of the Tin Circle and went off close enough to the structure to throw dirt, mud, and rocks all over us. Surprise at the audacity of such an unprovoked attack, Emmet's henchmen hustled toward to center of the Circle to protect their High Priest.

"What kind of foul deceit have you planned?" Emmet bellowed.

"It's not my people," I barked. "Maybe the Coven wants your ass back."

Another explosion rocked the penal colony, shaking the ground so hard, I almost lost my footing.

The thing that LaRue and I are best at is making a bad situation pay off. I glanced into the shadows to see my partner taking advantage of the noise and confusion by striking the short fuse on an M-80. He returned my look and chucked his chin past me, a silent command to draw my shotgun. I pulled the weapon with a flourish of my cape and went for broke as he tossed the cherry bomb into the center of the pentagram. When it exploded, the noise reverberating off the tin walls practically blew Emmet's anointed underwear off. Leaping clear, I decided it was time to set the so-called magic in motion. Rolling toward the point of the pentagram, I came quickly to my feet and grabbed Emmet's precious Book of Shadows.

A second after I kipped the manual, I charged for the exit. The sentry, alarmed by the explosions, forced open the door in time for Gibson to swing around and skewer him through the chest with a harpoon. I blasted one of the attendants, cutting him in half and splashing his innards all over the High Priest. The others rushed in, but LaRue popped off another bomb, pushing the bastard into retreat and allowing us enough time to cross the bridge and run like our past lives were chasing us.

FIFTY-EIGHT

Upon reaching the *Delora,*, we found her engines thrumming. The boat was moving full ahead even before Russo retracted the plank. Neilson, Curran, and Hogan manned the deck, taking potshots into the night. I didn't even stop to catch my breath. Instead, I led my comrades to the bridge to confront the captain. Imagine our surprise when we opened the hatch to see Riverman Harvey pointing a carbine at Ritter. Yarrow steadfastly faced ahead as though her concentration on the wheel might prevent her from being killed by a stray bullet.

"Glad to see you made it back alive," Harvey said. "You were set up, in case you didn't figure that out."

"What's going on?" LaRue barked.

"He called Zoltana and told him you were meeting Emmet at the Tin Circle."

"Those are guards doing the shooting?"

"You can bet on it."

"What tipped you off to this piece of shit?"

"I caught him coming out of sick bay with four gel cells under his arm and a pocketful of pearls," Harvey said. "It looked like he was going to do some bartering on his own."

LaRue grabbed Ritter by the collar and twisted the ma-

terial, cutting off the pee-trap for his incoming air. "You
know what, Captain?" he said ominously. "I hate snivel-
ing, spineless cowards."

Ritter clawed at LaRue's neck tourniquet, but could not
dislodge my partner's steely fingers. "Where were you going with all that booty?" he asked.

The man didn't answer and so my partner increased the
squeeze. It looked like his victim might burst an eyeball or
two, but before that happened, LaRue relieved the pressure
by releasing him so he could take a breath. Ritter came
clean immediately. "I was supposed to meet Stirling," he
wheezed. "We were going to trade the stash for safe passage back to the district."

"Where's Stirling?"

"I don't know. We were going to get together at Vivian
Narrows. He had a contact. But when we pulled in, he
wasn't there."

"He was there. He was aboard this boat." LaRue
grabbed his collar again and twisted. "Let me guess. Stirling felt he had to leave before we sniffed out who he really
was. He stumbled across Kleege's body before I did and
he stole the pilot's scrimshaw charm. Stirling hid the gems
in the sick bay, thinking he could retrieve them at any time,
and when we anchored, he came back to collect them. I'll
bet it gave him quite a start when he realized they weren't
there. Maybe he blamed you."

Ritter protested in moans and whimpers before hissing.
"Stop. Please."

There was a moment there when I could tell my partner
was weighing the options—choke him to death or throw
him overboard. "Why were you going to jump ship?"

Ritter hesitated again, but when LaRue pulled his fist
back to cuff him across his face, he hurried to answer.
"Zoltana knows we've been collecting dead man's chests."

"Is that so?"

"I suppose you were using the hydrotomography unit to
decide who carried what," Gibson said.

"Yes," he answered.

"How long has this been going on?" I asked.

"For years."

"What did you do before the unit was installed on the boat?" Gibson asked.

"Hit or miss. Random selection."

"How many prisoners did you kill?"

"Not me. Stirling. He always did it. Zoltana would deliver a group to him in a compound somewhere in the labor camp. I got a percentage because I changed the records back at the district dock."

"You changed things like prisoners' blood types," LaRue said. "Why?"

"Because I made a mistake. I was working after hours in a restricted database. I did something wrong and the computer crashed."

"So, when it was up and running, you tried to cover your ass, and filled in the blanks on the deleted records."

"Yes. I didn't have any backup files. I had to guess."

"And for this aggravation you wanted more compensation."

"I was taking a lot of chances."

Harvey interrupted his confession by charging at him. "You piece of shit! You've endangered all our lives!"

LaRue swung Ritter out of the way, and with his free hand, he grabbed the riverman by his uniform. He used Harvey's momentum to toss him backward and the riverman landed with a thump, ending his performance wearing a surprised expression. "What the hell are you doing?"

"Shut up," LaRue ordered. "I'm asking the questions here."

Before the man could respond, Ritter belted Harvey with an accusation. "Why don't you stop with the indignant crap? You knew what was going down. Admit it, you were hoping to talk Zoltana into a little deal, yourself."

"That's a lie!" Harvey growled. "I was sent here to watch you."

At that admission, we had another standoff. "There's a bold wind blowing through this crew," I said. "And it's pushing their sails the same direction."

"You don't understand," Harvey said.

"Enlighten us," I answered.

He tried to do his own sidestep by not answering immediately, but I was still riled from our narrow escape and so I went nose to nose with the riverman. "Who do you work for?"

This time Harvey stuttered over words in his haste to answer. "I w-work for the Prison Reform Committee."

"There's no such thing," Ritter said.

"Yes, there is," Harvey countered. "We were formed by the District Council to uncover evidence supporting allegations concerning murder and fraud. The PRC wants to get Zoltana out and turn this place into a properly run labor camp."

"Won't that be a trick," I muttered.

He snorted. "It will be impossible."

Ritter jumped on his explanation. "You've worked at the dock for years."

"I didn't say when the PRC was formed, now, did I?"

"I take it the PRC needed you in the field," I said.

"Yeah," he answered. "When those crewmen came up dead, I was sent as an independent observer."

"Knowing that a couple of marshals would be aboard to do the dirty work."

He shrugged. "I only follow orders. I'm on your side."

I couldn't help laughing at the insanity of that last statement. Glancing back at him, I said: "How can you be on our side when we don't know what side we're on?" I interjected a sigh and turned to Ritter. "Well, come along, Captain. I want you to send a message to ol' Zol."

"A message," he said. "Why?"

"Because I want you to tell him we have Emmet's Book of Shadows."

FIFTY-NINE

My idea was that the rumor mill would churn out new scuttlebutt immediately and Neal and Wheeler would find out I had the book and come after it. I'd intended on luring them into a trap of my own making, sprung at my own time. Unfortunately, the law of cause and effect was in operation.

Superstition is not my cup of tea, but then, I occasionally find out that what has been relegated to the realm of invisible magic may indeed have a basis in reality. Take divine retribution, for instance. Acts of God happen with startling regularity and the next day we awoke to a red-sky morning and a strong wind gusting downriver. By evening, the fog had come in with rain squalls. Visibility was limited to a few meters and the boat horns kept up the hoots and toots.

LaRue, Gibson, and I sat in the mess with Harvey, trying to eat a sailing delicacy known as SOS and ignore the dicey traveling conditions.

"Those folks who attacked the Tin Circle were carrying enough firepower to riddle us," I announced. "I checked the *Delora*'s ammo cabinet to find it empty. What's this all about, Harvey?"

"It's one of the problems that the PRC was formed to

handle," he answered. "The River Patrol has been sending in regular supplies, but they haven't been getting to the guards."

"Zoltana?"

"We think he's sending the ammo to other districts."

I suddenly got a queasy feeling. That happens, especially when I consider what might become of LaRue and me if the district government lost its hold on the citizenry. Yes, I complain with the best of them, but I do have a regular paycheck and a place to live. The rumors of civil war had escalated in the last few months and to think that Zoltana was fueling the hatred and discontent that might change my life pissed me off. "I take it the River Patrol is still bringing in new loads of ammo?"

Harvey nodded. "Before I shipped out, I dispatched a go-ahead for delivery of handguns, bullets, and grenades."

"Why don't you just pick this guy up?" I demanded.

"Because it would cause a riot like none before it."

"Well, what the hell is the PRC going to do to get rid of his ass?"

"We were hoping to do it quietly."

"Slip someone in there to replace him? Why would that work?"

Harvey shook his head and spooned up some slop. "There are PRC agents planted all through here. They're trying to sway the population to join a more traditional task force that is organizing to wipe out all this witchcraft stuff."

I couldn't help smiling into my food. That would never happen. It would be like trying to run invisible magic out of the district.

In the very next moment, though, I was no longer smiling. The *Delora* groaned and seconds later we rammed into something, the impact throwing us out of our chairs and sliding the dishes off the table behind us. Dead time followed, that familiar lull when the world turns silent. It's that moment when divine retribution makes the final decision to send your butt straight to Hades. This pronouncement came, heralding itself with the ominous sound of metal scraping stone.

The bulkheads buckled and the overhead bulged as the boat listed toward port. We rolled with the *Delora* and the furniture until the cutter came to a final, shuddering stop.

No one said anything for a minute. I've always been the brave one, and after pushing a chair off of me, I asked if we had any injuries.

"Only to my dinner," Gibson answered, wiping at a splatter of chipped beef decorating his cammies.

"What did we hit?" LaRue asked.

Harvey rose and pulled me to a stand. While I shook down, he headed for the hatch. "I'll check the bridge."

"Wait," I called. "We'll come with you."

I was last in our shinny up the ladder, so I paused when I was high enough to survey the situation. We had somehow made a wrong turn in the fog. The river had narrowed into a creek that eventually rushed off down a sheer, rock gorge. The *Delora* had plowed aground, finally stopped by an outcropping of boulders.

We stormed onto the bridge to find it a mess of glass, sparking wires, and smoking computer equipment. Yarrow manned the helm alone, standing at the wheel and staring out the porthole as if nothing had happened. She nodded when we entered, but beyond that, she didn't have much to say by way of explanation. Of course, it might have been because she was stewed.

I don't mean a little drunk. This woman was ready to be poured into a jar and put on the shelf. Her every breath was ignited with vodka and she was forced to lean heavily upon the wheel to keep her balance. Stepping closer, I heard her mumbling the words to "Blow the Man Down."

LaRue glanced toward me and then spoke to Yarrow. "What have you done?"

Before her next breath, she was sobbing. "We're doomed, doomed, doomed," she chanted. "I followed the song of the naiads and I lost my way."

SIXTY

I heard shouts and crunched through the wreckage to look out the cracked observation porthole. The *Delora*'s crew had gathered on the main deck to discuss the damage. From where I stood, I could see the water gushing into a large tear along the hull at the bow seams. It was then I remembered that Jasper Finn was lounging in the lockup.

I forgot the bridge and rushed off toward the dungeon. Unfortunately, the impact had not only caused the breach in the *Delora*'s hull, but it had also caused injury to her internal integrity, and the companionway hatch was jammed. I trotted toward an entrance at the stern and thankfully found it open. Slipping down into the bowels of the boat, I found myself in the flooding engine room, and then desperately searched for an exit that would get me out of the bilge and into the hold. It took me a couple of minutes to kick aside spilled tools and loose diesel drums, but I finally found the deck hatch. As if my day wasn't already hard enough, the damned thing was stuck and the wheel was greasy. I grabbed a rag, and summoning every bit of strength I had, I twisted the latch and broke the seals, slipping through the narrow opening along with the rush of water.

I ran toward the lockup, where Finn huddled against the rising water.

"Help me," he whined. "I can't swim. I'm gonna drown."

"Hang on, Finn," I answered, fumbling with my key ring. After a couple of bad guesses, I found the right key and liberated the prisoner. He clanked out behind me and struggled up the ladder into the engine room, grunting and groaning about the load the shackles put on his arms and legs.

"Hurry up," I ordered. "The water is starting to flood the hold." I pushed up the ladder and set my shoulder against his ass, shoving him until he squeezed through the overhead hatch. Following him through, I stopped to lock the flood down below.

Finn gasped for air. "Thanks for coming to get me," he whispered.

I didn't reply. Instead, I dragged him topside, where I chained him to the railing while I sought out LaRue and Gibson, finding them on the bridge in a confab with Harvey. By the time I caught the gist of the conversation, I began to realize just how desperate our situation was.

As destiny would have it, Yarrow had not only driven the *Delora* aground in the middle of the largest cell block of the labor camp, but she'd also headed up a lonely tributary of the Black River. We listened with dismay as Harvey gave us a rundown of our possibilities, but every sentence he spoke was a further prediction of our doom.

"Even if the hull hadn't been breached, there's not enough water to launch the boat."

"Then our only option is to send someone in a skiff to fetch a rescue team," I answered.

"That's just asking for trouble from the locals."

"We don't have any choice, do we?"

Harvey shook his head. "We've had it. We've got to be miles from the main river. A skiff will never make it out of here."

"Do you have any better ideas?"

He snorted, shook his head, and dropped his gaze toward

the deck. "Let me see if I can get the radio working. If anything, we should button up tight and wait for help. We're bound to get on the search-and-rescue list when we don't report in at the delta station."

"We've got an energetic killer on our hands, who probably has friends," LaRue said. "We better take care of that matter as soon as we can, or none of us are going to be alive when the new list is issued."

SIXTY-ONE

At the very core of LaRue's personality, you'll find a flamboyant man who barely restrains his own criminal tendencies. In the fading light of day, he proved it by bravely climbing down to the creek bed, where he stood in a foot of water to spray graffiti on the hull of a government boat. His labors produced a big, red swastika.

When I joined him with my own spray can, he stood back to admire his work. "I hope Emmet and the Coven see attacking this boat as a bad move."

In the district, the swastika was a symbol of supernatural alliance, so I could understand where my partner was going with this. "I don't think Emmet will do anything in a big way. Does he want the camp to know that I stole his precious book? He'd be better off to keep it a need-to-know secret. Denying it would still give him some operating power."

LaRue added a finishing touch to his artwork before answering. "You're scraping off pieces of hope, Ty. Zoltana has spread the news far and wide. Emmet is going to have to put up or shut up at some point. The question is: Who will get to us first?"

True. The odds sucked. Until help floated down that

creek, we were going to be sized up for possible inclusion
in the shrunken-head economy. I turned to one of the sheer
walls of the gorge to decorate the bare rock with my own
spray paint, but my concentration went out ahead of me.
LaRue had spoken of the water witches' belief in the threefold way. It boiled down to instant karma times three. Put
grief into the world and prepare to find yourself sandwiched
between pain, fear, and unrelenting heartburn.

As much as I hate to admit my compliance with metaphysical ideas, standing there, adding more scars to the
world, I wondered if my problem had always been the result of my former choices. It was hard to accept the possibility of living through incarnations filled with equal
turmoil, but given my current disabilities, it seemed likely
I fashioned my own path from the anger I've held since
childhood. This rage has rubbed the steel edge of my days
until they are sharp with violence and discontent. Had I
chosen my final destination, then, a place where I would
offer fate the invisible sword of my consciousness?

I shivered at the thought of an untimely demise and immediately realized that reincarnation did not address such
considerations. Death came when our choices led us to that
point; there was never anything premature about our last
hours in flesh. From this angle, a walk-in was not possible,
because the mind of the host body had already edited the
initial soul with the desires and decisions that had brought
it to the day of judgment in the first place.

Look where my life had led me—a huge pearl in my
pocket and a bad situation. If I had it all to do again—
would I? Could I?

According to LaRue, the instant grace comes into a person's life, he makes sharp left turns despite his efforts not
to. He is forced to accept this intervention in the law of
karma and many times he allows it to proceed under the
delusion that the outcome is preordained on some cosmic
level. Still, the problem with the explanation is this: If you
don't recognize the intercession of divine grace, how do
you know it has touched you? Can a person's soul sense
this divine change? Does it know the person has built up

some karmic merit points? Can it grandstand the next big flop in a person's earthly incarnation and alter the outcome for the better? Or is it just a bowling card that can only be redeemed during league night in Summerland?

I've seen some creative scams involving reincarnation, but the folks in the labor camp employed them in ways I wouldn't have considered. Zoltana played these options with force, using the concepts to build up his power like a Roman emperor looking to convert Christianity to his own ends. He strong-armed the wicked and the oppressed and that made him a beast in his own right. If man's inhumanity to man extended into the next life, then it had further opportunity to develop evil. Thinking in such terms gave the observation ''he was a bad seed'' new meaning.

One thing was certain. Ol' Zol had all the power here and the government was impotent through funding, bureaucratic bungling, or just plain apathy. Any way you turned, it was not a good idea to get on the warden's bad side. That said a lot for Wheeler, Neal, and Emmet. It said that the disease they lived with had rotted their brains to the point of recklessness.

''We certainly have consigned a lot of people to this paradise,'' I said as I adorned a large rock with a mystical design.

''Yeah,'' LaRue answered. ''Do you think we're paying in kind?''

At first I didn't think so, but then, I saw Ol' Zol riding a gunboat down the creek and I was forced to reevaluate my answer.

SIXTY-TWO

Zoltana ordered the pilot of the gunboat to drop the anchor. He debarked, walking straight up the creek with five armed guards flanking him. Watching him march toward us, swarthy and swaggering, I got a very bad feeling and didn't bother to hide the fact that I unbuckled my thigh holster. LaRue went a step further and drew his sidearm.

"Well," Zoltana greeted. "It looks like the pilot lost her way. On purpose, would you say?"

LaRue glanced at me before answering the warden. "It was an accident caused by bad weather."

"Are you here to help us?" I asked. "Or were you responding to our little announcement?"

Zoltana nodded to his guards, and then paused to pull a cigar from his uniform pocket. He spent several moments ceremoniously lighting his stogie before finally answering. "I must admit, your announcement intrigued me. I was on the river when you called it in. So sorry it took me a while to locate you."

"Then you're here to render assistance?"

"In a way," he answered nonchalantly. "I want to make certain, first and foremost, that my investment remains secure."

"The dredge."

He blew a smoke ring in response, grunted, and studied our artwork. Pointing to LaRue's swastika, he said: "This is a violation of the penal code, but I'll let it pass by this time."

"How generous," I said. "Why don't you just lay it on the line so we know where we stand with you."

Zoltana stared at me. "They said you had spunk."

Spunk? This guy was completely lost where I was concerned. "And you're good at dancing around answers."

"Can't you figure out some of what I've come to do?"

"Yeah," LaRue said. "You want the book."

"Score one for the district flatfoot," Zoltana said. "You will give it to me now."

"And if we refuse?"

He demonstrated his ethics by pointing to one of his guards, who raised his automatic weapon in our direction. "Tom is a very good shot. He'll send you to Summerland with a ratta-tatta-tatta echoing in your ears. Now, Marshal Merrick, don't misunderstand me. I don't usually threaten law enforcement officers. Without you to supply the dregs of society, where would I be?" Zoltana sucked on his cigar and pointed to the *Delora*. "If you please. And no funny stuff. Not only are my guards good with guns, but they're used to dealing with prisoners and I'm afraid they can be a bit trigger-happy."

Prick. I'd complicated the scenario too much and had underestimated Zoltana. He'd been following the *Delora* the whole time. In fact, I now knew for certain that it was his guards who'd attacked the Tin Circle. So I stalled with a question, hoping to come up with an answer to pull our butts out of the bear trap. "Did you catch Eldon Emmet?"

He smiled. "Emmet is dead and vying for a berth in Davy Jones's locker. Now move."

I glanced at LaRue, who solemnly stowed his sidearm in its holster. With jerky steps, we headed up the gangplank. By the time we reached the main deck, I was still out of ideas and so kept talking instead. "I guess you'll want Jasper Finn, too."

"Yes. And Ritter. You see, I already have his partner."

"Stirling?"

"That's right."

"What did Stirling do to you?" I asked.

"He sold medical technology that I helped to bring about."

That had a nasty, familiar ring to it. "And he wasn't going to share the profits with you."

"That is correct."

"Are you referring to a cure for this leprosylike disease the prisoners have?" LaRue asked.

Zoltana took another puff. "Yes. Stirling first developed a viable vaccine that worked with the guards and then he came up with a verifiable treatment." He pointed in the general direction of his men. "You'll notice they don't have any outward signs of the debilitating malady."

"Outward signs," LaRue said. "What's going on inside?"

Zoltana shrugged. "They grow. We all grow. Can't seem to stop that."

"Why don't you help the prisoners?" I asked.

"Why should I?"

"Compassion comes to mind."

"Compassion? You forget, Marshal Merrick, these animals deserve to be here. They've killed, raped, and maimed. You and your partner have sent many a man up this river. Why should I find compassion in my heart to heal them? Karma puts them in this situation and suffering is their redemption."

Obviously, this man had never heard of liquid grace. "Also, you would lose one of the best handles you have on their fear."

"Reincarnation and the fear of death go hand in hand." He turned to two of his thugs. "Secure the *Delora*."

They barked their compliance and stomped off to hold folks at gunpoint. Try as I might, I still couldn't find any options to salvage the day. I hit him with another question while I worked over possibilities, none of which were feasible. "Aren't you afraid someone on board the *Delora* will challenge what you're doing?"

"No," he said. "In some form or the other, I've got their allegiance. I pay well for their services. They wouldn't think of standing against me."

"Sounds like a lot of spit, Zoltana."

He chuckled and I found the sound to be obnoxious. Then, turning deadly serious, he said: "I want the Book of Shadows. Now."

"It's in my cabin," I answered.

"Tom will accompany you."

I nodded and headed for the bunk room with this watchdog hounding my footsteps. Just as I reached the hatch I saw the dispatched guards drive Gibson and Curran down the main companionway. The good doctor threw a confused look my direction.

"Cooperate," I called out to him.

The guard nudged me with the barrel of his death piece and pushed me into our quarters. I headed for the locker, opened it, and rifled through my duffel bag. Normally, I stash a pistol in my stuff, but despite the firepower at my fingertips, I feared retribution that would see my partner and my lover killed. I grabbed the Book of Shadows and stomped back toward the deck to find the entire crew looking as stunned as Gibson had.

When I returned, I heard LaRue unloading his ideas on Zoltana's scheme. "Let me see if I read it right," he said. "You're going to take Ritter and leave. What are you going to do? Pin him to stakes somewhere and peel the flesh off his bones to make a point?"

"Very good," Zoltana answered.

"What about your precious dredge?"

"When word gets out that I have the Book of Shadows and the Coven in control, I won't have to worry about the safety of the dredge. I can come back after I arrange a scow to unload it. Simple, isn't it?"

"What about us?" I asked, tossing him the book. "Are you going to kill us or let us hang around for someone else to do your dirty work?"

He laughed. "You still have to have your day of reckoning with Neal and Wheeler," he said. "I don't want to get in the middle of that. I know for a fact that they will be here soon. They won't surrender and you'll have to kill them, because if you don't, they'll murder you. It's impossible to reason with a bogeyman."

SIXTY-THREE

LaRue and I didn't even bother to protest Zoltana's plans. It wouldn't have done a damned bit of good, anyway, and despite our armed status, he purposefully took momentary control of our lives.

"What the hell is going on?" Gibson demanded.

"Warden Prefect Zoltana is doing what every government official we have ever come across does," I said. "Lying, cheating, stealing, and killing."

"No one invited you into my kingdom," Zoltana answered. "Now you have to play by my rules, and my rules say you have to help me before I'll help you."

"And what if we don't get Neal and Wheeler?" I asked.

"If that happens, I'll be too busy trying to find them to worry about you."

Before I could say another word, Zoltana's bulldog returned with Ritter and Finn. The prisoner flashed me a helpless expression and all I could do was shake my head and raise my hands in surrender. Ritter openly blubbered about his fate and fell to his knees begging for mercy, but Finn remained stoic, gathering what ragged dignity he had left to him. We continued to stand clear, though I knew LaRue was itching to blast away like an old-time matinee movie hero. Still, we have learned over the years that misplaced compassion usually gets a person killed and at the moment I was trying to find a way off this rock and back home. I was sorry for their fates, but their decisions had brought them to this point.

We watched in silence as the guards loaded the prisoners, and after signaling their readiness, Zoltana turned back to drop his final commandment on us. "I want Neal and Wheeler dead. Double-cross me, and you better have some mighty fine karma, because you're going to need it to get out of here alive." With that, he stomped away, unconcerned that we might try to aim around his guards to shoot him in the back. He stepped aboard the gunboat and waved gaily before he ordered his men to shove off.

"Are you okay?" Gibson asked me.

"We're fine," I answered. "Any injuries inside?"

There was a chorus of "no's" and then Harvey spoke up. "Zoltana thinks Neal and Wheeler will come tonight. He's probably right. Red sky at morning, sailor take warning." Harvey stared at us for a minute as though he suspected collusion on our part, but wisely he didn't say anything, instead slipping back through the companionway hatch with the other crew members.

Zoltana's admission about paying off the rivermen gave me the willies. We were forced to bunk with real rats, it seemed. Was everyone on the take? Either way, we would never know.

Gibson returned to the sick bay and LaRue and I stayed outside painting magic symbols on the rocks, simply because there was nothing else we could do but wait and fret. We worked until the sun dipped behind the walls of the gorge and the night bugs started their evening concert. My thoughts had stayed with Ritter and Finn, who were by that time fish food.

"Are you about done, Ty?" LaRue asked, stepping over to me.

I nodded, intent upon adding the finishing touches to my fancy swastika. Unfortunately, I messed up my design, because a stretch came on and I froze, unable to take my hand off the spray-paint nozzle. A minute of dead time followed before I collapsed in a heap, doing my best to keep my screams crushed to my breast by curling into a fetal position. LaRue was on me in an instant. He held me like a lover, but I knew his attention was on our surroundings. You see, I could feel the cold steel of his sawed-off shotgun barrel as he hugged me. If a surprise attack came from the left, he would use my trembling shoulder to balance his aim.

Finally, mercifully, the stretch ended. LaRue felt it leave and he pulled back to allow me a moment to absorb my new form. I'd grown, more than usual, and my muscles had popped. My hearing had sharpened and the shape of my eyes had changed. The sparkling Van Gogh view I had on the world was transformed yet again by my sense of smell as the bright colors and patterns pulsed through my optic nerves. It was LaRue's odor I detected, and for a second I stared dreamily at the shimmering blue drops dripping into my vision.

With his help, I sat up and realized that I could also feel changes in my throat. My next words would have a gravelly edge to them, but upon testing my communications ability, I realized I was in deep trouble. Aphasia had struck.

Bleach my bones! My brain had failed me after all. I had a good chance of going to my grave without ever being able to say a sentimental good-bye or understand one in return. If predeath trauma trapped the spirit in the Davy Jones's locker, then I'd be haunting this hell for an eternity.

LaRue said something and sighed, but I understood what he meant just through his body language. My stretch had left me an unreliable ally.

He helped me to a stand just before Gibson jogged down the gangway. The good doctor took one look at me and turned to LaRue, who confirmed my disposition with words that were composed of nonsensical sounds. After hearing this explanation, he swung his wild-eyed squint my direction again. It was enough to make me walk away, but try as I might, I couldn't haul off my embarrassment. I had the odd feeling it had stayed behind to shout out its presence.

Gibson stalked after me. I was only a yard or two from
the plank when he caught me by the arm. One thing is for
sure, he didn't miscalculate my lycanthropic vigor. The bastard used every bit of strength he had to keep me from
pulling away and it didn't take long before I surrendered.
Wasn't dealing with regret and fear enough? Did he have
to give me hell for something I couldn't control?

I was sure I was in for a chewing-out, but Gibson fooled
me. His grip relaxed when I looked into his eyes. He drew
me into an embrace, and instead of speaking, he kissed me
passionately on the lips. If there was ever a moment when
I could have believed LaRue's claim that the good doctor
and I were soul mates down through the ages, this was it,
for the enforced silence between us only heightened the
feeling of familiarity.

Gibson released me and I realized that he did, indeed,
smell like a rainbow.

SIXTY-FOUR

Gibson thinks that my environment and situation determine the severity of my lycanthropic changes. He also believes it's a weapon that I routinely call upon. His theory suggests that I have some idea of the supernatural artillery I will need and then my subconscious sets about to bring it to fruition. Unfortunately, the truth from my perspective is far different, and this hypothesis has a question that begs answering. How could my subconscious have saddled me with aphasia when I required all my faculties to properly maim and kill?

Far worse was the fact that I'd become an unpredictable liability. I'm sure LaRue and Gibson must have discussed just this subject, but I was helpless to defend my position in the argument growing between them. They finally threw down the boxing gloves and urged me up the plank. With the help of Neilson, they paused to manually retract the gangway and then we took up our posts at designated points on the *Delora*.

Gibson hid at the bow with Harvey while LaRue and I huddled in the stern near the dredge. The other rivermen were to assume their places and wait for the attack that would surely come.

My partner and I had been in bad situations before, but communication had never been a problem. As we sat on the deck, glancing over the railing to watch the night flow down the creek like a giant dumping a huge jar of liquid darkness, I tried to put my worries behind me, confident that when the time came I would act appropriately.

As evening approached, the scraggly oaks decorated in streamers of Spanish moss winked with the ethereal sparkles of lightning bugs and flick jiggers. The naiads began their enticing song, but with my lycanthropic hearing, I sensed the aria behind their tribute and after several minutes I realized I heard the beat of metal drums far in the distance. It filled out the noise, making me pause to wonder if the passing of scuttlebutt relied upon old-fashioned means. I'd not heard this ancient rhythm before. Perhaps, it was some strange gift caused by the aphasia, but sadly, I had no good way to tell my partner and no way to know if it was important.

I took a deep breath as if this might clear my head, and then attempted to find the center of my self-absorption. Despite my screwed-up language processor, LaRue used the moment to whisper to me. I could only guess what he spoke of—everything from water witches to ideas on how to reincarnate his beloved Trabi. I let him talk, mainly because I didn't know how to shut him up. As it was, it didn't take long before he did that on his own.

No sooner had the moon risen than LaRue was rudely interrupted by the most inhuman roar I've ever heard. The noise reverberated through the gorge and into my skull. It was so sharp, it brought me to my knees and made me drop my shotgun on the deck. I squeezed my ears, but nothing would block out the sound. If I'd expected help from my partner, I was shit out of luck, because he was busy trying to cover his own head. We hung on until this supernatural trumpeter was done serenading the stars.

When the screeching assault ended, I shook my head to clear it and discovered that the sound had somehow propelled me into a different mode of comprehension. I can't tell you how it happened; I just know that my brain's warring neurons had finally called a truce. Whatever caused it, I had a moment of clarity when I realized that I could see LaRue's fear because I could smell it. Gone were the shimmering blue drops. In its place, my synesthesia picked up the musky odor of his anxiety and transported it into my awareness as shivering sapphire circles. Even against the darkness, the patterns were annoying and forced me to glance at the rising moon to dilute the images with brilliant light.

I know I should have been more concerned about the approaching bogeymen, but my mind ran off my concentration and layered my confusion with questions. Did these color and pattern variations mean my blended senses operated on a sliding scale, picking up the nuances of emotion and reflecting their levels in the patterns and colors I saw? If so, what signified the different plateaus? Was the stale smell of periwinkle dots a sign of moderate fear? Or the stinging smell of turquoise beads an indicator of uncertainty? What, then, did the killer's odor of golden squares represent?

For several minutes with muscles straining and trigger fingers itching, we listened for footsteps, grunts, or the noise of a dislodged stone. I took a leap of faith into the lycanthropic dimension by relying upon my synesthesia to give me an olfactory warning of our intruder's approach. Sadly, my nose was stuffed up and my long-range sniffer didn't work, because I didn't detect the presence of the giants before it was too late.

SIXTY-FIVE

When I did, I got a snoutful of golden squares. The smell was so overwhelming to my blended senses that for a panicky few seconds I was literally blinded by the patterns and strong colors. I heard LaRue yell, and as my vision leaked back to me, I saw it was a pirate attack.

Several giants armed with machetes, pipes, clubs, and pure, unmitigated gall stormed the boat. Someone hit the switch on the generator and flooded the scene with the atomic glow of halogen light, placing us in surreal circumstances. There were strange beings, odd shapes, and flashing implements of death.

LaRue screamed at me and shoved me to the deck. This wallop pushed me completely out of my reverie and into the midst of the melee. My partner unloaded a round of buckshot into an advancing bogeyman. He hit him square in the chest, but the giant kept coming, swinging a sledgehammer. Two steps and he was on us. I rolled clear and drew my own shotgun, adding to the hole LaRue had started. This blast finally stopped the prisoner. He howled with agony and then, like the Viking god Thor, he chucked his weapon at us. We both jumped clear, watching in disbelief as the inmate struggled to pull back the hood of his cloak. Upon his success, we saw the frightful pain of a creature who had curling fangs and a lifetime of regrets. He stared at us before lifting his head toward the moon and wailing the litany of his sorrows. Then, falling like the timber of a ship's mast, he gave up the ghost to Davy Jones.

Gunshots and shouts were going off all over the *Delora*. I suddenly feared for Gibson's current incarnation and grabbed LaRue by the shoulder to rush him off to the gouging taking place in other parts of the boat. We passed attackers skewered by harpoons, finding one who had been killed by his own machete. Russo had bought his ticket to Summerland and Yarrow was down for the count. At each dispatch, my blended senses pummeled me with the acrid odor of golden squares.

Could it be that the smells I picked up with my synesthesia belonged to the very life force? If so, did it mean I detected the degradation of this power and the smell of impending death?

It was too bad this moment of my enlightenment came crashing down around me as one of the bastards reached through the confusion to try to yank my gun from my hands. LaRue shot wild and nearly grazed Gibson as he valiantly battled with a creature twice his size. The beast charged the good doctor with an iron club. I screamed for Gibson to duck, but I knew my warning would go unheeded, so I pulled a hardy lycanthropic breath and roared my lungs out. My noise drew off the bogeyman while LaRue went to Gibson's aid. The giant chased me, our noise drawing the attention of others and shifting the weight of the fighting until the combatants followed us toward the stern of the boat.

Before scraping against a dead end, I turned on the monster and pumped the shotgun, but as with everything else in my current life, the sucker jammed. Still, Davy Jones must have been with me, because the bogeyman stepped into friendly fire, taking a round from a water rifle. It split his head in two and gave me just enough time to pull my sidearm and crawl toward the dredge. My movement proved to be the deciding moment of the showdown, for

stalking through the madness was a giant among titans—
fanged, furry, and furious. This Goliath lumbered up to me
and introduced himself. Yes, he introduced himself and I
understood every word.

I didn't have time to figure out how this was possible or
whether I was hallucinating, but instead I babbled at him
in a vain effort to buy myself some time. With the caliber
on my pistol, the best I could hope for would be to push a
bullet into his eye.

"I am Tidus Neal," he thundered. "I own my soul,
kami. Get your own."

"I don't want your stinking soul, you piece of filth," I
yelled. "What good is your karma?"

He screeched into the night like a wounded lion. My
sensitive hearing suffered from this display, but as I turned
my head to blot out the dizzying noise, I saw my hope—
the dredge pump. The *Delora*'s stern was stranded in three
feet of water and the dredge's suction hose was submerged.
It was a possibility. In fact, it was the only one I could
think of that might save our asses.

I took the opportune moment and unloaded my pistol at
Neal. It struck him in various places, but not one of the
plugs hit a lethal spot. Neal screamed in pain, brought his
rifle down, and shot a stream of electrified water my way.
I jumped clear, and using the speed and vigor of my lycanthropic nature, I flipped the switch on the dredge. Russo
had done his job and the machinery fired to life instantly.
I spun and grabbed the suction hose, yanking it from the
storage housing. Neal sent another rifle blast my way. It
singed my cammies as I swung the nozzle toward him and
punched the button that armed the pump.

The crap from the bottom of the creek rumbled up the
hose, shooting out with tremendous force. It was all I could
do to tame the whipping action caused by the suction and
aim the business end at Neal. He shot at me again, but I
defended myself by deflecting this lethal arc of electricity
and water with a stream of rocks and dirt. I then turned my
nasty mood on the bogeyman.

The dredge siphoned all sorts of debris, jettisoning the

trash on the deck. I manhandled the hose and prayed for a victory, ready to jump over the railing in case the litter it spewed clogged the nozzle. Neal fired at me again, but his volley fell far to the left. I returned fire with the hose and hit him straight between the horns with a rock. He went down, but his finger must have been on the trigger because he sprayed the night with electrified water. The shot lanced the pump, making my weapon useless.

LaRue and Gibson battled the surviving bogeyman by drawing him in my direction. It was like a telecast of *Wrestling for Dollars* with the two of them slamming the guy with kicks and punches while staying clear of the bad side of his rifle.

I was out of ammo and helpless, because at that very moment when I might never see my lover alive again, I had another stretch.

The seizure raged through me. It reamed me to the core, but for some silly reason, I didn't double over with the pain. In fact, I couldn't move—not one muscle. The burn continued into my nerve endings, tracing up my spine and into my brain. For a minute I was totally immersed in the agony, unable to differentiate between normality and this exquisite feeling of molten energy. My head felt inordinately heavy as though my skull had been tapped like one of LaRue's homemade wine kegs and someone was busy pumping in supernatural slime that would eventually harden around my brain. I was sure that I was having a stroke, positive I would die under this lycanthropic weight without getting a chance to sell my beautiful pearl.

SIXTY-SIX

I must have collapsed and passed out in the middle of this horrendous event, because the next thing I remembered was the sting across my face. Gibson. What a nice way to welcome someone back from Summerland.

In my daze, I still had my wits enough to grab his hand as he came around for another strike. "I'm okay," I mumbled. It took me several odd moments to realize I could understand his reply.

"Thank St. Ophelia," he growled. Wincing, he pulled from my lycanthropic grip.

I glanced around, trying to clear my vision. It was still night, but the battle was over. "Did we win?" I asked.

LaRue joined us and smiled. "Yes."

Gibson helped me sit up. It was then I noticed he had a large gash on his forearm. I touched him gently and my action pulled his attention to his wound. "I'm all right. It's not as bad as it looks. I guess I'm just not much for hand-to-hand combat."

"You better doctor yourself before it gets infected or a mosquito shits in it," I said.

He nodded. "Don't want that to happen. I need both arms to hug you."

When he said it, I reached for him, but our embrace was cut short by the appearance of Riverman Harvey and Jasper Finn. For a second I thought I was hallucinating the return of the prisoner. "What the hell are you doing here?"

"He was our savior," LaRue said.

"I thought Zoltana had made a pie of you already. What happened?"

"I suppose I was right scared of dying," Finn answered. "Zoltana was just gonna shoot me like a dog for the dead man's chest. I couldn't let him do that."

"He overpowered the guards," Harvey said. "That's when Ritter made a break for it. They killed him, but Finn used the moment to get one over on Zoltana."

"Did you kill him?"

"Let's just say I took care of ol' Zol," Finn said. "He won't be bothering anyone anymore."

"What about the guards?"

"I aimed the boat's cannon on the screws and the sons of bitches dropped their guns and ran away. They're a right cowardly lot when you get down to it."

"Why'd you come back?" I asked. "That gunboat would have made you a powerful man. At least for a little while."

He shrugged. "What good is power, Marshal? I just want to live my remaining days in peace and quiet." He paused, snorted, and then added to his confession. "I wasn't going to come back, if you want to know the truth. In fact, I had the boat going the other way." He glanced at Harvey. "I guess I had an attack of conscience."

"Thank you, Jasper," I said.

"Hey, you saved me. I owed you."

Gibson interrupted us by assuring himself I was fit, and then he helped me stand. "It seemed that Wheeler and Neal had a little coven of their own. They weren't attacking this boat alone."

I nodded, letting my attention wander over the carnage. They were strange, hairy beasts, sinners who had paid into the coffers of redemption by giving up their humanity. "Is Wheeler among them?"

"Yeah," Finn said. "It's a real shame what happened to him."

"Well, let's hope with Zoltana out of the way, the government will clean this place up."

"Can I go?" he asked suddenly.

"You got family members in this cell block or something?" I said, with a grin.

He smiled. "As a matter of fact, yes. I'd kinda like to see them, too."

I waved him off. "Have a good life, Finn."

"Take care of yourself, Marshal," he answered. With that, he jumped over the side of the boat and headed down the creek until he disappeared into the rising mist.

"I'll get the crew assembled," Harvey said. "We should get out of here as soon as we can. If our luck holds, we'll be able to reach the main tributary by dawn."

Gibson left us to scrounge supplies from sick bay while LaRue checked the bodies. I lingered by the dredge, lost in thought and hopefulness, happy to have my pearl and my miserable life. It's a known fact that I don't place a lot of stock in fate and destiny, but at that moment of gratitude, I was presented with the possibilities that a person really could be in the right place at the right time, for lying on the deck in the midst of the mud and rocks, I saw a shiny stone. I picked it up, wiped the crud off of it, and holding the rock to the light, I realized that I had found a chunk of gold.